Praise for *Body Work*

"*Body Work* is the kind of book that sucks you into the pages and won't let you go until the end. It's edgy and different, with a strong hero and heroine who don't fit the usual mold."
—*New York Times* bestselling author
Linda Howard

"Brand tells a disturbing, engrossing tale of murder and madness, adding her own unique touches of eroticism and humor. An excellent read."
—*Romantic Times BOOKreviews*

Praise for *Touching Midnight*

"Brand's extraordinary gifts as a storyteller are very evident here. This story is a rare and potent mixture of adventure, mystery and passion that shouldn't be missed."
—*Romantic Times BOOKreviews*

Also by

FIONA BRAND

BODY WORK
TOUCHING MIDNIGHT

Watch for Fiona Brand's upcoming novels

KILLER FOCUS

Available December 2007

and

BLIND INSTINCT

Available February 2008

DOUBLE
FIONA BRAND
VISION

MIRA®

ISBN-13: 978-0-7783-2546-8
ISBN-10:   0-7783-2546-6

DOUBLE VISION

www.MIRABooks.com

Printed in U.S.A.

Thank you to Jenny Haddon, a former bank regulator, for her invaluable advice and her fascinating insight into the world of international banking, Eileen Wilks for giving me the inside running on how to get a driver's license in Texas, and Claire Russell of the Kerikeri medical center for help with the medical details. Thank you also to Miranda Stecyk of MIRA Books for her editorial expertise and direction, and some really great ideas that helped make this story sing. You ladies are fabulous!

To Robyn and Don, and Keith and Daphne, who truly gave me my start in writing. Thank you for all the years of support and friendship, the teaching and advice, the cups of tea, the shared meals and those wonderful weekends at the Kara School of Writing.

Part 1

Prologue

December 1944, Lubeck, Germany

The steel arm of a crane, pockmarked by rust and salt, swung across the frigid decks of the *Nordika*. A heavy crate, a swastika and a number stenciled on the side, hung suspended, straining at aging steel hawsers as the freezing northerly gale increased in intensity.

Gaze narrowed against the wind, Erich Reinhardt, captain of the cargo vessel, watched as the delicate process of lowering the crate into the hold commenced. Loading cargo under these conditions was an act of stupidity; putting out to sea was nothing short of madness, but lately, everything about Germany was madness. To the east, Russians were massing along the border. In the west, the British and Americans had launched their offensive. There was no heating, no food; his family was starving and they all lived in fear that British and American bombers would kill them while they slept. For months he had expected to die that way or, failing that, to be torpedoed at sea. Perhaps that was better than a bullet in the brain from a cold-eyed Schutzstaffel.

"How much longer?"

The question from the SS officer who had commandeered his ship was curt, but there was no disguising the accent. Bremen, maybe, Hamburg at a stretch, and straight off the docks. Himmler might be scraping the bottom of the barrel with this one, but Reinhardt still had to be wary. Oberleutnant Dengler might have working-class roots, but he knew ships and had taken control of the *Nordika* with ease. "Fifteen minutes, maybe half an hour if the conditions become more difficult."

And Reinhardt expected the weather to deteriorate. A storm front had been pounding the coast all day; a Force ten gale was predicted before dawn. He watched as another crate was lowered into place. Garish spotlights lit up the feverish activity in the hold and on the dock as the final truck was offloaded, a stark contrast to the blackout of the city behind, and all along the coast. Even the navigation lights along the channel were turned off. Loading cargo was dangerous, but attempting to navigate the channel in this weather, with no lights, was tantamount to suicide.

Dengler strode to the railing and roared an order.

The doors of a truck were flung open. Seconds later, people poured out—passengers, Reinhardt realized—and began to embark.

The first was a tall, elegant woman, bent against the wind as she clutched a baby to her chest and held the hand of a toddler. A group of older children followed, hustled on by a straggling group of women and the tall, authoritative figure of yet another SS officer. Counting the two who held his crew at gunpoint in the dining room and the four supervising the loading of the cargo, that brought the total number of SS officers on the *Nordika* to eight; more than Reinhardt had ever seen in Lubeck at any one time, and seven more than was needed to keep him and his aging crew in check.

A small girl, blond ringlets streaming from the hood of an expensive fur-trimmed coat, stopped when she reached the top of the gangplank and stared up at Reinhardt, her gaze expressionless, before she was hustled below.

The wind picked up, scattering ice. Cold stung Reinhardt's cheeks and flowed around his neck, finding its way through cracked and thinning oilskin and the threadbare layers of the muffler beneath. The image of the little girl's face stayed with him as he watched another crate swing in the wind. She had been maybe six or seven, the same age as his granddaughter, Bernadette, but for a fragmented moment he hadn't been able to see any difference between her and the SS officer who had scooped her up and taken her below.

A gust of wind hit the starboard side of the ship. Saltwater and ice sprayed across the decks. A split second later, the crate slammed into the side of the hold. Wood splintered and Reinhardt held his breath as the damaged crate was buffeted by the wind.

The first mate joined him on the quarterdeck, huddling in the lee of a cable housing, leathery face reddened by wind and ice. His gaze was glued to the frayed hawser. "What have they got in those crates?"

"I don't want to know." The less they knew, the more likely they were to get out of this alive.

A second gust sent the crate spinning. Fatigued steel groaned, the hawser snapped and the crate dropped like a stone, the contents exploding across the floor of the hold, scattering the loading crew. Hidden on the quarterdeck, Reinhardt had a moment to feel utter disbelief and fear as he stared at the strewn contents of the crate. Seconds later, the SS officers who were overseeing the placement of the crates stepped out of the gloom and the flat spitting of Schmeisser machine-gun pistols punctuated the pressurized whine of the wind.

An hour later, the hold was secured and the bodies of the loading crew were disposed of over the side. The spotlights washing the decks of the *Nordika* were extinguished and the small glow of a kerosene lamp on the bridge became the only point of reference in pitch-blackness.

Reinhardt ducked his head as he stepped onto the bridge, a sense of fatalism gripping him as he saw Dengler and another SS officer, this one a full colonel, studying a map of the channel. He had known the three men who had been executed in the hold most of his life. Konig and Holt had both been in their late fifties, with large families to support. Breit had been a gunner in the First World War. "Where is it you want to go?"

In the glare of the lamp, Reinhardt noticed for the first time that Dengler was barely old enough to shave. The Oberst was a different matter. His cheekbones were high, his mouth thin, his gaze coldly amused. It was the colonel who spoke.

"Somewhere warm. How about Colombia?"

One

Forty years later, San Francisco

The sound of the gun was an insignificant pop. The entry wound was even less startling, a hole about the size of a nickel.

FBI agent Lance Williams blinked, but the surprised flicker was a reflex only. The instant the .22 slug ploughed through his temple, slicing at an angle that sectioned both right and left hemispheres of his brain before lodging in his occipital lobe, he was clinically dead.

Agent Edward Dennison watched as Williams crumpled with an angular sideways grace, his shoulder brushing one of the potted palms that was positioned either side of the wide, elegant portico of one of Nob Hill's most prestigious addresses. Methodically, he wiped the gun and slipped it back in his shoulder holster. The weapon was a Saturday-night special, the most popular handgun in town and the most difficult to trace; every career criminal and junkie—not to mention a lot of ordinary citizens—owned one. He would dump the gun and the body later, somewhere they would both be found after a decent interval had passed, in which time he would be able to voice his concern about his missing partner and maybe even raise the alarm.

He pressed the doorbell for the second time and tensed as the door swung open, startled when Alex Lopez answered the door himself. But then, he was aware that he and Williams had been on camera from the moment they had driven through the electronically controlled entrance gates.

Lopez studied the body, his expression bland, and Dennison felt a chill that was becoming familiar penetrate even his cynical exterior. He'd worked for Lopez on and off for the past eighteen months, but the kid had been busy since the last time they'd met. The baby-faced handsomeness had grown into the trademark cheekbones and heavy jaw that made his father, Marco Chavez, instantly recognizable, but some of the changes weren't natural. Dennison knew enough about facial reconstruction to recognize that Lopez's nose had been thinned, his cheekbones shaved, the distinctive hollows beneath filled. Even the slant of his eyes was subtly altered. The jaw hadn't been touched, yet. He guessed that was a more complex procedure.

Despite the extensive surgery, Lopez was still recognizable as the heir apparent of one of Colombia's most brutal and successful drug cartels, but the changes were enough to create uncertainty.

Lopez bent and touched Williams's throat, checking the carotid. As the sleeve of his jacket slid back from his wrist, Dennison noted that the small tattoo on the back of his right hand had been removed. The patch of skin was noticeably lighter and faintly pink, which meant he'd gone for a skin graft instead of laser treatment. Given Lopez's plans, the removal of the tattoo was expedient.

When Lopez was satisfied Williams was dead, he straightened. Not for the first time, Dennison wondered if Lopez saw anything more than the potential to satisfy his own needs when he looked at another human being. Williams had had a wife and two kids. On the drive up the hill, Dennison had heard it all, chapter and verse. Both of his boys had graduated from college, one was teaching math, the other had gone into the academy, following in his old man's footsteps. With both his boys working, Williams had been looking to quit the bureau and sink his pension into a small business. Then he'd had the misfortune to stumble across Joe Canelli.

Canelli was a petty criminal and, when money was tight, a hit man. He was also an unfortunate link between the murder of a number of organized crime figures and the sudden boost in the amount of cocaine being trafficked along the West Coast by the new boy on the block, Lopez.

Dennison had dispatched Canelli, neatly tying off that loose end. He hadn't wanted to kill Williams, but he'd had to be pragmatic. With the capture of Canelli, Williams had been on the verge of implicating Dennison in the series of killings, and that was something he couldn't allow. After twenty years of climbing the slow, slippery ladder in the bureau, what Dennison needed was simple—money, and lots of it.

Murder didn't sit easily with him. He had always walked a measured path between what the bureau wanted and his own personal needs, but lately his needs had become paramount. Lopez was dangerous, but the rewards were enough to make his head spin. Whether or not he lived to collect was another question, and that depended directly on his usefulness to Lopez. Dennison intended to be very useful.

Lopez met his gaze, dark eyes subtly amused, as if he knew exactly what had just passed through Dennison's mind. With a jerk of his head, he indicated Dennison should precede him into the house.

A queer thrill ran up Dennison's spine. He had passed the test. He was in.

Seconds later, Dennison stepped into a dimly lit reception room, and any thoughts of backing out of the deal he'd just contracted died an instant death as he made eye contact with a four-star general and a key official with the San Francisco Police Department. A wealthy financier and property developer recognizable from the society pages rose to his feet.

The fact that Cesar Morell was here surprised Dennison. "Mr. Midas," as he was known, was money, not power.

The door clicked shut behind him as a fourth figure rose to his feet and Dennison's stomach contracted.

Becoming Alex Lopez's mole in the FBI had always been a risk. He had negotiated the money; the initial down payment alone had made him a wealthy man and had relieved the financial pressures that had squeezed him dry. The money had enabled him to make ample provision to get out. He had formulated three separate identities. The passports were secured in a safe-deposit box, and he had deposited large sums of money in offshore accounts. He had done everything possible to ensure his survival and the survival of his wife.

Now the fail-safe escape plan he'd formulated seemed entirely useless.

Lopez had been a step ahead of him all the way. The man who had just risen to his feet knew everything there was to know about Dennison practically from the moment of his birth, including fingerprint records and his blood type. For all he knew he had Dennison's inside thigh measurement.

And he knew where Anne was.

Dennison could escape. He could alter his identity and leave the country within a matter of hours, but Anne couldn't. There was no way he could organize a quick flight out and a change of identity for a woman who needed around-the-clock care and a nurse in attendance at all times. There was no way Anne could even be moved without risking her life.

His wife had been a quadriplegic for almost three years. The accident that had caused her disability had been relatively minor, an intersection snarl that hadn't done much more than shunt her car a few feet, but somehow the jolt had broken her neck. With only partial mobility in one arm, she needed help to feed herself, to wash and dress and go to the bathroom. She needed help to turn over in bed and, periodically, to clear fluid from her lungs. Some days she needed help to breathe, and only twenty-five percent of the costs were covered by insurance.

Lopez made the introductions. The tall, clean-cut man stepped toward him, and Dennison wondered that he'd ever thought of him as a straight-down-the-line career man.

He held out his hand and accepted the handshake. The eye contact was acute and faintly amused, reinforcing the facts. Dennison wasn't the pinnacle of Lopez's incursion into the FBI. He was just a subordinate.

Two

The afternoon sun slanted through open French doors, gleaming on cut crystal and silver cutlery as Esther Morell checked the place settings for dinner. Eyeing the lush arrangement of scarlet roses and glossy green leaves in the center of the long table, she paused to straighten a fork. As she continued on through a large, airy sitting room, she glimpsed her ten-year-old daughter, Rina, sitting out on the patio, eyes half-closed and dreamy as she stared at the setting sun, the ever-present easel and paints beside her.

Stepping out onto the patio, Esther paused to ruffle Rina's dark hair and examine the unfinished watercolor. As always, she got lost in the image. She had an analytical mind, a mind that grabbed numbers and chewed them up. Usually she got caught up in financial reports and stock options, occasionally in the purity of Mozart, but when she looked at Rina's paintings something else happened. Her mind stopped and her chest went tight. As adept as she was at grasping concepts, she couldn't understand the ephemeral, ever-changing quality of the way Rina arranged paint on canvas. It simply grabbed her inside.

Somehow, she knew that if she could explain what happened, if she could break down the spectrum of light and turn the transparent drifts of color into an equation, she wouldn't *feel* it. And lately, feeling something—anything—had become increasingly precious. "What are you looking at, honey?"

Rina's finger traced a shape in the air, as if she could see something that Esther, and everyone else, couldn't. "The light."

"Why don't you paint it?"

"Can't."

Esther didn't try to extract a logical explanation. Rina was special, so gifted that sometimes Esther panicked that she wasn't doing enough, providing enough, to feed and stimulate her talent. Cesar had money and he lavished it on his only child, but expensive day school and tutors aside, for the most part Rina remained oddly separate, her focus inward. When she was a toddler, Esther had taken her to a specialist, worried that she might be autistic, but the specialist had put her fears to rest. Gifted children were often misunderstood, and Rina was gifted on more than one level. She was normal, as far as "normal" went; she just had a different way of viewing the world, and a different agenda to most people. The reason she retreated was the acute sensitivity that made her gifted. Parts of her brain were highly developed. In essence, the incoming data could be overwhelming. She could see more, *feel* more, than most people. With time and a more adult perspective, she would adjust more fully to the "normal" world, but in the meantime they should hang on to their seats. Esther's daughter would never be Joe Average.

Rina stretched and straightened, the dreaminess abruptly gone. "You look nice. Red suits you, but you need different earrings. Those long dangly ones with the diamonds."

Esther lifted a brow at the autocratic assessment. Rina might be gifted and a little introverted, but more and more she was being reminded they had a precocious almost-teenager in the house. "I'll tell you what. You go and get changed, *then* we'll discuss earrings. Don't forget we've got guests."

Rina's dark gaze sharpened, reminding Esther of her husband, Cesar: demanding, and with a stubborn, ruthless streak. "I'll eat in my room, thanks."

"Not tonight. Your father wants you at the dinner table."

Which reminded Esther that she needed to check on the kitchen. Carmita was short-staffed tonight and Cesar wanted to make a big impression.

Frowning, she strolled back through the dining room and headed for the kitchen, not for the first time uneasy about the new business partnership Cesar was researching. She'd met Alex Lopez once, very briefly, and she didn't like him. There was nothing logical about her response to Lopez, like the effect Rina's paintings had on her, the emotion had simply been evoked.

But there was something more. It had been nagging at the back of her mind for days. She was certain she had seen Lopez before, and she was equally certain Lopez wasn't his name.

Normally it didn't take her long to track down the reference and figure out what was wrong. Before she'd married Cesar, she'd worked as a consultant for a Swiss international banking conglomerate that dealt with billions of dollars of offshore funds. Her job had entailed investigating business connections and clients, anything that could threaten the bank's reputation. Esther's success at her job came from more than just having a knack with figures. She had a photographic memory. It was a detail that her employers, and Esther, had made sure was kept secret.

It had been more than twelve years since she'd worked in international banking, but she never forgot a number, and she never forgot a face.

The sun had set, but the air was still warm and pleasantly laced with summer scents as their dinner guests filed into the foyer.

Cesar made introductions and Esther moved smoothly into her role as hostess. Lopez was young, definitely Latino, as his name suggested. He was no more than mid-twenties at most, and on the surface he was charming, personable and obviously wealthy. According to Cesar he was also a little on the reclusive side, which Esther had to assume was the reason she hadn't yet been able to track down any information about him.

Lopez's fingers closed briefly on hers, and the uneasiness she'd felt the first time she'd met him grew. Charming he might be, but there was a bite behind the charm, despite his youth. And he didn't like women. The thought dropped into Esther's mind, irrelevant, maybe, but interesting. Every other man in the room responded to her long red dress, the faint hint of cleavage and the diamonds, and no doubt the stereotypical image the media had always projected of her as the glamorous, pampered wife of "Mr. Midas." But Alex Lopez hadn't wanted to touch her. When he'd met her gaze, fleeting as the contact was, his eyes had been flat and opaque.

On the surface he was an all-American male, right down to the Boston accent, handsome except for an overly heavy jaw, but his attitude didn't fit. Idly, she wondered if he was gay, then dismissed the notion. She had no doubt women had a place in his life, but, like everything else, sex would be coldly controlled and only on his terms.

As she greeted the second man, Dennison, the

annoying sense of recognition lingered. She had seen Lopez before. She couldn't put her finger on where or when, but it would come to her.

The third guest was a different matter. As she extended her hand in greeting, a newspaper article popped into her mind. The photographs had been grainy black and whites, the incident, just over twelve years ago, horrific. The article had been part of her research into a client attempting to move an extraordinarily large sum of money.

Esther's breath stopped in her throat, every cell in her body on high alert. She couldn't place Alex Lopez, but she had no problem placing his accountant.

The handclasp was brief, but even so her stomach turned, and for a moment she wondered if she was going to throw up. She remembered the village in Colombia—Los Mendez. Families casually machine-gunned; a baby left crying in the mud.

The accountant might call himself Mike Vitali, but his *real* name was Miguel Perez, one of a coterie of men surrounding Colombian drug lord and all-round cold-blooded murderer, Marco Chavez. It had been Chavez who had been attempting to move the funds. They had turned him down. An investigation by Interpol wasn't the best credential in the international banking community.

Cesar threw her an annoyed glance. "Are you all right?"

"Fine." Esther forced a smile. Touching Perez had been like dipping her hand into a sewer. She needed to wash, and she needed to get him—all of them—out of her house. But she couldn't afford the simple luxury of ejecting them; she would have to tread carefully. Perez was a butcher. If he suspected that she knew who he was, she would place them all in jeopardy. "I just felt dizzy for a second."

She sent Cesar a hard stare, indicating she needed to talk with him *now,* in private.

His brows shot up as he misinterpreted her expression, and for a moment the distance that had grown between them over the past few months dissolved and she caught a glimpse of the "old" Cesar, the arrogant financial wizard who had swept her off her feet. The only time in her life she had been dizzy had been when she was pregnant, but they were both well aware it couldn't be that. Lately, they had been either too preoccupied or too busy for even casual conversation, let alone sex.

They had problems. Big problems. Over the past year almost everything they had touched had fallen through. Their net worth had more than halved. In the past two months their position had worsened, unbelievably, to the point that they now faced losing everything. Esther had abandoned her own projects and had been working overtime, researching the labyrinthine twists and turns of the contracts Cesar had signed in an effort to stave off a massive loss on a development that had collapsed when a major investor had withdrawn. Cesar had gambled heavily on the failed Ellis Street project—they both had, throwing all of their resources behind the mall complex in a bid to recoup their losses. He should have succeeded; she had checked the deal herself. Incredibly, he had lost. Now they were facing the imminent failure of a second project. Even liquidating her own considerable assets, they were so close to bankruptcy she could feel the chill at her back.

Drinks were stilted. Cesar was unruffled, always the elegant host. Esther forced a smile and circulated with canapés, trying to isolate Cesar, but he continued to ignore her signals.

Frustrated by Cesar's stubborn refusal to wangle a few seconds alone with her, Esther deliberately spilled wine on his sleeve. Seconds later, in the privacy of a downstairs powder room, she grabbed a bunch of tissues and sponged the wine. "Do you have any idea who Vitali is?"

"Lopez's accountant."

Jaw tight, she filled him in on Vitali's real name and history. Cesar went pale, but something about his expression was just a little too wooden. "Please don't tell me you knew that already."

His gaze flashed. "Of course I didn't. I didn't pay him much attention—he's Lopez's accountant. I've met him briefly, maybe twice."

She tossed the tissues in the trash can. "After tonight, cut ties. Don't get involved with any of them, including Lopez."

Cesar's expression was evasive. "There's a problem. Remember the Pembroke Project?"

How could she forget? It was the second of their major property developments that was threatening to pancake. If that went down, they would go with it.

"Lopez wants in on the deal."

"Does he know about Ellis Street?"

"He knows. Now do you understand my position? I can make Lopez get rid of Perez, but *not right now.*"

Not if there was a chance of salvaging Pembroke. Unpalatable as it was, Esther had to back down. If either she or Cesar made an issue of Perez now, Lopez might pull out of the project altogether. Esther didn't like the idea of partnership with Lopez—the man was a snake—but in this instance Cesar was right. They were fighting for survival.

Dinner proceeded at an agonizingly slow pace. Carmita was harried because not one, but two of the kitchen hands she had employed for the night hadn't turned up. Esther, unable to stomach small talk, helped Carmita serve and clear.

As she moved smoothly from table to kitchen, serving first an appetizer then the soup, she kept a weather eye on Rina, who had taken one look at the three visitors and retreated like a turtle withdrawing into its shell. Her baby might be quiet and a little dreamy, but the girl had instincts.

For the past half hour Rina had eaten what was placed in front of her and answered when spoken to. Other than the usual pleasantries, no one had paid her any attention, for which Esther was relieved. She didn't like the ability Rina had to shut herself off at will, but at the same time, she didn't want any of their guests to find anything at all interesting about her child—especially not Perez.

Every time she looked at his dark, narrow face, she thought about the dead children and her stomach turned. Accountant he might be, but he had been in Los Mendez when almost an entire village had been gunned down, allegedly on Chavez's orders. The only survivors had been villagers who had been able to escape into the jungle. Horror-stricken by the attack, they had provided eyewitness reports, but, despite that testimony, Chavez hadn't been indicted. Perez and a number of other members of the cartel had disappeared, escaping certain jail terms, but Chavez had remained in Colombia. According to a Reuters report, his influence within the government and more important, the military, had made him untouchable.

After the formality of the dining room, the kitchen was alive with heat and sound. Steam erupted from a pot as a lid was lifted and dishes clattered as bowls of vegetables and salads were loaded onto a serving trolley.

Dumping a tray of dirty dishes onto the kitchen counter, Esther stepped outside, took a deep breath and let it out slowly. It wasn't often that she envied Carmita the hustle and bustle of her job, but tonight she did. From the second she'd laid eyes on Perez she'd been a bundle of nerves. Her stomach felt tight, she had barely been able to eat, even her skin felt tense. She'd taken every excuse to leave the table and distance herself from him, but the few minutes she'd managed weren't enough.

Stepping farther into the garden, she breathed in the rich scent of gardenias and willed herself to relax, her gaze automatically drawn to the limpid surface of the lit pool.

Lifting her hair off the back of her neck so the air could cool her skin, she strolled closer to the pool, gaze drifting over jardinieres of trailing ivy and the glossy leaves of palms. On impulse, she slipped off her shoes, dragged the clinging silk jersey of her dress around her thighs and lowered herself to the tiled edge of the pool. As her feet slid into the water, a small shudder went through her. The water was tepid, barely cooler than the surface of her skin, but it was enough to provide relief from the heat and give her a few moments to assess exactly what was going on between Cesar and Lopez.

Cesar had said the dinner was simply a social "warm-up" while he and Lopez assessed their compatibility as business partners, but nothing about the evening felt warm. Lopez wasn't going out of his way to charm anyone, and Cesar wasn't himself. If she didn't know better she would think—

A shadow flickered, jerking her head around. Esther frowned, more at her own jumpiness than the fact that some small animal or a bird might have taken up residence in the thick grove of palms. The movement had been at the periphery of her vision.

It was possible it had been a shadow generated by someone in the house moving in front of a lamp, but with everyone seated in the dining room, that left the sitting room—the only lighted room that faced the patio—empty. Unpalatable as it was, the movement had more than likely been made by a rat. They loved the thick subtropical undergrowth. Carmita's husband, Tomas, was forever setting traps.

The clash of a dropped pan and the sharp edge of Carmita's voice broke the balmy quiet. Shaking off her tension and the growing anger that, desperate or not, Cesar had allowed a man like Perez into their family home, Esther swung her feet out of the water and straightened, her shoes dangling from her fingers.

The branch of a magnolia quivered. She frowned. The quivering branch was some distance from the first disturbance. The obvious answer to the small movement was the breeze. But there was no breeze.

Eyes unblinking, she probed the shadows, but the glow from the pool destroyed her night vision. She couldn't make out much more than the outlines of shrubs and trees.

A further flickering movement sent her heart slamming hard against the wall of her chest.

The breath drained from her lungs when she realized the movement was a leaf dropping into the pool. For long moments she stared at the leaf where it floated, and the fine shimmer of concentric circles forming around it.

Nothing could have demonstrated more clearly

that she was becoming paranoid. The estate was security-fenced and monitored twenty-four hours a day. If any of the alarms had been breached, either Tomas or Jorge, Tomas and Carmita's son, who lived with his parents in a cottage on the estate, would have rung through to the house.

With disgust she strode back into the kitchen just as the main course trolley was finally wheeled through to the dining room.

Within an hour dessert was cleared and Carmita was circulating with the coffeepot and a dish of her homemade chocolates.

Cesar refused coffee, instead refilling his wineglass. Esther noticed he was drinking heavily and talking too much, which wasn't usual. Normally he kept a clear head when they entertained because he was well aware that his strength lay in playing stocks and his ability to make a failing business soar, not in dealing with people. That was where Esther's expertise was invaluable. Cesar weeded out the bad risks; she weeded out the bad people.

Rina, who must have sneaked her Walkman to the table while Esther was out of the room, despite the fact that she was expressly forbidden to do so, abandoned listening to music, attracted by the silver dish of chocolates. Carmita pushed the dish into Rina's hands and urged her to take them around the table. Normally, Esther would have been more than happy for Rina to lend a hand, but on this occasion she wished Carmita had stuck to etiquette.

As Rina drifted past with the dish, Cesar's arm curled around her waist, halting her. Rina stiffened, clearly not in the mood for a public display of affection. Cesar, usually more sensitive to his daughter's moods, refused to take the hint, and for the first time Esther realized what was behind Cesar's uncharacteristic behavior: he was afraid.

She'd been so preoccupied with her own perceptions, her own *knowledge*, she hadn't stopped to think about Cesar's state of mind. Usually, the bigger the monetary challenge, the more he relished it. He was like a general in battle, every deal a campaign to build his empire ever larger. She had always admired his courage and his audacity. Normally his instincts were good and, more important, he was *lucky*. Or, he had been.

Cesar's smile widened, a sharp edge to the grin. "C'mon, honey, show our guests what you can really do."

Esther's smile slipped as the focus turned on Rina.

Suppressing the urge to hustle her daughter from the room, she pushed her chair back, rose to her feet and began gathering dishes. "Mr. Lopez and his friends aren't interested in school tricks."

Cesar frowned at the clatter of plates. "A photographic memory isn't a school trick."

Esther ignored him as she moved around the table, deliberately adding a swing to her hips. The impulse to preserve her child was knee-jerk and primitive. Perez made her skin crawl, Lopez didn't make her feel much better and Dennison had about as much charm as a piranha. She didn't want any of these men looking at Rina or focusing on her. She didn't want any of them remembering one thing about her daughter.

Cesar produced a sheet of paper and a pen and began writing figures in bold print. "Here, honey, you get five seconds to look."

Rina stiffened. Her gaze automatically connected with Esther's, the communication clear. She had stopped enjoying performing in public at age five and she was in no mood to start again now.

Grimly, Esther jerked her head in assent, indicating Rina should go along with her father. As much as she wanted to get her daughter out of the room and away from Perez, she would have to wait another few minutes. Things were tense enough. If Rina dug her heels in there would be a scene, and after the reversals of the past few weeks, a dinner table brawl with his daughter was the last thing Cesar needed.

Her expression set, Rina deposited the dish of chocolates on the table and glanced at the sheet her father handed her. Esther's stomach tightened as she watched her daughter do what had always come naturally to them both. From as early as she could remember, Esther had had a photographic memory. As long as the material was visual the process was simple; she told her mind to remember, then she let it. If she interfered with the process and concentrated on one part of an image or one number, that was all she remembered, but if she distanced herself and let her gaze slide down the page she had total recall. It was a weird process that didn't make "normal" sense, but it worked.

When Rina was finished, Cesar handed the sheet to Lopez. Something about Alex Lopez made her skin crawl, but he was fascinating in an odd way. All through dinner she'd tried to figure out exactly what it was that was wrong about him. Dennison was dull, more interested in slicing up his food than making conversation. Perez was quick and darting, like a snake. In comparison to everyone else at the table, Lopez was still. He didn't move or gesture much, and he didn't bother trying to promote the fiction that he was having a good time.

Rina began repeating the numbers in sequence, her voice flat. When she was finished Lopez placed the sheet of handwritten numbers on the table, his eyes on Rina. "One hundred percent accuracy. An interesting talent." Lopez's gaze was still fixed on Rina. "Where does she get that from?"

"Her father." Esther cut Cesar off with a cold, warning glance. "Cesar's always been dynamite with figures."

"That's not news," Perez inserted smoothly. "He didn't get the nickname 'Mr. Midas' for nothing. We're hoping the golden touch will rub off on us."

Dennison laughed as if Perez had said something hilarious and Lopez's gaze swiveled. He muttered a sharp comment, cutting off Dennison's mirth. Esther noticed Lopez's accent had slipped. Even more interesting. Something had finally gotten under his skin and he'd revealed some emotion and the fact that, *surprise, surprise,* Boston wasn't his natural home.

Esther forced another tight smile as she smoothly redirected the conversation back into a general discussion about the economy and away from Rina. Her daughter had fitted the headphones of her Walkman back over her ears and was staring back at Lopez with a fixed, unblinking gaze.

Rina was so mature in her outlook and so exceptional in her talents that sometimes Esther forgot she was still a ten-year-old kid. Cesar hadn't noticed what she was doing yet, because she was sitting right next to him, but it wouldn't be long before he realized his daughter had targeted Lopez for eyeball extinction.

As much as Lopez deserved it, someone had to call her off. Smothering a grin, Esther walked around the table and shook Rina's arm. There was no point trying to catch her eye, because when Rina identified a victim she locked on like a heat-seeking missile. She never voluntarily gave up on a stare until her victim was a quivering jelly. "Bedtime."

Rina didn't shift her stare. "Another five minutes would be good."

Which meant she had already gained the ascendancy, now she wanted the victory lap. "Uh-uh. You're finished for the night."

With a shrug, Rina abandoned the stare and gracefully exited her place at the table. "It's okay." She sent Esther a sly wink. "My work is done."

Making her excuses and sending Cesar a hard glance, Esther hustled Rina out of the room and watched with an eagle eye as she got settled for bed, allowing Rina to spin out the process in the hope that Cesar would get the hint and make moves to get rid of their guests. When she returned to the table, the evening was finally winding up. Cesar had had too much to drink and so had Dennison, but she couldn't help noticing that Lopez and Perez were both stone-cold sober.

Seeing them to the door, she watched as they climbed into a low, sleek Cadillac. A second vehicle, a gleaming black Chevrolet truck with tinted windows, glided behind the Cadillac as it nosed through the security gates, and she tensed. She had been aware they had a driver, because she had suggested he eat in the kitchen if he was hungry, but not that there had been a second vehicle. The only possible reason for a second vehicle was security, which meant Lopez had had additional men loose on the property that she hadn't known about.

Suddenly the interlude in the garden began to make sense. There *had* been someone there, maybe more than one. Cesar must have been aware of their presence, because otherwise Jorge and Tomas would never have admitted the second vehicle.

As the gate closed behind the truck, Esther turned on Cesar. She didn't care if they did go bankrupt. "Finish with them."

It wasn't often she demanded, but in this case it was too strong a reaction to deny. She was itching to go to the police, but she was going to have to wait until Cesar got clear. Perez was a wanted man, but as much as she needed to see him behind bars, she wouldn't allow Cesar to be dragged into the investigation or the media storm that would follow when Perez was picked up.

"I can't—not yet."

"Why not?"

"I've already made arrangements for Lopez to look at the project. He's a new player in the market and he's got cash. We can't afford to throw away the opportunity." He indicated for her to precede him into the house, the gesture normal and courteous, but the fact that he was avoiding her gaze made Esther's stomach plunge.

She stepped into the foyer, her heels rapping on the marble floor. "What have you signed?"

His gaze was rapier sharp, a glimpse of the old, imperious Cesar. "Relax. Like I told you, I'm just researching options. Lopez has got some heavy-duty connections."

"I don't like Lopez, and Perez is a wanted criminal."

He locked the front door and set the alarm. "Ease off, honey. Like I said, Perez can go, just not yet."

She watched as Cesar crossed the foyer, heading for the stairs, his gait very slightly unsteady. "Promise me you'll get out of whatever it is you've gotten involved with."

She was like a terrier with a bone, but she couldn't let it go. It was panic, pure and simple. Her stomach was tight and her eyes were burning. She was on the verge of crying and that was something she hadn't done in years. Something was happening that she couldn't control and she needed to find out exactly what had gone wrong.

Business—money—had always been an exciting game, one that she and Cesar were very good at. They took risks and lived like kings. That was part of the excitement and the reward of what they did, but in no way did they break the law. She didn't tolerate underhanded business ethics, and she wouldn't tolerate involvement with criminals. With everything they did, there was a moral line between greed and good business practice, and Esther believed in staying on the right side of that line. She'd seen too much ugliness and too much dirty dealing to ever want to join those ranks. Naive or not, she believed that if she behaved with integrity she would always prosper. *They* would always prosper.

Until tonight, she was certain Cesar had shared that view. With a sudden chill, she wondered if that was what had gone wrong. Cesar had gotten tied up with criminals and their luck had dissolved.

She shook off the thought, which was patently ridiculous. Cesar had said he wasn't committed. There would be logical answers as to why so many of their ventures had failed, one after the other. Lately, she'd been working overtime to find the key to the failures and a definite pattern was emerging, but she needed more time to find her way through the paper companies and isolate exactly who it was sabotaging the deals.

"Promise me, Cesar. These people are dangerous." Images from the newspaper article flickered through her mind. "Perez was tied in with Marco Chavez."

Just speaking the name aloud made her feel sick. For a moment she thought Cesar was on the verge of telling her something, then the soft burr of the phone broke the moment.

Esther watched as he changed direction and strode into the office to take the call. She listened long enough to ascertain that this was "normal" business, not Lopez, before she strolled through the house and back out into the garden.

The kitchen was darkened, and the patio and the pool area were quiet now. Only the hum of the pool filter disturbed the peace. The leaf was still floating near the center of the pool. Directing her gaze upward, she checked the nearest trees, most of which were palms or subtropicals with large, fleshy leaves, nothing like the small, square leaf in the pool.

Strolling around to the far side of the pool, where

a small shed was concealed behind a screen of plant-ings, she located one of the pool scoops. Seconds later, she examined the "leaf," which wasn't a leaf at all, but the torn-off cover of a small book of matches emblazoned with the name of a bar on Grant Avenue.

A chill roughened the surface of her skin. She had watched as it had landed in the water. Someone *had* been there, and they had enjoyed playing a cat-and-mouse game with her.

Three

An hour later, Esther eased out of bed. Cesar was sound asleep, his breathing heavier than usual, courtesy of the amount of alcohol he'd sunk during the evening. Normally, she hated it when Cesar drank, but tonight his comatose state provided her with the opportunity she needed.

Slipping on a silk wrap, she padded through the house and downstairs to the office.

The fact that Cesar had failed to advise her that Lopez had personnel loose on their property kept playing through her mind. Normally any extras were invited into the kitchen or the staff lounge, where they could have a meal and watch television if they wanted, and where Jorge and Tomas could keep an eye on them. Security was important. There were priceless works of art in the house, not to mention her jewelry, and they had Rina's safety to consider. The risk of kidnapping wasn't high, but it was always there.

She began to search Cesar's office, carefully leafing through files and replacing them. An unfruitful hour later she sat down at the computer and booted it up, but was stymied when she was denied access. Cesar had changed his password and hadn't advised her. It was possible he had just done it that day and had forgotten to tell her, but Esther didn't think so. Cesar hated computers with passion. Normally, he got her to change his password and load any new programs. She had her own separate office and her own computer, but she had always had unlimited access to Cesar's.

Feverishly, she searched the desk drawers, examining notepads and loose papers, just in case he had written the password down. On impulse, she searched the trash. Halfway down the basket she hit gold, a crumpled piece of notepaper with the word *chameleon* written across it in bold print. Holding her breath, she typed in the word. A split second later she had access to Cesar's directory.

The alarm bells that had been ringing ever since Cesar had invited Lopez to dinner sounded even louder as she opened a file labeled "Lopez" and began to read.

Together, with her sharp logistical mind and photographic memory and Cesar's genius for business, she and Cesar had made a great team. *But not anymore.* He wasn't researching a possible business venture with Lopez; he was already involved.

Shutting the computer down, she sat back in the chair and stared at the blank monitor. She needed to sleep, but now she doubted that she would. Cesar had lied about his involvement with Lopez and hidden the facts from her. He had already signed a deal to salvage the Pembroke project.

Financially they were safe, which meant Cesar had also lied about that this evening, and the lie was unforgivable. He knew how worried she was about their financial position and the fact that a predator had targeted them. If he had made a deal he should have told her; it was her neck on the line as well as his.

The sheer scale of Cesar's deception made her stomach churn. She was beginning to have a horrible feeling about who Lopez actually was, but that research would have to wait until the morning. She still had contacts in international banking, but if Lopez was who she suspected he was, all she would need was an hour in a library.

Hidden in a corner of the San Francisco main library, Esther scrolled the microfilm until she found the newspaper article about Perez that she had researched more than a decade ago. The article didn't contribute much more to her knowledge, but it provided her with a definite date to work from and a list of names. When she'd scrolled through to the end of the reel, searching for related articles, she selected another film and threaded it into the machine. An hour and three more reels later she found what she was looking for. A rare photo of Marco Chavez filled the screen. She skimmed the brief article and the suspicion that had kept her awake all night coalesced into reality. The reason she hadn't been able to remember where she had seen Alex Lopez was easy—she *hadn't* ever seen him before, but she had seen his father. Alex's name wasn't Lopez; it was *Chavez.*

Minutes later another article followed and Esther's skin went cold, the chill sinking deep as she read. At first she thought it was a recap of the Los Mendez story. She checked the date, in case the newspaper had been incorrectly archived, but the article was correctly placed. Less than three weeks after the initial massacre in Los Mendez, men, women, children—*babies*—had been slaughtered indiscriminately; lined up and shot. The pattern had been repeated in three villages all along the Guaviare River, an isolated region inland from Bogotá. Four villages decimated. Then, abruptly, the killing had stopped.

Mind working feverishly, Esther began to search for any other news reports from Colombia within that period. It didn't take long. The killings had stopped the same day a murderer had been released from prison, pardoned in recognition of the prisoner's juvenile status and the significant charitable contributions his father had made in donating a hospital to the poorest region of the country. The name of the prisoner was Alejandro Chavez.

Esther stared at the grainy black and whites that accompanied the story, one a standard mug shot, another of Alex handcuffed as he was taken into custody under armed guard. She noted the small tattoo visible on the back of his right hand and her blood ran cold. Alejandro Chavez had been a baby-faced twelve-year-old when he had been jailed for the murder of his own bodyguard.

Alex Lopez was the only son of Marco Chavez, the head of Colombia's paramount drug cartel. Marco was a clever, astute businessman, his operation smooth by any standards and fronted by a raft of legitimate business enterprises. Its tendrils reached into the highest echelons of South American government. Normally, the powerful and influential Chavez family never made the front pages of any paper unless it was for a charitable donation—until Alejandro Chavez had removed his bodyguard's gun from his shoulder holster and shot him at point-blank range in a busy mall.

Alex Lopez didn't dislike women; he didn't like humanity, period. The emptiness she had seen in his eyes was utter amorality.

An hour later, Esther picked Rina up from school. When she reached home, Cesar wasn't there, but she hadn't expected him to be. Normally, he spent the day working from his downtown office. Six o'clock, when Cesar normally returned home, came and went. Carmita served dinner. Afterward Esther helped Rina with her homework and saw her to bed, then went to the sitting room to wait. Cesar didn't walk in until after ten. His lateness was as uncharacteristic as his bad manners in not phoning to say he wouldn't be home for dinner, but Esther no longer expected normality.

Stomach tight, she followed him into the office, watching as he set his briefcase down on his desk and removed his jacket. "I know about the Pembroke deal, and I know about Lopez."

He went still, his expression oddly blank, and she had to wonder if he'd been drinking again.

"It's too late. I've accepted the deal. The money's in the bank."

"What money?" She hadn't seen anything on the computer file that indicated that cash had changed hands.

Cesar shrugged. "It's not directly connected with the deal. It's his money. I just facilitated the transfer."

Panic surged. Esther flipped the catch on his briefcase and began to search. The implications made her blood run cold. Money laundering, fraud, possibly even treason. She hadn't checked the finer points of the law, but she was certain that helping a foreign drug cartel establish an organized-crime syndicate on United States soil was a treasonable offence.

When she didn't find anything in the briefcase, she started on the desk, just in case he'd slipped something in the drawers since she'd searched last night. She knew Cesar, or thought she had. He was meticulous about keeping records; the paperwork had to be somewhere. "Where is it?"

Cesar shoved papers back into his briefcase, his face flushed. She could smell the alcohol now, which accounted for his passivity. He had moved the money, then anesthetized himself.

And what better financial pipeline for the Chavez cartel to utilize than the Morell Group? On the surface Cesar was solid gold, a business prodigy with the Midas touch. Until recently his assets had rivaled those of some of the most powerful men in the States. She yanked open a drawer.

He slammed it closed. "Don't bother looking, there's nothing here."

"Liar." Whatever he had done, he wouldn't be stupid enough to store the records in his office downtown. Carmita had said he'd been home briefly at lunchtime. He would have hidden the papers then.

She began opening drawers that held hanging files. Not bothering with the contents, she searched instead between the files. She hadn't thought to do that last night. Cesar had a good brain, usually— he was analytical with just the right amount of greed and ego to ensure success—but his mind wasn't serpentine. If she hadn't been so panicked, she would have thought about searching between the files last night.

She pulled the final drawer open. Her fingers walked through the files. Nothing.

Her temper erupted. With a jerk, she hauled the drawer off its runners and let it fall to the floor. A neat manila folder was stored at the base of the cabinet.

Cesar grabbed, but he wasn't fast enough. Papers scattered, numbers leapt at Esther, the configuration as familiar to her as her own name. An account number in the Cayman Islands. Her gaze flowed down the page and stopped, the chill congealed into ice.

Not seven figures. *Eleven.*

Her heart stopped in her chest. More than thirteen *billion* dollars.

Numbly, she transferred her gaze to Cesar. *"What have you done?"*

The blow was short and vicious, an openhanded slap that caught her on the side of the jaw. She staggered back, almost tripping over the drawer she had pulled out of the filing cabinet. Her hand shot out, connected with solid wood, clutched at the edge of the desk to keep herself from falling. Sucking in a breath, she wiped blood from her mouth and waited until the room stabilized. It was the first time Cesar had so much as raised a hand to her, but Esther barely registered the blow.

They were dead.

She knew it as surely as she knew her marriage to Cesar was over.

Lopez—*Chavez*—was using them. They were his doorway into the States. He was the predator who had systematically ruined them. He had set them up with breathtaking brilliance, his plays elaborate and perfectly executed, turning them into puppets. When he no longer needed them, he would kill them: *all of them.*

Fiercely, she stared at Cesar, no longer seeing the brilliant man she'd fallen in love with and married, but the man who was responsible for putting her baby in danger. She had been thirty-four when she had given birth to Rina. She had lived life to the full, but never more so than that first moment she had held her own child in her arms. The thought of all that bright promise, of Rina's quirky intellect, the fun and the dreaminess being snuffed out, was wrenching.

She couldn't allow it.

With everything that was in her, she would stop that process, but she was going to need help. Lopez had gone too far, done too much; she was out of her depth.

Cesar's hand closed on her wrist. She wrenched free.

Something cold and feral flashed in his gaze, and Esther fought down another surge of panic. It was tempting to ignore Cesar, but she couldn't forget that he had made this deal. He had climbed into bed with the Chavez cartel, and if anything was precious to Cesar, it had always been his own skin. His quick instincts and visceral reactions had made for good business decisions, but right now she was in almost as much danger from him as she was from Lopez.

She clenched her jaw as she rubbed at her wrist, the words she wanted to spit locked at the back of her throat. She would stop this madness, and if she had to lie through her teeth to do it, then that was what she would do. "Don't worry, I'm not going to do anything. I can't, it's too late."

"Okay." Some of the feral tension abated. He let out a breath, dug in his pocket and handed her a white linen handkerchief. "I know it doesn't look good. It's not what I planned, but I'm handling it." He turned away. "If I hadn't signed with Lopez, we would have been out on the street within a week."

Esther blotted blood from her mouth as he shuffled papers and slipped them back into the manila folder.

Fool. Lopez was the one who had put them there.

Four

Esther locked the door of her office and crossed the room, blind to the morning sun flooding through the French doors and gleaming off the rich hardwood floors. Cesar had finally left for work, an hour later than he usually did, and Tomas had just pulled out of the drive with Rina in the passenger seat. Esther had asked Tomas to take Rina to school on the pretext that she was feeling unwell after slipping on the steps of the pool, the piece of fiction Cesar had devised to explain her split lip and bruised jaw. She had iced her jaw before going to bed, and a few minutes spent applying makeup this morning had hidden most of the damage.

Bending, she opened the doors of an exquisite Louis XV bureau. Reaching inside, she pressed on a section of paneling and a secret drawer at the side of the bureau slid open.

The address book in the drawer wasn't secret—Cesar knew about it—but it was sensitive and entirely her business. With the media's interest in Cesar, and now her, it was expedient for the stability of their business that certain details of her past were never revealed to the press, and one relationship in particular.

The book in hand, she walked to the French doors and stared in the direction of the garage, which was partially hidden from her view by a screen of shrubs and palms. Cesar had said he would be out all day, but she didn't trust that he wouldn't turn up unexpectedly to check on her.

The previous evening she had convinced him that she was prepared to go along with his partnership with Lopez. By the time she had gone to bed they had reached a fragile accord, but she had no illusions that would last. Cesar had promised to give her breathing space to allow her to "adjust." The offer had made her skin crawl and she had finally given in to the fact that Cesar was no longer operating in a normal way.

Despite his formidable business talents, Cesar couldn't work out an equation that to Esther was obvious. She and Lopez existed on different sides of a very stark line; it was a truth that had been acknowledged on a subtle level the first time they had met and that had been reinforced at her dinner table. Lopez could control Cesar—to the extent that he had entrusted him with the bank transfer—but if he didn't know it already, he would soon know from his research into her background that he would never be able to control her. The second Lopez knew she had unmasked him, it was game over. By her calculations she had bought herself a day, maybe two, three at the most.

When she was satisfied that Cesar had gone, she took a seat behind her desk and flipped through the address book until she found the entry she wanted. It wasn't the telephone number she was searching for, it was the small color snapshot that slid out from between the pages. Heart pounding at the step she was about to take, she studied the lean, tanned features of a man she had once known very well. As it had turned out, far better than she had ever known Cesar.

Xavier le Clerc was an intellectual, a frighteningly clever man who would have been at the very top of his field in international banking…if he had chosen to stay within the bounds of the law. When he had transgressed more than a decade ago, he hadn't done it by half measures. A skilled trader of stocks and shares, in a two-pronged assault he had engineered the financial collapse of the Swiss bank that had employed him—a bank he claimed had, in connivance with a former banker and SS officer, illegally transferred money out of the accounts of Jews who had been sent to the death camps.

Hours after the financial disaster had hit the front pages of European newspapers, it had been discovered that an inordinate proportion of the cash and art treasures stored in the bank's vaults by alleged Nazi war criminals had also been stolen.

Xavier's actions had caused a furore. A Jew himself, he had been labeled a thief *extraordinaire,* a Nazi hunter and a revolutionist. Despite the magnitude of what he had done, his crimes had been almost universally applauded, his sense of justice viewed as biblical. Not exactly an eye for an eye, a tooth for a tooth, but close enough.

Esther had dated him a few times when she'd worked in Bern. The hours she had spent with Xavier had been challenging and addictive. She had come close to falling in love with him, but when his name had appeared on her list of people to investigate, she had immediately cut all ties. Shortly after the scandal had erupted, her contract had finished and she had returned to the States.

She didn't know where Xavier lived now. He had gone to ground years ago and, to her knowledge, had never surfaced, but she could still remember the address of his sister in Bern.

Sliding the snapshot back into the address book, she put a call through to the number, not expecting to connect with Eva le Clerc after all these years. When the woman who answered the call confirmed in French that she was Xavier's sister, Esther's stomach contracted. It was the point of no return.

Despite the fact that Eva remembered her, she was abrupt and dismissive. "You're wasting your time. I don't know where he is. No one does."

Esther stopped her before she could hang up. "Just tell him I need to talk to him. Urgently."

There was a bleak silence. "He won't call you."

"Just tell him. Please."

It was close to three-thirty in the afternoon when the phone finally rang. Tomas, who was picking Rina up from school, was due to arrive home any second. Esther picked up the receiver. A premonition prickled along her spine as she waited for the caller to speak.

The voice was male, the French rapid. *"A qui appartient l'argent que nous allons valer?"*

Whose money are we stealing?

That was Xavier, sharp as a tack. Cut to the chase with no preliminaries. He had always been too clever for everyone, including her. It had taken her hours of frantic thought and discarded plans before she had finally arrived at that particular option: get Rina to safety, steal Lopez's money, then go to the police. That way she would cut Lopez off at the knees, and she would have the money as a bargaining chip if anything went wrong. She had tossed up going to the police straight off, but if she did that Lopez would have time to get away, and she couldn't discount the fact that he could have law-enforcement people on his payroll. "You don't have to know who we're stealing from yet."

"I'll find out."

That was true enough. Once the process was initiated, Xavier would be in control and she would merely be a passenger. The thought made her mouth go dry and her heart pump so hard that for a moment she couldn't breathe. Xavier would have her cold. He could steal the money himself or expose her.

Either way, she reminded herself, it didn't matter. All she was doing was improving her and Rina's odds of physical survival. Lopez was a killer, le Clerc was a thief who lived by his own code; the choice was literally the lesser of two evils. "Okay. The name he uses is Alex Lopez. His real name is Alejandro Chavez. He's the only son of Marco Chavez, and he's banking with RCS. I have an account number, and not much else."

"Chavez. You do like to walk on the wild side."

"Not by choice."

"If it's not your choice then it must be Cesar's." There was a brief silence. "You should never have married him."

For a split second the knowledge of what could have been, and almost *had* been, hung between them, and with it an unexpected cocktail of emotions she thought she had dealt with years ago. Her options had been cut by Xavier's choices. He had chosen his path; she had chosen hers. As it turned out, they had both ended up in exactly the same place: on the wrong side of the law. "Will you help me?" Instinctively, she used the personal plea, not one that included Cesar.

There was a pause. She could hear the faint rhythm of his breathing and somewhere farther away the cry of gulls, which meant he lived close to the sea. That fitted with what she remembered about him. Xavier had come from a well-heeled family. His father had been a banker. He had always liked the good things in life, particularly fine art and yachts.

"I'll think it over. If I decide to take the job, I'll be in touch."

"Wait. I need to—" The phone clicked in her ear, followed by the sharp sound of the dial tone.

Hand shaking, Esther put the receiver back in its cradle. She had no idea where Xavier had been calling from. He could be anywhere in the Mediterranean, or even South America. He could be sitting in the Florida Keys or out in San Francisco Bay.

He would be in touch with her.

Her heart was pounding again, her stomach tight. She had to calm down. If Xavier didn't want the job, he would have said so. The fact that he had contacted her at all and was now taking the time to think over her proposition meant he *was* considering helping her.

Despite needing his help, hooking up with Xavier in any capacity carried almost as much risk as dealing with Lopez. She had worked with him, dated him, then investigated him. She assumed that he had been attracted to her all those years ago. She also had to consider that he had known all along what her bank had employed her to do and that his interest had been a way of getting an inside track on any investigation.

By the time she had reported the anomalies it had been too late, the damage had been done. Still, she couldn't help thinking that if Xavier had a hankering for revenge, now would be the perfect time to exact it.

An hour later the phone rang again.

"I'll take the job, but I'm going to need help from you. RCS isn't top-of-the-line, but they do have dual controls, which means I'm going to have to bring someone else on board."

Esther's stomach sank. Most banks operated on a dual-controls system, where one person instigated the transaction, and another authorized and confirmed it. There was also the problem of transferring the funds out of one bank and into another. That transaction would have to go through a clearing bank, which would require more signatures. "Can you do it?"

"At a cost."

Esther went still inside. He couldn't have any idea of the enormity of the sum Lopez had in the bank. Then again, if he already had a contact in RCS, maybe he did. The thought was sobering. Despite the fact that Xavier was a thief, she hadn't expected his motivation to be greed. "What kind of guarantee do I have that you won't steal it all?"

"You don't have any."

Her ace in the hole was that she didn't care if he did take the money. Esther had no interest in it other than removing it from Lopez in order to break his hold over Cesar and shatter his power base. Once she and Rina were safely in hiding, she intended handing the money over to the authorities.

"Relax," he said smoothly. "It's information I want, not the money."

She frowned. "About Lopez?"

"And some of the interesting people he and his father do business with."

Her fingers tightened on the receiver. "Whatever you're up to, it can't impact on this. I have a daughter to protect."

"Don't worry, my interest in Lopez is a separate issue. We steal the money, you and your daughter get to safety. Then I get what I want."

The flatness of the statement sent a small shiver down her spine. He made it sound cut and dried, as if the theft itself was just a detail, when the mere thought of what they had to do made her break out in a cold sweat.

"If we're going to succeed, I'm going to need you to use that remarkable talent of yours."

Xavier required information. However, obtaining computer passwords and access codes to Lopez's accounts was as likely to land her in jail as stealing the money.

Redan Capey Securities wasn't a bank she had ever worked for, but she knew of it. RCS traded in what she liked to call "the banking twilight zone." Their rates were cutthroat and they weren't too choosy about their clientele. Based in the Cayman Islands, they ignored the regulatory procedures in place in Europe and the United States and made their own rules, practicing a policy of nondisclosure, which made them a big favorite with clients who had something to hide.

When she checked with a contact in the business, she discovered that over the last decade RCS had expanded, taking on a more respectable facade. They had branches in London, New York, Florida and, *surprise, surprise,* San Francisco. Although, the fact that RCS had a branch in San Francisco shouldn't have been unexpected. It made sense that Lopez would choose a bank—and a banker—that was physically within reach.

The increasing respectability of RCS created difficulties, because that meant stiffer controls, but there was one ray of hope. An ex-colleague worked there. As advantages went, it wasn't much, because Esther had never been particularly friendly with Dana Jones, but it was going to have to be enough.

The next morning, she dropped Rina off at school, drove home and dressed with care, applying makeup to minimize the split in her lip. Half an hour later, she parked her car just off California Street in the financial district and walked the block to the RCS building.

The bank itself was surprisingly spacious, with a large reception area for clients. The receptionist rang through to Dana's office, then indicated that Esther take a seat.

What she had to do made her mouth go dry. If RCS practiced conventional banking routines, the passwords and access codes would be changed regularly, perhaps even daily. As efficient as Dana had been when they had worked together in Bern, she had never been able to keep track of the numbers. It was an illegal practice, but Dana used to write the codes down on the back of a business card and slip the card under her keyboard for easy reference.

Her plan was almost ridiculously simple—get into Dana's office and get a look at the codes—but the number of things that could go wrong were legion. First off, Dana might direct her to an anonymous interview room instead of her office. Secondly, even if she got into Dana's office, it had been twelve years since they had worked at Bessel Holt. It was a long shot by anyone's standards that Dana still carried out the same bad practice and hid the access codes beneath her keyboard.

The gleam of a coffee machine in the corner of the reception area released some of her tension. There *was* a coffee machine. If there hadn't been coffee, she would have faked a dizzy spell and requested water.

Making a beeline for the machine, Esther half filled a foam cup, not bothering with either sugar or milk, and strolled to the nearest couch.

A woman exited an office, pausing to engage the

security lock before she continued on to reception. Esther recognized her almost immediately. Dana was a small, elegant blonde, forty if she was a day, but she looked closer to thirty. When she'd worked with Esther, she had been an established banker, with a solid, although unremarkable, track record. Despite twelve years, she hadn't progressed in the banking world, slipping sideways and, in Esther's opinion, down. RCS had always been known as an "untidy" offshore center. They had moved up a few notches, but the preliminary research she had done into their client base had informed her that, respectable facade or not, RCS was still trading on the fringes.

When Dana saw Esther, her expression was surprised but pleased. She had never shown any particular warmth toward Esther in Bern, but Esther was hoping that Dana was still ambitious enough that the carrot of snaring a chunk of Morell investment capital would smooth over the past.

Her own smile felt tight and forced as she rose and shook Dana's hand. She kept the chat light, and in the vein that she was researching short-term investment opportunities and since she'd heard Dana was with RCS, she'd decided to start here.

Dana's gaze followed Esther's hand as she lifted the coffee to her mouth and sipped, or more correctly, she followed the flash of her ring. Esther had worn it for effect. It was a rare pink diamond that matched her Chanel suit, a totally off-the-wall gift

Cesar had given her when Rina was born. The ring
was four carats and usually resided in a deposit box
in the bank, but it was perfect for this. No banker in
their right mind would have a discussion in a reception area with a client whose clothing and jewelry
alone totaled seven figures. Dana's career may have
flatlined, but she had been trained by the best, and
Esther knew that she loved jewelry. If the status
value of the ring didn't get her into Dana's office, she
didn't know what would.

Dana gave her a direct look. "We can't talk out
here. I don't have any appointments scheduled in the
next half hour. How about we adjourn to my office
and I can take you through some options."

Seconds later, Dana pressed the security code for
her door. Automatically, Esther watched her fingers,
but they moved too rapidly for her to get all of the
code. Suppressing the urge to roll her eyes at the ridiculous notion that even if she got the door code she
would be in a position to do anything about it, she
followed Dana into her office. A little spying was her
limit, not B and E. If they had to physically break
into the bank to get the codes, then that was in
Xavier's ballpark, not hers.

Esther preceded Dana into the room. The office
was small but nicely appointed, with an original
painting of the Bay area on the wall and a glossy
plant occupying one corner. A large L-shaped desk
took up most of the space, with two comfortably
padded chairs positioned near the desk. The bad

news was that even if one of the chairs was pulled up as close as possible to the computer, the keyboard was still inaccessible. To reach it, Esther would have to lean diagonally across the desk, and there was no way she could do that without Dana noticing.

To minimize the distance she would have to reach, Esther pulled her chair up as close to the keyboard as she could get on the pretext of needing a clear space to set her coffee down.

Dana frowned as she moved a computer printout, obviously not comfortable with the coffee on her desk, but too polite to insist that Esther remove it.

"Sorry about the mess." Dana stacked the papers Esther had pushed to one side and found a clear spot for them at the end of the desk. "I'm in the middle of a systems rehash. I don't need to tell you what a nightmare that is." She made a face. "The managing director wants more detailed reporting. Although, I don't know what more he expects to see, other than the color of our clients' underwear."

"Could be an interesting database."

"It might be, if there was anything in it but Y-fronts." Dana reddened, realizing she'd made a borderline offensive comment to a potential client. "I'm sorry, I shouldn't have said that. I missed breakfast and I'm on late lunch. My blood sugar is way down."

Esther forced a smile. "No problem. At a corporate level, Cesar doesn't allow Y-fronts."

Dana's blush deepened. "You *are* kidding."

"Unfortunately." Esther rummaged in her handbag on the pretext that she was searching for something.

"I was sure I put business cards in here this morning." Looking distracted and faintly annoyed, she set her bag down and leaned forward with enough swing that her elbow caught the coffee cup. Hot liquid splashed across the desk.

With a yelp, Dana shoved back in her office chair a split second before a wave of coffee slid over the side and dripped onto the carpet.

Already on her feet, Esther snatched a handful of tissues from a box on the desk. Apologizing profusely, she dropped them on the puddle, then, in a smooth motion, leaned over and lifted the keyboard away from a trickle of liquid.

The card was there.

Pretending to overbalance as she swiped at the coffee, she managed to flip the card around with the soaked tissue. The codes and the password were written in clear, bold black ink.

Dana grabbed at the card before a second stray trickle of coffee reached it. "Busted." She flushed bright red as she slid the card in her drawer. "I guess you don't have to remember access codes anymore. Not that you ever had a problem. They change them twice weekly here, Monday and Thursday. That was one of the reasons I left Bessel Holt, I couldn't stand the twenty-four-hour turnaround and my supervisor was constantly breathing down my neck."

She grabbed a handful of tissues, dropped them on the carpet and blotted more coffee. Her face was still flushed, her voice jerky with embarrassment. "I lived in fear of him checking beneath my keyboard. I'm all for security, but those people were anal."

Esther resumed her seat and worked to control her own breathing and the steady pump of adrenaline that was making her hands shake. She was more than happy to listen to Dana's nervy conversation, anything to distract her from realizing she had gotten a look at the codes. She didn't think anyone but her immediate superior at Bessel Holt had known about her photographic memory, but she didn't want to take any risks. It was an unhappy fact that somehow Xavier had found out about it. "Two years was enough for me. I couldn't keep up with the young computer nerds."

Dana tossed soiled tissues into the trash. "Tell me about it. There's a kid almost young enough to be my son running this place. Not," she said quickly, "that he isn't qualified, he is, but—"

"I know what you're saying. It's hard to credit it."

Her smile was relieved. "Exactly. Kids seem extra bright these days. The way their minds work is frightening." Her gaze lingered on the ring. "I hear you've got a daughter."

"That's right, Rina. She's ten." Esther extended her hand so the sunlight slanting through the window flashed off the diamond, more than happy to change the subject. "Cesar gave it to me when Rina was born."

"Tiffany's?"

"Cartier."

"Nice." Dana brandished her own wedding band and diamond solitaire engagement ring. "I've got a twelve-year-old, going on thirty. While her father was around, he didn't give me anything but trouble."

"Divorced?"

"I would have been if he hadn't widowed me."

"I'm sorry." Dana's personal circumstances explained what Dana was doing at RCS. With a bad marriage behind her and a daughter to care for, she hadn't had the luxury of choosing where she worked.

Feeling uncomfortable at the glimpse into Dana's personal life and guilty at the way she had used her, Esther gathered up soiled tissues and the empty cup and tossed them in the trash. Seconds later, the desk restored to order, she checked her watch. Only fifteen minutes had passed since she had walked into Dana's office, but now that she had the codes all she wanted to do was leave. "I'm afraid I'm going to have to go. Time's gotten away from me and I've got a lunchtime meeting."

After a brief discussion, Esther confirmed an appointment time she never intended to keep and walked quickly out of the office. She hadn't enjoyed manipulating Dana or flaunting the ring, but she hadn't had a choice.

When she reached the sidewalk, San Francisco's midday heat hit her like a wave. After the dry chill of air-conditioning, the humidity made her break out in an instant sweat. Fumbling in her bag she slipped dark glasses on the bridge of her nose and made her way to her car. Hot air blasted out of the interior as she opened the door. Sliding into the driver's seat, she started the engine and turned the air-conditioning on full. For long minutes she simply sat there, waiting for the shaking to stop.

She had done it. She couldn't believe it. She had the access codes and a time schedule and it had all gone more smoothly than she'd ever imagined. All she had to do now was act. It was Tuesday, which meant Xavier had a window of one and a half days. If RCS followed the same procedure as Bessel Holt, the codes would be changed at the beginning of the new business day on Thursday.

An hour after passing the codes on to Xavier, he rang back.

"There's a problem."

The amount in Lopez's account was so huge the bank had slapped extra security precautions on the account. Any movement of funds over five figures needed verbal approval from Lopez.

Xavier's solution was simple. "We steal his phone."

Or, more precisely, he would steal Lopez's phone number for a very short time. What he needed her to do was supply a recording of Lopez's voice.

When Xavier hung up, she pressed the rewind button on the answering machine and skipped through the messages. Alex Lopez's recorded voice floated over the phone, so real adrenaline shot through her veins.

She set the phone down, ejected the tape and slipped a fresh one into the cassette. It wasn't much. She didn't know if Xavier would be able to get an actor to do a realistic impersonation based on a few clipped words, but unless she called Lopez herself and recorded the call, it was their only option.

There was no way she could risk calling Lopez. He already knew she disliked him. If she rang, no matter how smoothly she handled the call, he would know something was up. His next step would be to talk to Cesar, and Cesar, in his current shell-shocked state, wouldn't be able to hold out against Lopez.

Gripping the edge of the desk, she forced herself to breathe until the pressure in her chest loosened and her pulse evened out, but there was no way she could banish the sense of raw panic that underscored every waking second.

With the extra security checks on Lopez's account, the funds transfer couldn't take place until tomorrow. That meant another twenty-four hours in the Sea Cliff house: twenty-four hours she couldn't afford, because time was running out.

It had been two days since she had confronted Cesar about Lopez. According to her most optimistic timetable, she had one day left at most before Lopez discovered that she knew.

The only problem was Esther wasn't an optimist;

she was a realist. Even if Cesar didn't cave, Lopez would unmask her. He had already demonstrated his predatory brilliance in the business arena. To achieve that result he had concentrated all of his attention on Cesar, not her, but the dinner party had signaled a change. She realized now that Lopez had been there specifically to observe her.

The second he focused that cold, precise intellect on the years she had spent in Bern, he would find out what Bessel Holt had employed her to do. He would realize that she had been instrumental in blocking a huge transaction made by his father and facilitated by Perez; that it had been her job to identify criminals.

That, potentially, there was no one more dangerous on American soil to the Chavez cartel.

Five

The tape in her purse, sealed in an envelope, ready to be dropped off at an address Xavier had given her, Esther slid behind the wheel of Jorge's aging Chevy and nosed down the drive. Maybe she was paranoid, but her own silver-gray Saab was distinctive, and it had passed through her mind that Lopez could be having her watched or even followed.

Cesar was out all day, supposedly at a meeting at the construction site of the development that had fallen through. Before she had left the house, Esther had checked with his secretary and found out that he hadn't showed. In fact he hadn't made an appearance at the office at all. If she had needed any further confirmation that she was out of options, that had been it. Cesar didn't normally let any detail of a business deal slip by unchecked, let alone miss appointments.

After dropping off the package in the lobby of an anonymous block of apartments, Esther drove around the steep, picturesque suburbs of Russian Hill until it was time to pick Rina up from school. The slow circling of blocks, aside from filling time, had also given her the opportunity to check if she was being followed. So far, she hadn't noticed anything suspicious. Minutes later, with Rina strapped into the front passenger seat, Esther took a left onto Leavenworth instead of turning onto California Street, heading for the expressway and home. According to Cesar's file on Lopez, he lived barely five minutes from Rina's school.

Checking out Lopez's address was a risk, but it was one that needed to be taken. Just because Lopez claimed he lived at an address didn't mean he actually did. She needed to find out for certain where he lived so she could give the details to the police. Once Xavier transferred the funds out of Lopez's account, the window for physically apprehending Lopez would be small. If the police didn't move quickly and raid the right address straight off, Lopez would slip the net.

There was no guarantee that doing a drive-by of his house would enable her to verify anything but she had to try. At this time of day, with the streets crammed with cars ferrying children home from school and driving Jorge's Chevy, she would be close to invisible.

Esther took a turn onto Hyde and slowed as she

counted numbers. She wanted to get a good look at the property as she drove past, and she could only risk doing it once.

Slowing even further as the number loomed, Esther craned, looking over Rina's head in an effort to see a vehicle or anything else that might indicate that Lopez actually lived there.

An ornate set of wrought-iron gates guarded the entrance, but otherwise, the property wasn't what she had expected. There was no fortress-style house, no high walls and no sign indicating there were roving guard dogs. It looked like any one of a hundred expensive addresses, with nicely landscaped grounds and tantalizing glimpses of a pool area. While the house was large and sprawling, it wasn't in the extreme-wealth bracket; it could have belonged to any number of prosperous families.

She took in the proportions of the house again. Oh, he was clever. He wasn't making a splash; he was blending.

The garage was closed, but she glimpsed the rear of a black truck parked at the side of the garage, almost obscured by a shade tree. It was the unexpected second vehicle she had seen the night Lopez had come to dinner.

Rina craned around, her expression openly curious. "Who lives there?"

Distracted, Esther took her gaze off the house and concentrated on the road. She should have done the drive-by before she picked Rina up, but she hadn't been able to risk it until she had been certain she wasn't followed. "Alex Lopez."

There was no point in not telling Rina that, and in a way it made sense. A little foreknowledge would prepare her for what was going to happen.

Rina settled back into her seat and dragged her Walkman out of her schoolbag, which was propped on the floor by her feet. "So that's why we're undercover."

"We are *not* undercover. My car's being serviced, so I borrowed Jorge's."

Rina flipped the Walkman open and examined the tape. "I would have taken Dad's 'Vette."

"Maybe the 'Vette was out."

"The 'Vette's in the garage."

"How did you know that?"

"Dad got picked up this morning. I saw him leave from my bedroom window."

Esther frowned. Cesar did use a driver occasionally, usually if he had a lot of stops to make in places where it was difficult to get parking, but according to his secretary he had had just the one meeting today, which he had missed. "How come you know so much about the 'Vette, anyway?"

Rina's expression was smug. "Dad's already let me drive it."

"What?"

Rina grinned. "Uh-huh. I'm on the road."

"Not with me you're not. And I'll be having a word to your father about that." The words were automatic, but with a pang she realized she wouldn't be having a word with Cesar about Rina, or anything else, in the conceivable future. For the next twenty-four hours, she would be staying quiet and keeping her mouth shut. Every ounce of energy she had would be directed into helping Xavier pull off the funds transfer and making arrangements for both Rina and herself to disappear.

Grief she hadn't had time to feel hit her like a fist in the chest. She had been so busy trying to find out what had gone wrong and figure a way through the mess, she hadn't had time to count the personal cost, and it was huge. She and Cesar had had twelve good years together. The pull of those years, of living and working side by side tugged at her, sharp enough to cause actual pain. At times they had fought—each as stubborn as the other—but the relationship had been exhilarating and Esther had been satisfied. Rina had completed them, filling the gaps that occasionally loomed, bringing softness and the sense of family she craved.

She turned a corner and accelerated away from the barbed territory of Lopez's house, shoving the misery down somewhere deep and dark until she had the time and the privacy to deal with it.

"Lopez is a problem, isn't he?"

Esther's gaze was sharp. "What do you mean?"

"I heard him and Dad talking." Rina made a face. "Don't look so surprised. Just because it looks like I'm not listening, it doesn't mean I'm not. Anyway, they thought I was listening to my Walkman, but I wasn't. Lopez was talking about the mall project that Dad's been worried about, the one that's threatening to go down the tubes. He owns the company that wants to pull out. Dad didn't look happy." She glanced at Esther, her gaze sharply adult. "I wasn't, either." She settled back in her seat. "He's got no color—he looks dark and flat—and his eyes aren't right."

And Rina would know, she'd stared at Alex Lopez for long enough. He had eyes like a shark, dead and cold. The skin at the back of her neck tightened, a sense of premonition that added to the urgency to simply cut and run.

"Do you want to hear?"

Esther braked for an intersection. "Hear what?"

Rina rummaged in her bag again. "The tape. I told you I wasn't listening to music, I was *taping*."

A horn sounded behind her. Jerkily, Esther accelerated through the intersection and pulled over. "You were *what?*"

"Taping." Rina pressed the rewind button on the Walkman then pressed Play.

Lopez's dark cold voice filled the car. Esther's skin crawled as she listened to evidence that Lopez was blackmailing Cesar, using the threat of bankrupting a company he had recently procured in order to collapse the Pembroke development, a run-of-the-mill project that had been solid.

The conversation must have happened while she was away from the table. Lopez had obviously thought he was safe in delivering the threat because he thought Rina was deafened by music. He had probably also made the mistake, like a lot of people, of assuming that because Rina looked disconnected she had no interest in what was going on.

Not for the first time Esther was reminded that beneath the disconnected façade, Rina had always worked to her own agenda. The only time she was really dreamy was when she was painting. The rest of the time she used the faintly "out to lunch" expression to buy herself leeway to do exactly what she wanted, and the tactic worked. She had Cesar wrapped around her little finger and she had outmaneuvered Lopez. Like Cesar and herself, Rina was a player, but on a whole other level entirely. If she ever got into business they would all be in for a wild ride.

Abruptly the voice was replaced with blaring pop music. Wincing at the assault on her ears, Esther stared at the Walkman. She'd been so busy listening to the content of the recording she hadn't registered its full value. The tape was manna from heaven on three counts. It was vital evidence—she would retain a copy of the tape to hand to the police—but it was also exactly what Xavier needed to help his actor replicate Lopez's voice. On top of that she was almost certain Lopez's unwitting testimony would buy Cesar some leeway in court when the feds closed in. "I need that tape."

Rina's gaze was wary. "I know I'm not supposed to tape conversations."

"No punishment, I promise." Relief at the discovery of the tape and the doors it opened made her feel light-headed. Cancel business; the kid could go into politics.

Dennison sat in his office, studying Collins's surveillance notes.

Esther Morell had had a busy day, but that was nothing unusual. For the past month Collins's daily report had contained a long list of appointments, lunch dates and trips to and from the fancy school the kid attended. However, the fact that Esther had left the house that morning, driving a battered Chevy instead of the Saab, had rung alarm bells. Collins had followed her, but he had lost her in a traffic snarl-up in town. He had picked her up just as she'd left the school, in time to catch her detouring from her usual route.

He slipped the security video for Lopez's house into the VCR, then rewound it and began skipping through until just before the time recorded in Collins's notes. Over a five-minute period, a number of vehicles had driven past the house, which was normal. At that time of day, with school just out, there was always plenty of traffic.

Dennison frowned. The quality of the security tape was abysmal. To avoid being spotted or stolen, the camera had been set back too far from the road, and the angle wasn't helpful. Consequently the film was grainy and it was difficult to read license plates or get any kind of accurate description of the occupants of cars. A brown Chevy appeared. Dennison could make out two people, but no more detail than that. Seconds later, Collins's charcoal-gray car appeared on the tape, confirming that the driver of the brown Chevy had been Esther.

Dennison picked up the phone and dialed through to Lopez's office, which was located on the first story of the house, then rewound the tape and played it through again. He didn't like the fact that Esther had driven by the house. Maybe there was a good reason why she hadn't used her own car today, but he didn't think so. More and more, he was beginning to believe that they had underestimated her.

Lopez arrived halfway through the segment of tape and took a seat. Dennison passed him Collins's surveillance report, rewound the tape and ran it through again.

When the relevant portion of the tape had played, he hit the stop button and ejected the videotape from the VCR.

Lopez got to his feet, his expression cold. What he wanted was old news: Esther watched more closely and researched more fully. He didn't trust her. Hell, neither did Dennison. Any woman that gorgeous…there had to be a catch.

He picked up the phone and put a call through to Collins. They were going to need a second man on the job, and a wire on the phone.

Lately he had been working 24/7 on Esther

Morell, but obtaining concrete information about her was difficult. When it came to business, Cesar was the head of the Morell Group, and every company report and legal document was signed by him. The only place Esther showed up on paper was in the private legal agreements that existed between her and Cesar, but those agreements in themselves were a piece of work. In terms of financial security, anything with Esther's name on it was ironclad. She didn't feature in the business—unless Cesar died, in which case she inherited everything—but legally she owned a sizable chunk of the Morell Group, and in the marriage, she definitely wore the pants.

If Esther and Cesar ever divorced, he got the Corvette and a whole lot of cold air. Mrs. Midas took all the real estate, including the apartments in Monte Carlo and London and the holiday home in the Bahamas. She also qualified for a solid cash payout, the Saab and the kid, and she retained her twenty-five-percent share of the Morell Group.

Morell was a clever man, unafraid of taking risks and with a knack for making huge sums of money, but he lacked the tough savvy and edge Dennison had been sure he would have. Dennison was now certain that "edge" was his wife. When he received the telephone call from Bern he was waiting on, he would have his confirmation.

The following day, Xavier le Clerc picked up the phone in his suite at the San Francisco Royal Pacific

Hotel, placed a call and waited while the receptionist put him through to Vincent, the telecommunica-
tions expert selected for this particular job.

At ten past one that afternoon, as arranged,
Vincent walked into a small café a block south from
his place of work. Xavier rose to his feet and waved
him into the booth he'd chosen, one well away from
the door. He had already ordered coffee for them
both, which tasted terrible. As soon as Vincent was
seated, Xavier got down to business.

He needed to "borrow" Alex Lopez's phone number for the few minutes it would take for the bank to
ring and satisfy Lopez's security requirements for
the transaction. He wrote the number of the new
phone line he'd set up on a sheet of notepaper, along
with the exact time he needed the swap to take place,
and slipped it across the table. "I need twenty
minutes exactly, no more." Any longer and it was
possible Lopez would understand that his telephone
line had been hijacked.

He slid an envelope across the table. It contained
a substantial amount of cash. Half now, half when
the job was done.

Xavier unlocked the door of an empty apartment
with a pleasant but distant view of San Francisco
Bay. The young actor he'd hired to impersonate
Lopez followed him into the cramped sitting room
and leaned against the wall while Xavier picked up
the receiver of the cheap phone he'd previously had

installed and dialed Vincent's extension. After a short conversation, he set the phone down.

Minutes later, Vincent rang back. The switch had been made. Lopez's phone was still active, but he would be operating on a different number for twenty minutes. Lopez would be able to call out, but all of his incoming calls would be directed to Xavier's phone. Xavier had twenty minutes, and counting.

Xavier set the receiver down, then picked it up again and dialed. He checked his watch as he waited for the first person to pick up: two-fifteen. The next few minutes would be an interesting and intricate dance. Success depended on the precise timing and the greed of the people he had paid.

Dennison paced the floor of Lopez's study, avoiding his cold stare and Vitali's raw impatience. He checked his watch—two twenty-five—and resisted the urge to jerk at the collar of his shirt. The temperature was in the nineties, but that wasn't the only reason he was sweating. They were waiting for a call from a source in the FBI, and confirmation about a two-year period Esther Morell had spent overseas.

Frowning, he tried his contact's number again and received the same reply. Johnson was away from his desk, which he already knew, since he hadn't been able to reach him for the past half hour. Johnson had driven to a pay phone to make the call, and if Dennison were in his shoes, he would do the same. There was no way he would use his office or his home phone to pass on information that could be incriminating, but that kind of logic didn't help Dennison where Lopez was concerned.

He set the phone down. Almost immediately it rang.

He snatched up the receiver and hit the speaker-phone function. "What took you so long?"

Johnson's voice filled the office. "I've been trying to reach you for the past fifteen minutes. Your line's been engaged."

Dennison frowned. It was possible Johnson had tried to call at the same time he had been calling him, but that only amounted to a couple of minutes over the past half hour. They hadn't had any other incoming calls. He should have gotten through.

Lopez spoke. "What have you found out?"

Johnson hesitated, no doubt put off his stride by the different voice. "Uh…all the records I have show what we already knew, that she worked as a banking executive mostly around the L.A. and San Francisco areas, but for two years while she was overseas she worked for a big international banking conglomerate. The reason we had trouble getting a job description was that she was never on their payroll. She set up her own consultancy company and billed the bank. The money was paid to a numbered account in Switzerland. No income was ever registered under her name or reached U.S. shores."

Johnson's voice flattened out as he repeated the information he had received from his source in Bern.

Like he'd said, Esther Morell hadn't been involved in day-to-day banking, she had been contracted by Bessel Holt to investigate their client base. Apparently, she had a photographic memory and a knack for research, with particular regard to South America. He could also confirm that Esther *had* been instrumental in blocking a number of offshore transactions out of South America, including a substantial movement of funds by the Chavez cartel. "And get this. She used to date le Clerc. As in *Xavier* le Clerc."

Dennison's stomach did an odd little flip-flop. Some agents talked endlessly about their "gut." They would have a hunch about this, an instinct about that. As far as Dennison was concerned, human desires and sheer greed, along with good information, were a much more reliable map to follow than some airy-fairy premonition, but suddenly the weird feeling he'd had all day that something was wrong made sense.

Le Clerc's name wasn't big here, but it was legendary in Europe. He was a coldly efficient thief who had done the unthinkable: collapsed a Swiss bank that had refused to disclose or release funds allegedly belonging to Jewish families that had survived the Holocaust. Simultaneously, he had engineered a bank heist that had removed certain items from the vault and safe-deposit boxes, all of which were said to have belonged to Nazi political leaders and war criminals.

López terminated the call, cutting Johnson off in midsentence. He handed the receiver to Vitali. "Check the account."

The whiplash command jerked Vitali out of his seat. "There's no way we'll get access to her Swiss—"

"Not her account. *Mine.*"

Six

Esther parked her car outside Rina's school, slotting into a space beneath a shady tree. She slipped dark glasses on the bridge of her nose and strode to the school's office. The brief flash of her reflection in the glass doors told her that outwardly she looked cool and collected, despite the steamy heat, but ever since Xavier had rung with a bogus message from the school that Rina was unwell—the prearranged code for her to get out of town—she had been a bundle of nerves.

When she had left the house she had followed Xavier's instructions to the letter. It seemed ridiculous to place her trust in him, but his precise list of what to do—and what *not* to do—had helped. As soon as she had hung up, she had informed Carmita that she was driving into town to pick Rina up from school. Xavier's logic was that it was best to construct a story that allowed her to stay within the bounds of normality, so that if she was being followed her movements wouldn't be perceived as out of the ordinary until the last moment, when she took the turnoff to San Jose and the airport.

She had changed into a lightweight linen pantsuit and stepped out of the house, taking with her only the things she normally carried, her handbag and briefcase, nothing that would signal that she was leaving town. The previous evening she had placed a suitcase of clothes and personal items in the trunk. They were due to fly out in just over an hour in a chartered private jet, not a scheduled flight. She had taken the precaution of also booking a regular flight, though, just in case anyone checked the airports.

The receptionist consulted the school timetable, then found someone to escort her through manicured gardens to Rina's classroom. After making excuses to Rina's teacher for removing her from class a few minutes early, Esther hurried Rina out to the car. An internal clock told her that everything was taking too long. The holdup at the office had been longer than she'd anticipated, then Rina's class had been at the far end of the school grounds, taking more precious time.

Rina dumped her schoolbag in the backseat and strapped herself in. "What's wrong?"

Esther shot her a glance as she pulled out of the school gates and turned in the opposite direction than they usually took, frowning as she noticed the huge bank of clouds that had rolled in off the sea. It was early in the day for fog, but the weather had been extra hot and humid, and cloud had been slowly building all day. "We're catching a flight out."

She frowned. Already a fine gauze of mist was filtering out sunlight. It was just as well they were flying out of San Jose; San Francisco and Oakland airports would be closed within the hour.

Rina's gaze was sharp. "Is Dad coming?"

"Not right now. Maybe later. Don't worry," she said quickly.

"What's wrong? Are the police going to arrest Alex Lopez?"

The accuracy of Rina's observation and the mention of Lopez's name made Esther's fingers tighten on the wheel, sending the Saab over the centerline. A truck swerved, its horn blaring. Heart pounding, she corrected her course and forced herself to slow down. She had to remain calm and take care not to draw any attention. She couldn't afford the delay an accident or a traffic ticket would entail. With jerky sentences she explained what had gone wrong and why they had to leave town. "The police will arrest Lopez, after we're gone."

An intersection loomed. Esther braked, jaw clamped, fingers tapping on the wheel as she studied the thickening fog while she waited for the lights to turn green. A car nosed close behind and she frowned, trying to remember if she had noticed the charcoal-gray sedan before she'd stopped off at the school. In the murky light, colors could be deceptive. Seconds later, she accelerated smoothly across the intersection.

When she got to the airport she would ring Cesar and tell him to get out, but she wouldn't do that until just before they boarded the flight. She couldn't risk being stopped, or found. Despite the danger he was in, Cesar had forfeited any right to her loyalty. Rina was her priority.

Vitali's face was oddly blank as he handed the receiver to Lopez. "It's gone. The account's empty."

Dennison's gaze sharpened as he listened to Lopez's clipped conversation and the replies, which were audible on speakerphone. Paperwork authorizing the transaction had been received via special courier just after two that afternoon. The signature matched the sample they had on file.

Lopez's expression hadn't changed, but his eyes looked strange, the pupils fully dilated, blacking out the irises. "Who rang to clear the transaction?"

"You did, sir. We followed the instructions." There was a pause. "I spoke to you myself, just a few minutes ago."

"I haven't called you. I didn't authorize the movement of any funds and I haven't received a phone call."

"The call was made." He cleared his throat. "We have it on tape. I'll play it back for you."

Dennison listened, studying the taped conversation. The sound quality wasn't great, but whoever it was, he was good. The voice was almost indistinguishable from Lopez's own; close enough to match the sample tape the bank had been instructed to keep as a check.

With cold precision, Lopez ended the call, disengaged the speakerphone and made a number of calls in quick succession.

Dennison retreated a step, on the pretext of propping himself on the edge of the desk. He had never viewed Lopez, who was lean and slight and had an aversion to physical contact, as physically dangerous, but he was revising his opinion. The change in Lopez's eyes had literally made the hairs on the back of his neck stand on end.

Dennison wasn't normally privy to Lopez's financial arrangements—that was Vitali's area—but what had happened was now clear. Approximately thirty minutes ago, someone with the expertise and knowledge to access Lopez's bank account and security details had stolen an amount so huge that when he'd heard the figure, Dennison had broken out in an instant sweat.

The scam was multilayered and complex. Given the bank's dual controls and the extra security measures Lopez had put in place, it shouldn't have succeeded—and wouldn't have, if the phones hadn't been tampered with.

The reason for Johnson's inability to ring in was now clear. They had been outmaneuvered. Whoever had stolen the money had gotten into the phone system and rerouted the number to another address for the brief window of time in which the bank's security call had been made. Lopez's phone hadn't been disconnected, so a new number would have been issued for the few minutes required, which was why Dennison had been able to ring out but no one had been able to contact him.

When Johnson had tried to call him, claiming the line was engaged, it had been because Lopez's number *had* been busy; the funds transfer had been taking place.

Lopez stared at Dennison, sending an involuntary shudder down his spine. *"Where is Esther Morell?"*

Dennison checked his watch. That, at least, was covered. Mistakes had been made, but not by him. "She should be on her way home from school."

The phone rang, breaking the eerie intensity of Lopez's stare. The call was for Dennison. Stomach suddenly tight, he took the receiver. Seconds later he barked out a precise set of instructions and set the receiver down. "Collins just lost her on the Bay Bridge in fog. He thinks she could be headed for Oakland International."

Esther glanced in the rearview mirror. Adrenaline pumped. Despite a few unscheduled twists and turns, the charcoal-gray sedan she thought she'd managed to lose had slotted back into traffic behind her. The probability that whoever was driving the vehicle was taking the same route out of sheer coincidence had just played itself out.

For the first time, she faced the very real possibility that they weren't going to make it. "There's a notepad and a pen in the glove compartment. Get them out and write down the numbers I tell you."

Rina, who had been silent and unnaturally still, retrieved the pad and pen.

Esther checked the rearview mirror as she recited the numbers of two Swiss accounts. The first was the Swiss account she had arranged Lopez's money to be transferred into, after Xavier had stolen it; the second was her own private account. If Cesar had gone broke, the money in her Swiss account would have been the capital to start again, but now… "Recite the numbers back to me."

Rina read the numbers out: they were correct.

"Okay. Now look at the sheet and remember the numbers. When you've done that, put the pad in my handbag." At the first opportunity, she would destroy it.

She waited until Rina had slipped the pad inside her handbag, then pressed her foot more firmly on the accelerator and overtook a slower vehicle. Her gaze moved rapidly over buildings and road signs as she tried to figure out exactly where her evasive tactics had taken her and how quickly she could get back onto a state highway. The fog that had blanked out downtown San Francisco had also drifted in here, gradually blotting out the landscape and making it even more difficult to pinpoint her position.

The gray car loomed closer. She pressed her foot on the accelerator, widening the gap again. Ahead she could see an interstate sign and the symbol for the airport. She could also see two cars parked across the on-ramp, one with a flashing light. Traffic was already backing up.

Braking, she jerked the wheel and darted down a side road. The car behind shot past the turnoff. She didn't know what the blockade was for, but she wasn't going to risk it. The car tailing her was confirmation that Lopez knew she was headed for San Jose Airport, and that he had found out his account had been emptied.

Esther spared a glance for Rina, who was half out of her seat, craning around, studying a second car that had come up close behind them, this one a light bronze in color. The stark terror on her face made Esther's chest go tight. Rina understood that Lopez was a criminal, the importance of the evidence on the tape, and just why they had to disappear. She had even accepted that they would have to be separated from Cesar. Esther had taken pains to reassure her that everything was under control—that they were safe—but now it was patently obvious that they weren't and there was nothing she could say to change the situation. All she could do was act. "Sit down, honey. Make sure your seat belt's tight."

A corner loomed. Esther braked and wrenched on

the wheel, hauling the car over as a school bus appeared. Seconds later another country lane provided her with the opportunity to drive back the way she'd come. The problem was she was caught in a narrow section of land, hemmed in on one side by mountains, on the other, a river. If she could get back onto the interstate her options would improve.

The jet in San Jose was on standby, but with Lopez's men so close behind, flying was no longer a viable option; they would have her before she made the terminal building. She would have to cut back into the city and hope to lose the cars following her in the chaos of rush-hour traffic. Once she and Rina were free and clear she could ditch the car, hire a rental and head south for L.A.

A car materialized out of the mist, parked across the road ahead. Esther jammed her foot on the brake in a desperate bid to avoid a collision. The Saab slid sideways, punched into a fence post. She had a fractured glimpse of the driver's face. *Perez.* Then the car was in the air.

Seven

The Saab's air bag slammed Rina's head back against the headrest. The seat belt bit into her chest, pinning her in place as the car spun through the air in eerie silence.

The car hit the ground with a bone-cracking thud and continued to roll, faster, harder. She couldn't breathe, couldn't think; she felt like she was looping the loop on a roller coaster, but the grinding crunching sounds in no way resembled anything she had ever heard at a fairground.

Something hit her wrist and punched the side of her head. When she opened her eyes the sickening whirling had stopped, the car was stationary and the world had turned red. It took long seconds for her mind to accept that the color splattered on the deflated air bags, coating what was left of the windscreen and soaking into her clothing, was blood.

She couldn't see her legs, and for a frightening moment she wondered if they were still there. The front end of the car was buckled like a concertina, the hood snapped up in the air and hanging at an odd angle. Experimentally, she wiggled her toes in her school sandals, then tensed her calf muscles and realized that part of the weird feeling was that water was lapping at her feet. Her heart pounded faster as she realized that the car had slid partway into the river.

Esther reached behind her to the backseat. Her hand fumbled at the strap of her handbag. It was then Rina noticed blood welling from a frightening cut in her mother's chest. Esther pulled the bag into her lap, grimacing as she did so, and Rina saw a jagged piece of twisted steel the size of a knife protruding from her shoulder. Raw fear exploded. "Mom, you're cut—"

"It's all right, baby." She reached inside the bag, then with a frustrated sound upended the bag, which was empty.

Swiveling in her seat, Rina saw that most of the contents of the handbag were strewn across the backseat. It was then she realized the reason her right hand wouldn't work was that her wrist was broken.

Esther's fingers closed on her good hand. "I need you to do two things for me. I had a gun in my handbag. I need you to get it for me. Then I want you to find the notepad you wrote the numbers on and throw it in the river."

Blindly, Rina depressed the button that released

her belt, not questioning why her mother needed a gun, or even that she had one. Her whole being was centered on doing exactly what Esther wanted.

"Hurry, baby."

Esther's voice had gone funny, soft and a little blurry, and she was sitting quietly, as if she was too tired to move. Rina hurried. Her head felt weird, heavy and hot as if she had a fever, and sharp pains shot up her right arm every time she moved. Holding her broken wrist against her stomach, she wriggled through the gap between the seats. Even back here there was blood, soaking the leather upholstery and the tangled mess of objects strewn across the seat and floating in the water that covered the floor.

The notepad was easy to find, it was in the water, the ink smeared, the numbers already dissolving. The gun was wedged in a crumpled corner of the backseat.

Climbing back into the front seat, she handed the weapon over, then threw the notepad out through the gaping hole in the windscreen, watching to make sure it went into the river.

With a slow movement, as if she was so tired she could barely move, Esther set the barrel of the gun on the buckled rim of the window. "Repeat the numbers I gave you to remember."

Blankly, Rina repeated them once, then, when Esther insisted, a second time.

Esther's gaze was fierce. "The first set of numbers

is for the police, no one else. That second set is for you, *only you,* do you understand?"

Tears squeezed out from beneath her lids. "Yes."

Esther's hand closed on hers and gripped hard. "Good girl. I love you, baby."

Seconds later, the narrow face of Vitali appeared. There was a loud explosion and Vitali disappeared.

Rina blinked, her ears ringing. Someone said, "She's got a gun," but the words sounded like they'd been spoken through a long pipe. Another explosion followed. Esther's head rocked back, then flopped sideways onto her shoulder.

Rina stared with horror at the hole in her forehead. Her eyes squeezed shut and her torso shrank inward in mute denial. She shook her head, every cell in her body utterly rejecting the image.

That wasn't right. Her mother didn't look that way. She refused to see it. She refused to *know* it.

The heaviness in her head increased, the pressure crushing. She felt weird and floaty. Then, as abruptly as if someone had just flicked off a light switch, everything went dark.

Confused, she stared at the thick, impenetrable blackness. She was still awake; her eyes were wide open. She could feel her arms and legs, the soreness in her head and her wrist. She could hear voices.

The heaviness in her head increased, as if she was caught in a vice and someone was winding it tighter and tighter. Her chest ached and dimly she realized her mouth and throat were clamped so tightly shut she couldn't breathe. An odd buzzing started in her ears. The pain in her chest and throat grew sharper, tighter. Then suddenly she couldn't hear or feel, either.

Dennison dove into the water and surfaced, wallowing out of his depth. His fingertips brushed the notepad; it spun, moving out of his reach. The ink had almost dissolved but he could see numbers: two sets.

River water filled his mouth; he went under. He flailed, trying to get his footing but the current was too strong. Clamping his mouth shut, he surged toward shore. His feet finally found hard ground and he bobbed up, gasping for breath. Blinking, he scanned the surface of the river. In the middle, the current was moving like a freight train; the notepad was gone.

He waded from the water and used a tree branch to haul himself up the lip of the bank. Sucking in a breath, he surveyed the wreckage of Esther Morell's car, which was partly submerged. The Saab was totaled, but then it wasn't designed for aerial stunts, and for the first part of the crash it had been spectacularly airborne. The air bags had deployed, saving Esther and her daughter. If Esther Morell hadn't produced a gun and shot Vitali, the situation just might have been salvageable.

Now Lopez was going to go ape, but Dennison didn't think there was anything he could have done that would have saved her, even if she hadn't had the gun. The driver's side had taken a big hit. The door had been punched in and the engine block had shoved back, pinning her in the seat. Blood was everywhere, coating what was left of the interior of the car, and coating the kid.

Bending, Dennison checked Esther Morell for a pulse, although he didn't expect to find one. He'd seen plenty of dead bodies, and Esther Morell was dead on a couple of counts, between the piece of steel that had pierced her chest cavity and the bullet hole in her forehead.

It was regrettable, but in shooting her, Dennison had made the only decision he could. She had known she was dying and she'd had nothing to lose; she had been protecting her kid.

He wasn't happy. The order had been to bring her in alive, but with arterial bleeding that close to the heart, there had been no chance she would survive more than a few minutes. Lopez would be upset at the outcome, but Dennison was pragmatic. Sometimes shit happened, and in this case it was a given. After stealing Lopez's money, there had never been any question that Esther Morell was going to give up easy.

Dennison signaled to Collins, who was crouched over Vitali. By some strange quirk, she had shot Vitali through the heart. It wasn't often he saw a shot as clean and instantly fatal as that. Usually, when someone got hit there was a lot of noise and mess before they finally died, but Vitali had barely shed a drop, and most of it was staining the front of his shirt.

Esther Morell had stopped Vitali's heart dead and saved him a major headache. The last thing he needed was for the cops to find a blood grouping that didn't match either Esther or Rina Morell's at the scene. "Open the trunk of my car, then give me a hand."

Pulling on a pair of latex gloves, he leaned into the car, picked up the gun and slid it into his pocket. With a jerk, he wrenched the door off its hinges and let it drift away in the water. Reaching into the interior of the car, he lifted Esther into his arms, strode up the bank to his car and placed her in the trunk. Slamming the lid closed, he sat in the driver's seat, picked up his car phone and called Lopez, who was already en route. Then he went back for the kid.

She was unconscious but still breathing. Feeling sick to his stomach, he checked her over. She had a broken wrist, a few cuts and bruises. Unless she had internal injuries, she would survive. As Dennison hauled her out and laid her on the grass, he couldn't help thinking it would have been a lot simpler if she had died.

Collins stared at Rina Morell. "What are we going to do with Vitali?"

"Put him in the trunk of your car."

Collins swore beneath his breath.

Dennison hooked his arms beneath Vitali's knees

and waited for Collins to take his shoulders. "What do you think you're paid for? To sit on your ass and drink coffee?"

"I didn't think it would be like this. That's a *kid*."

"It's a job."

Collins gripped Vitali beneath the shoulders, hauled upward and straightened his legs. "I've got a daughter."

Dennison could feel himself going red in the face as they moved awkwardly up the slope; Vitali was a lot heavier than Esther had been. He was having trouble breathing and the blood was pulsing through his veins in thick, labored strokes. He had high blood pressure; carrying Vitali up the bank would probably give him a heart attack, but was he bitching?

Collins leaned his hip against the rear fender of his car while he juggled supporting Vitali's weight and unlocking the trunk. The lid sprang open. Seconds later, Vitali's body was neatly folded on his side; he looked like he was sleeping.

Dennison slammed the trunk closed. "You know what? I never had kids, because I knew this was *exactly* what it would be like."

Minutes later, Lopez arrived, pulling in behind Dennison's car. So far, only one other vehicle had used the country lane, and it had barely slowed. The fog had thickened, blanketing the countryside, but even if it hadn't rolled in, the Saab, which lay at the bottom of the slope, wasn't visible from the road.

Dennison gave Lopez his report. He had finished cleaning out the car, and with Collins's help they had pushed it farther into the river. The water would wash away most of the evidence, and they had been wearing gloves. They couldn't do much about the muddy trampled area or the tire tracks their vehicles had made, but the chance that the cops would be able to find anything to connect either him or Collins to the accident was remote.

He had searched the car and removed everything, including all of Esther Morell's and the kid's luggage and personal possessions. So far he hadn't been able to find any trace of an account number, or anything relating to an international banking transaction on either Esther, the kid or any of the possessions that had been strewn about in the car and on the ground. It was possible the information was there and he had missed it. The only way to be thorough was to take it all with him.

The only item he had missed had been the notepad. Collins had taken a quick walk downstream and checked out the riverbank, but with no luck. At the speed the current had been going, the notepad would be in San Francisco Bay by now.

Lopez stared at Rina Morell. "Are you sure there were numbers written on the notepad, not words?"

Dennison rose to his feet. "Numbers, two sets, although I couldn't make them out clearly because the ink had mostly dissolved. What do you want done with the girl?"

Lopez's expression was cold. "We need her alive."

Dennison's stomach did a queasy flip. Lopez had actually imagined that he had just offered to *shoot* Rina Morell. A ten-year-old kid.

Suddenly the gulf between Dennison and Lopez yawned wide. He'd thought he was a hard-ass. On occasions he'd been certain he had scraped the bottom of the barrel of human behavior, but Lopez was operating on a whole other level. Lately, when Dennison looked into his eyes, he didn't see anything he recognized.

Collins looked like he was going to throw up. He sent Dennison a sideways look. "She was conscious when Dennison shot Esther Morell."

Lopez barely acknowledged Collins's presence. Ever since Dennison had told him about the notepad and the figures, his gaze had been fixed on the kid's face. "It's a risk we'll have to take."

Dennison watched as Lopez walked back up the bank and disappeared into the mist. The money Esther had stolen was the power base of Lopez's operation. According to Vitali, very little of it had been his. The money was loaned to Lopez by his father, Marco Chavez. Losing it had effectively cut Lopez off at the knees and had likely signed his own death warrant.

Esther had taken the secret of where she'd stashed the money with her to the grave, but if Rina Morell had the key to the Chavez billions, then there was no way she could be allowed to die, and no way Lopez would let her go until she spat the key out into his hand.

Eight

Cesar stared at Esther's body where it lay in the trunk of Dennison's car. He hadn't believed Dennison when he had called him about the accident, but he believed him now. Grief speared through the haze of alcohol that had gotten him through the afternoon, and would have driven him to his knees if it hadn't been for the barrel of the .38 shoved into his side.

Dennison's hand shot out and gripped his throat, choking off his breath as he pushed him back against the wall of Lopez's garage. "We know your wife had a photographic memory, just like the kid. So why would she write down details of account numbers?"

Dennison's fingers tightened, grinding on his trachea, then abruptly released. Cesar gulped in air and massaged his throat. The snick of a blade jerked his head up. Lopez stepped out of the shadows. Warily, he studied the flick knife in Lopez's hand.

Lopez repeated Dennison's question.

Cesar's stomach rolled. The amount of money that was "missing" was nightmarishly large and right now it was balanced against his and Rina's lives. Even drunk, the logic was clear. It was too late for Esther, but if he could make Rina remember, he could get the money back.

His gaze flickered to the body in the trunk. He began to shake. Dennison had shot Esther. Lopez would have no compunction about ordering Rina's death, or his. Their only chance for survival lay in the fact that Lopez believed she had something he wanted.

Maybe his logic was flawed. He hadn't been thinking clearly for weeks, but with Esther dead and Rina lying unconscious in hospital, there was only one strategy: bluff, delay for time while he tried to think of a way out of this mess. "Esther has—*had*—a photographic memory. If she wrote numbers down, there is only one reason. She would have given them to Rina so she could memorize them." He let out a breath. "As insurance."

Bluff or not, nothing else made sense. She must have known Dennison was following her and panicked, otherwise she wouldn't have risked involving Rina.

"Why didn't you tell us about Esther?"

Lopez's voice was soft and sibilant, his Colombian accent abruptly strong. Adrenaline shoved through Cesar's veins, making his pulse thud jerkily and his fingers twitch. "I didn't think it mattered. She didn't know—"

But she had.

With a shock he realized that when Esther had confronted him on Monday night and the manila file with Lopez's account details had scattered on the floor of his office, she must have gotten a look at the account number. It had only been a split second, but for Esther it had been long enough. He had been stupid, *stupid*—

"When did she find out?"

"Monday."

There was a deadly silence. Cesar rushed to fill it. "I didn't know she'd seen the account number, if I had—" He swallowed. Just seconds before he'd been cold, now sweat was pouring off him. "She asked for time. She was my wife. I *believed* her."

The fist caught him in the jaw. When he came around he was lying on the concrete floor and music was playing.

Dennison was crouched a few feet away, systematically going through the luggage from the Saab, which included a small antique music box Cesar could remember Esther buying for Rina's first birthday. The presence of the music box hammered home the fact that Esther had not only stolen the money, she had been leaving him and taking Rina with her.

Dennison upended the box with the lid open and shook it. The music stopped. A small compartment slid open. After a cursory inspection, he placed the box on the floor and picked up Esther's jewelry case.

"What do you know about Xavier le Clerc?"

Lopez's question cut through the dim shadows of the garage. He was leaning against the open trunk of the car.

Cesar pushed to his knees. His head spun and his stomach cramped, the pain agonizing, and for a moment he thought he was going to throw up.

Le Clerc? For a moment the name meant nothing, then comprehension hit. He swallowed the sour taste of bile in his throat. "Esther knew him in Bern years ago, when she investigated him for Bessel Holt. Aside from the stories in the paper, that's all I know."

"Your wife rang a number in Bern on Monday."

Cesar used the wall to brace himself as he staggered to his feet. Lopez wouldn't bring up le Clerc's name unless he was somehow implicated, which was crazy; le Clerc had disappeared more than a decade ago. "I didn't know that."

"We tried the number. It belonged to le Clerc's sister. She's since disappeared and the number has been disconnected." There was a pause. "Do you know how to reach le Clerc?"

"Why would I have any connection with him?"

Lopez's gaze was unblinking. "Your wife had a meeting with a former colleague from Bern on Tuesday. Dana Jones. She works at RCS."

Shock reverberated through Cesar. Now, finally—too late—he could see the pieces of the puzzle falling into place. "I've never heard of her."

"Dana Jones was in Bern at the same time Esther and Xavier le Clerc were there. Don't you think that's a coincidence?"

"Yes. *No.*" Cesar shook his head, trying to clear away the heavy ache. "I don't know. If I did, I would tell you." He rubbed at his face. "If you can't find le Clerc, maybe this Dana Jones knows something."

Lopez's expression was cold. "Finally, you're beginning to think."

Annoyed at being kept late when she needed to be home for her daughter, Dana Jones lifted her head as the branch manager strode into her office.

Jeremy Prattwurst—Pratt for short—didn't look happy. His mouth was tight, and his expression cold. There had been whisperings all afternoon that someone had slipped up, big-time, and signs of stress showed in the unusual length of time spent behind closed doors in meetings, but so far none of the executive staff had spilled any details. The lack of information was, in itself, worrying. In this place, rumors spread like wildfire.

"You saw Esther Morell two days ago."

"That's correct." She had made sure that was no big secret. If she managed to pull even a fraction of the Morell resources under the RCS umbrella, it would be a major coup.

"Esther Morell's dead."

"What?" For a second Dana thought he wasn't serious. When his expression didn't change, she shook her head. "I don't believe it."

"A car accident. The thing I'm trying to work out is why she came to see you when the Morell Group banks with Bessel Holt."

Dana blinked. The fact that Esther still dealt with Bessel Holt was, to put it mildly, shocking. Dana had had the distinct impression that she had cut her ties and was dealing locally. "She said she was interested in making some investments."

"She wasn't interested in making an investment. She stole a client's money."

By the time Pratt had finished detailing how Esther had managed to bypass the account security features and transfer the funds, Dana understood exactly what Esther Morell's visit had been about. She had been using her. She had remembered her terrible memory and her trick with the card. The whole thing with the coffee spilling, and Esther helping mop up the mess, had been staged so she could lift her keyboard and get a look at the access codes.

Pratt seated himself on the corner of her desk and hitched up a trouser leg. The movement was calm and studied. "What I'm interested in," he said slowly, "is how, exactly, she managed to get hold of our access codes. The only conclusion I can come to is that she got them from you."

Dana swallowed. "I didn't give her anything. *I wouldn't.* It's more than my life's worth—"

He leaned forward and lifted her keyboard. Adrenaline pumped and for a raw moment she couldn't breathe. The card was sitting right where she always kept it.

He picked up the card. "Della told me about your little habit. It looks like she wasn't the only one who knew."

Dana sucked in a breath, trying to control the rapid pounding of her heart. Della worked in the adjoining office. She must have spotted Dana slipping the card under the keyboard.

She swallowed and blinked. Her nose had begun to run. She couldn't believe it, she was crying. She hadn't cried in years. In a convulsive movement she grabbed at a tissue, and in that moment saw an instant replay of Esther Morell doing the same thing. "She spilt some coffee and lifted the keyboard. She saw the card, but only for a second. I grabbed it and slipped it in the drawer. There was no way she could have remembered that many numbers."

"Are you telling me that you didn't know Esther Morell had a photographic memory?"

Dana blew her nose, discarded the tissues and pulled some more, her mind frantic. *A photographic memory?* If Pratt had thrown a brick at her head she couldn't have been more stunned. "I didn't know that," she said tightly.

Pratt was silent for a moment. "If you really didn't know, that might be the only thing that saves you."

The door opened. A lean, dark man of average height entered the room. Dana had seen him before on a couple of occasions, but only fleetingly. Alex Lopez usually dealt directly with Pratt.

Pratt straightened, handed the man the card and left the room, closing the door behind him. Warily, Dana pushed to her feet. Lopez was young, in his early twenties, and expensively dressed in a charcoal-gray suit with a diamond tiepin. He was wearing gloves.

He stared at the card for a moment, then slid it into his pocket. "Because of you, Esther Morell was able to access my account and remove a substantial sum of money."

He mentioned the amount and Dana's head reeled. Despite working in banking for most of her life, she didn't know it was possible for any one person to hold that much money in liquid funds. If anyone did have that much *legitimate* personal wealth, it would usually be split into various forms: property, bonds, shares, blue-chip investments, mortgage funds. If a large amount of capital was available for even a few hours, it went on the overnight money market, or for longer periods on the short-term money market. For Lopez to have that amount in liquid funds meant the rumors in the office that he was involved in organized crime were true.

The slap came out of left field, snapping her head sideways. The back of her legs hit her office chair and she stumbled off balance, clutching at the desk to stay upright.

"I could break your neck." His voice was calm, even casual. "But that's not what I need right now."

Half-formed and horrifying visions of what he might possibly need made her feel physically sick. That amount of money could only come from one source: drugs. Despite the bank's reputation, she hadn't expected to deal with criminals. People wanting to reduce their tax bill, yes, but not real criminals.

Something warm trickled down her chin. Dana touched her mouth. Her bottom lip was stinging and she could taste blood. "What, then?"

His gaze flashed and she realized she'd pushed his buttons with that reply. A shudder worked its way down her spine. He had just assaulted her and threatened her; she could go to the police. She was sorry she had made a mistake, and sorry that he'd lost his money because of it, but hey, she only worked here. There was no reason she had to put up with any of this. She would lose her job, but that wasn't a problem. She no longer wanted anything to do with RCS.

"Where is the money?"

She flinched, expecting another blow. When it didn't come, she let out a breath. "I don't understand what makes you think I had anyth—"

"Where is the money that you and Esther and Xavier le Clerc stole from me?"

She stared at Lopez. Now she knew he was crazy. She had known Xavier, but years ago. She hadn't heard anything about him for more than a decade, ever since the tabloids had lost interest in a story and a trail that had gone cold. "What has le Clerc got to do with this?"

A flush stained his cheekbones. A gun appeared in his hand. He jammed the barrel against the side of her neck. *"Give me the account numbers."*

The instant cold metal touched her skin, she froze. "I don't know the account numbers. I don't know what Esther did with the money. And I don't know anything about le Clerc."

His gaze didn't waver. "I have your daughter."

Her heart slammed against her chest. Panic turned to sheer terror. *Taylor.* She should be at home, watching TV or doing homework, not—

Her jaw clamped. She had to stay calm, work this out. He could be lying. She had done a training course about coping with armed offenders. She knew the tactics: stay quiet, stay still, use soothing language, give him what he wanted. But in this case she didn't *have* what Lopez wanted. "I don't understand how I can help you. I made a mistake writing the access codes down, but I had nothing to do with Esth—"

The barrel jabbed into her throat, choking off her breath.

"I don't believe you," he said with deadly calm. "And until I'm satisfied that you don't know where the money is, you and your daughter will do exactly as I say."

Nine

Colombia, one week later

Heat enveloped Dennison as he stepped out of the Cessna onto the rough grass of a private airfield, the only clear strip of land he'd seen for mile upon mile of thick, impenetrable jungle, except for the arid moonscape that surrounded the Chavez stronghold.

Lopez exited the plane as a dust-covered vehicle came to a stop just beyond the inky shadow cast by the plane. Draping his jacket over one shoulder, Dennison waited for the pilot to unload his overnight bag and studied the vehicle, which looked remarkably like an ancient Rolls-Royce.

The driver, a young Latino, requested their weapons, then held the door. Shaking his head, Dennison waited for Lopez to take his place, then climbed in. As the Rolls-Royce bumped across the airfield, a second vehicle, this one a jeep bristling with a motley assortment of men and automatic weapons, fell in behind them. If he had needed a reminder that he'd left civilization as he knew it behind, that was it. The Chavez compound was situated at Macaro, hundreds of miles east from Bogotá on a mesa overlooking the Vaupés River, smack in the middle of coca country.

The Rolls proceeded at a slow pace through the small village, working its way ever higher. The blunt lines of the compound wavered in the distance; the heat shimmer giving the sprawling casa bounded by high, thick walls an almost mystical aspect.

Fifteen minutes later, the car rolled to a halt outside what could only be described as a *castillo*. From the air, it had looked impressive. On the ground, it was big enough to take up an entire city block.

A plump woman dressed in faded black, reminding Dennison of a dusty crow against the pristine white of the walls, hurried down the steps. The woman, who he guessed was Marco's housekeeper, opened the door for Lopez. Dennison opened his own door and stepped out of the creaking luxury of the Rolls, gaze narrowed against the glare of sunlight off the building as Lopez spoke to the woman. He noticed that she stepped back, her head bowed respectfully. The conversation was brief, the dialect difficult to understand, but Dennison was fluent in Spanish. The woman had indicated that Marco was waiting in the study.

After the glaring heat, it took Dennison long seconds to adjust to the dimness of the casa, which was built along medieval lines with flagstone floors, vaulted ceilings and enormous fireplaces. Dark, heavy furniture gleamed in clusters, decorating a seemingly endless succession of reception rooms and halls. Faded tapestries and what looked like the weapons and armor once used by the conquistadors hung from the walls.

A servant scurried ahead, dressed in what Dennison now recognized as a uniform of sorts—black pants and a white shirt with a black waistcoat. A set of double doors swung open and the servant backed away, melting into the shadows.

Despite all the research he'd done before this meeting, Dennison's stomach tensed as a white-haired man, much smaller than he had imagined, rose to his feet and walked toward them.

Despite having the heavy features and thick build of a peon, Marco Chavez traced his ancestry back to the first conquistadors, claiming that his blood was royal. He enjoyed the connection and the rich history, and he enjoyed the wealth of his empire, originally forged from Mayan and Inca gold and now rejuvenated with the new currency, coca. In a country dragged down by poverty, he lived like a king.

He had taken his obsession with royalty a step further by traveling to Spain for a wife. Maria Beatriz had been chosen for her bloodline, which could be traced back to the House of Aragon.

When Maria had eventually died after a series of miscarriages, Marco hadn't replaced her. He had been nearing sixty and he had what he had wanted, a son.

Lopez moved forward. Marco opened his arms for the traditional embrace, revealing the butt of a shoulder-holstered weapon, and Dennison experienced a curious moment of awareness.

The driver of the Rolls had taken his Glock and Lopez's knife. When they had arrived at the walls of the casa, the jeep load of armed men had peeled off. From the time they'd stepped into the dim entrance hall, he had noticed a number of people, servants mostly, and the security personnel who had kept pace with them as they'd walked. At no time had he seen a weapon on anyone within the environs of the house, and he had been looking.

He logged the movements around him, the weird sense of premonition strong enough to make him break out in a sweat. Two men were behind him, one in the far corner, and at least ten that he'd counted within calling distance.

With a smooth movement, almost in slow motion, Alex loosened off the old man's clasp, slipped his hand inside Marco's jacket and pulled out the automatic pistol. Jabbing the barrel against Marco's chest, he pulled the trigger and stepped back.

Shock reverberated through Dennison as he watched the old man crumple. Breath held tight in his lungs, his hand reached for a gun that was no longer there, the moment impossibly vivid as he tensed against the anticipated punch of bullets as Marco's soldiers reacted.

The silence following the detonation of the gun stretched, and the moment took on a surreal quality. Dennison was reminded of the first time *he* had killed; the thump of adrenaline almost stopping his heart, the weirdness of space and time when, for those few fractured seconds, everything had culminated in a series of freeze frames. But this wasn't a dealer in a back alley in Chinatown. They were in Colombia and this was Marco Chavez.

Dark eyes, blank with shock, centered on Lopez. No one could shoot except Lopez. He had the only gun in the house. Dennison studied the hole in Marco's chest. The lack of movement indicated that the old man had been killed outright.

The irony of the way he had died didn't escape Dennison. Marco had fallen prey to the one weakness in his rigid security regime. He had had the only weapon, but it had been taken off him.

Of all the scenarios he had projected when they hadn't been able to recover the money, this hadn't been one of them. In theory, the loss of billions of the cartel's cash reserves should have signed Lopez's death warrant. If he had belonged to a "normal" crime family, he would be dead already. But there was nothing remotely normal about either Marco or his son.

Dennison hadn't thought that Marco would kill Lopez. For the past twenty-four years, Alex had been

Marco's entire focus. The wholesale slaughter Marco had ordered to force Alex's release from a Colombian prison was a case in point. To preserve his son, Marco had destroyed his standing in his own country, necessitating that he live in a virtual state of siege. The hatred the massacres had sparked had been so intense, he had had to take Alex out of the equation altogether and remove him to the States under a false identity.

Unfortunately, the overprotective approach, mixed with the weirdness and isolation of Alex's upbringing, hadn't made the Chavez heir a balanced human being. The casual way he had just gunned down his father confirmed it.

Pedro crept forward, then crossed himself when he saw the blood staining the front of Marco's jacket and spattered on Alex's hand.

Alex leveled the gun at Pedro. "Don't worry," he said. "It's not mine."

All the hairs at the back of Dennison's neck stood on end. Any normal person would have been consumed with guilt or terror at killing a parent. Alex had smoothly sidestepped those emotions and instead was calmly assuring his father's servant that *he* was unharmed.

Alex stepped away from Pedro and the crumpled form of Marco. Glancing around the room, he began to speak.

The flatly spoken words echoed in the cavernous room.

He was the line; he had the blood.
He was their king.

Dennison watched the slow, deliberate way Alex ate and a shudder moved down his spine. All through this trip, he had been anticipating a downscaling of Alex's role in the cartel and a gold-plated opportunity for his own escape. Marco's murder had put a proverbial spanner in his plans. He had worked through his options and, unfortunately, come up with the same answer: he was back to square one. With Anne in the clinic, no matter how much he wanted to, he couldn't disappear. His only hope was that Lopez would be forced to stay in Colombia and oversee the coca operation, leaving him free and clear to make arrangements to move Anne and disappear off Lopez's scope.

Alex set his fork down and waited for a servant to take his plate and refill his glass of iced water. "I've made a decision."

Dennison almost choked on the odd concoction of reconstituted salted fish mixed with rice that had been ladled onto his plate. He had a sudden, all-too-familiar, cornered-rat feeling.

Alex sipped at the water, his movements as mundane and unhurried as if they were sitting by the pool at his house in San Francisco, but Dennison wasn't fooled. He had the unsettling conviction that, despite his preoccupation with the organizational chaos wrought by Marcos's death, Lopez could see right through him.

"Now that Marco's gone, I need you here. Someone has to run this end of the business," he stated flatly. "You're not going back to the States."

Xavier le Clerc studied the steaming carafe of coffee that room service had just delivered to his suite, along with a plate of hot biscuits served with curls of butter and a dish of preserves. The waiter deposited a folded newspaper beside the coffeepot. Ignoring the coffee and the food, Xavier tipped the waiter, then unfolded the newspaper.

Marco Chavez was dead.

Finally the information that had been communicated to him twenty-four hours ago via a source within the Colombian government was now official news. Interestingly, there was no mention of the fact that Marco had been murdered by his own son. Instead the story speculated that, as Chavez had been over seventy years of age with a history of heart problems, it was likely that he had expired from natural causes.

Turning to the back of the paper, he found the death notice he had been expecting, and any hope that Esther had survived the "accident" evaporated. When her body hadn't been recovered from the site, she had been presumed drowned. The river and parts of San Francisco-Bay had been searched, without success. For a while Xavier had thought it was possible she was alive and in Lopez's hands, but if Cesar had authorized a memorial service, that could only be because he knew she was dead.

His jaw tightened as he studied the formally worded notice. If Esther had entrusted him with her daughter, he believed he could have gotten them both to safety; they could have disappeared without a trace.

He turned to the business section. There was still no mention of the theft from RCS. Thirteen billion dollars had disappeared into thin air, and the crime hadn't registered.

He no longer knew where the money was. Esther had made arrangements for almost the entire sum— minus the amount he needed to pay off his people— to be transferred into an account she had set up at a reputable Swiss bank. He could guess at the bank she had chosen, but unless she had kept a record of the account number, to all intents and purposes the money was now lost.

The money, useful as it had been as a tool to expose Lopez and, more important, the cabal who backed him, no longer concerned Xavier. Marco's death had stirred up a hornet's nest in South America and in the States. Lopez was not only fighting for control, he was fighting for survival. The opportunity inherent in the struggle could finally provide the break he needed.

Finally, after years of patient searching, he was on the verge of picking up a trail that had gone cold, a trail that had started in Lubeck, Germany, in 1944.

Ten

Cesar stared at Rina's small, straight body as she lay in the private clinic Lopez had had her removed to. Her head was bandaged and her right arm was in plaster. Unconscious, her face smoothed out, she looked a lot like Esther and a little like him, but he didn't feel the usual rush of warmth and pride when he looked at her. Fear had squeezed him to the bone, and the jab of cold metal in his ribs reminded him that if he did one thing Lopez didn't like, he was dead.

Cesar was in shock. He knew it on an intellectual level, but that didn't begin to describe the reality. He couldn't sleep, he couldn't eat and he couldn't stop shaking.

He wouldn't ever be able to wipe the stark image of Esther's body or the sight of Rina lying pale and bloodied on a hospital gurney from his mind.

Or the fact that he had betrayed them both.

He stared at Rina through the glass panel of the door and felt panic rise.

Thirteen billion dollars.

There was no way back from that.

The raw fear of what Lopez would do, not to him but to Rina, made him break out in a clammy sweat. His own personal fear of death had been ground away by the past few days. He no longer cared if he lived or died, but Rina *had* to survive.

He had failed Esther; he wouldn't fail his daughter. He would do anything, say anything, to protect her. "I'll do whatever it takes to recover the money—or replace it."

The offer made his gut hollow out. If Lopez accepted, he had effectively sold himself into cartel bondage. Even trading in illicit drugs, it would take him a lifetime to amass thirteen billion dollars.

Lopez sent him a glance that was utterly lacking in humanity. "I'm afraid I'm going to require much more from you than that. The girl belongs to me."

Part 2

Eleven

Present day, Winton, Oregon

Just seconds short of midnight on the eve of her second wedding anniversary, Rina Morell Lopez walked into a wall. Blind since the age of ten, she literally didn't see it coming.

When she came to seconds later, her skull throbbing with a deep-seated ache, she had the sense to remain lying on the floor until her head stopped swimming.

The floor, she noted, was hard and very cold despite the West Coast town of Winton's warm midsummer temperatures. The chill bit through the tank top and cotton pants she'd worn to bed. Sensitive fingertips that doubled as her eyes when she sculpted traced a network of fine crevices: a mosaic, apparently. Rina didn't know for sure, and she could care less. The house her husband, Alex, had recently bought, and which he was in the process of renovating, was large and expensive, but she could be lying on bare concrete for all the difference it made to her. The visuals and how much they cost didn't matter so much as the obstacles, and this one had been huge.

The wall hadn't existed this morning, which meant it had only just been constructed. The problem was nobody, including her husband, had bothered to tell the blind person in the house.

Gingerly, Rina touched her forehead. There was a swelling dead center. When she'd fallen, the floor had given her a matching goose egg at the back of her head. Both lumps were painful enough to bring tears to her eyes, but at least there was no blood.

Wincing, she eased into a sitting position, her stomach churning at the thought of blood. Ever since "the accident," she'd been phobic about it. At first the tiniest cut had practically sent her catatonic, but as time had passed the phobia had toned down. Now she simply threw up and, if there was enough of the red stuff, she fainted.

Pushing onto her knees, Rina shuffled forward until she found the offending wall, braced her palms flat on the unplastered board and took a moment to reorient.

When she'd knocked herself out, she had been on her way to the kitchen to get a snack. She had left her bedroom, walked along the hall and down the stairs, then taken a left, past the dining room. By her calculations, the formal lounge should be off to the right and the corridor that led to the kitchen and laundry should be dead ahead.

In theory.

Walking into a wall seemed symptomatic of how her life had gone ever since she had gotten married, but in an odd way, the fall had cleared her mind. She had already gone out on a limb and way out of her comfort zone for Alex. She hadn't wanted to leave San Francisco and she definitely hadn't wanted to move to Oregon. The fact that Alex hadn't bothered to tell her about such a major change to the house plan after she'd spent painstaking days learning the layout of the rooms confirmed her decision to leave.

Marriage statistics were something of a joke, but her situation wasn't funny. The suspicion that Alex had been more interested in a business merger with her father than home, hearth and family with her, had just coalesced into certainty. The marriage had been a mistake.

Putting two fingers in her mouth, Rina whistled a high, piercing note that was almost silent. The effort sent pain stabbing through her skull, but it was a better option than calling out for Alex. When she had passed his suite she had paused to listen, even though she'd known the likelihood that he was actually in his own bed was remote.

Since they'd moved less than a month ago, Alex had spent even less time at home than usual. He traveled extensively, managing his property development company and the gambling franchises both he and her father operated, but that didn't account for all of his absences at night.

They were the second reason their marriage was over. Her husband was a very clever, very busy man, but he had forgotten something fundamental: his wife might be blind, but she wasn't deaf or dumb, and it didn't take a genius to work out he was having an affair.

A scrabbling on the stairs heralded Baby's arrival.

A wet nose nuzzled her cheek, sending another jolt of pain through her skull. Rina lifted a hand to keep the big golden retriever at bay. "Ease off, Baby."

With a whine Baby sat, his tail thumping the floor, and Rina turned in his direction, her heart pounding.

Mouth dry, she wondered if she was hallucinating. After years of pitch-blackness, of being able to see absolutely nothing, she could "see" Baby. Or, more accurately, she could see light where Baby was, a pale glow tinged with a warm smudge of candy-pink.

Rina stared until her eyes ached, reluctant to relinquish the soft beauty, even if it was a hallucination. She had to be suffering from a mild concussion, although she couldn't quite get her head around how she could see visual color effects when she was profoundly blind.

Unless she was regaining her sight.

Heart still pounding, she straightened, and found that when her focus was removed from Baby, the light disappeared. Panicked, she "looked" at Baby again. The sharp movement sent another throb through her skull, but she could still "see" the light.

Relief poured through her, along with a mounting excitement she knew she should squash. The phenomenon would probably go when her headache eased, but despite the logic, she clung to the spectacle, drinking in every detail. The glow was pale and diffused at the edges like mist, with a faint smudge of pink in the region of Baby's chest. She didn't know what was causing it, but she was going to hold on to the glow for as long as she could.

Experimentally, she turned her head and frowned. As before, the light remained only where Baby was, which didn't make sense. She opened and closed her eyes, and found that made no difference. She could still see the color with her eyes closed, which meant her optic nerves couldn't be involved.

The disappointment was acute. She *was* hallucinating, after all.

Twenty-two years ago, after the car accident that had killed her mother and left her with a broken wrist and head injuries, she had been CAT-scanned and exhaustively examined by neurological and eye specialists. Her head injury hadn't been severe and her eyes and the complicated system of optic pathways and nerves hadn't been injured. According to the experts, she should have regained her sight.

As time had passed, according to the neurological specialist who had continued to treat her, her chances of regaining any portion of her sight were as uncertain as the cause of the injury itself. Physically Rina was able to see—her retinas received light and transmitted it via nerve impulses to the brain. It was there that the process was interrupted; her mind simply refused to register the images.

At thirty-two, Rina had given up on any hope of a medical cure and she wasn't looking for a miracle. She preferred to deal head-on with the life she'd ended up with. Whatever the explanation, physical or psychosomatic, she was blind, period. She would take a couple of pills and get some sleep. In the morning, the light show, whatever it was, would be over.

"Sad but true, Baby. But at least being blind means I got you."

Baby snorted and cocked his head. Holding her breath, Rina cupped Baby's head and stroked one silky ear, and all the fine hairs at her nape stood on end. She couldn't see Baby, but the light where his head was had moved in such a way that she had instantly understood he was cocking his head. *She had been right.*

Adrenaline surged. She was still blind, but she could see *something.* Exactly what that something was, she wasn't sure.

Pushing to her feet, Rina leaned into the wall until she felt steady, then hooked the fingers of one hand through Baby's collar. "Okay, boy, let's go back to bed."

Her appetite was long gone, killed by the headache and the stunning discovery that she could see light. What that light was she had no idea. The only hard fact she had was that there was nothing normal about the phenomenon: she could see with her eyes closed.

All she wanted now was a glass of water and some painkillers, and both of those she could get in the familiar, *safe* surroundings of her own suite.

Rina repeated the order to walk on, but Baby refused to budge and Rina recognized the signs. Baby was a Seeing Eye dog; he was trained for "intelligent disobedience," to ignore her commands if he recognized danger or an obstacle. Right now Baby was blocking her.

Cautiously, Rina went down on her hands and knees and felt the floor ahead and around them with her hands. Her fingers hit the hallway wall to her left. To the right, just beyond where Baby was sitting, the polished mosaic ended in a raw edge. Cold gripped her as she traced the extent of the hole that she could reach. Now that she knew the hole was there, she could feel a draught flowing upward and sensed that the hole was large, possibly dug down into a cellar beneath, which was logical, since the kitchen and laundry were close.

With a shiver she pulled back from the edge. She had been lying just inches away, which meant she had come close to both walking into the hole and, after she had knocked herself out, falling into it.

Still on her hands and knees, she backed away farther, pulling Baby with her until her shoulder brushed up against the hallway wall. She had been out most of the day, coincidentally having a routine checkup, which had involved a return flight to San Francisco. She and Baby had both eaten before the evening flight home. When they'd returned, Rina had had no reason to go near the kitchen. She'd gone straight upstairs, showered and gone to bed.

Apparently, while she was away, Alex had either forgotten to inform the workmen who had been carrying out the renovations that she was blind, or else they had simply neglected to put a safety barrier around the excavation. Either way the error was inexcusable: she could have been badly injured.

Baby nudged her arm and stood; his message clear: he wanted to move away from the hole.

Using the wall as a guide, Rina rose to her feet and began the slow, careful process of negotiating the hole. She wasn't a wimp. She'd had her share of knocks and bruises, but for now, she was officially shaken. For a blind person, just walking to the shops in a strange town could be a near-death experience, but she hadn't expected to have one in the supposed comfort and safety of her own home.

Alex Lopez stood on the patio of a darkened penthouse apartment that overlooked Winton's deep-sea port, observing the unloading of the container vessel *Capricorn* through a high-resolution nightscope that had been developed for Special Forces.

His interest sharpened as a four-wheel-drive truck came to a halt in the parking area adjacent to the dock. A dark-haired man, above average height with a lean, muscular build, emerged from the vehicle. After a brief discussion with port officials and the ship's captain, he began checking the manifest as the cargo was unloaded.

The process was slow and methodical, but Lopez had no problem with the way the business was being done. James Thompson had come to his attention just months ago. He was a businessman with an import license for farm equipment from Australia that, interestingly enough, was shipped by a container vessel that made stops along the South American coast. Thompson also had business connections south of the border. Those two pieces of information, when combined, had interested him greatly.

The firm Thompson owned had been trading for several years with a clean bill of health from port and coast guard officials. Thompson himself was clean, except for one small incident Lopez had managed to unearth. He had covered his past well enough and didn't have a criminal record, but Lopez had had the patience to dig.

Several years ago Thompson, who was ex-military, had been stationed in Panama and had become involved in an incident across the border in Colombia. A village suspected of harboring a terrorist camp had been raided; several civilians had died, including women and children. In the process a coca plant had been uncovered. There had been more deaths and a large shipment of cocaine ready for export had disappeared. Thompson and his men had been held on suspicion for a month. Without witnesses prepared to testify, they had been released and given the option of voluntary resignation or a dishonorable discharge. Nothing had been proved, but the military report was damning. In the eyes of his superiors, Thompson was a cold-blooded murderer and a thief.

As Lopez watched, the last of six containers were trucked out. Satisfied that Thompson had delivered on his promise to provide low-risk container space and a clean bill with customs, Lopez took his cell phone out of his pocket and placed a call. "The delivery system is in place."

The voice that answered was dry and precise. Lopez had met the owner of the voice on two occasions in a business partnership that had spanned twenty-two years. In total, he had heard the man's voice only a handful of times, because direct contact was deemed hazardous.

It was a matter of operational procedure that they dealt only through previously agreed third parties unless there was an emergency. The fact that they were speaking directly now emphasized the high risk involved with the delivery of this particular package. The agreed protocol was necessary to protect the interests of all parties involved and to hide the existence of a secret cabal that had its roots buried deep in the political and military structure of the U.S. government. If Lopez became compromised, he was on his own. If he broke the protocol, his life was forfeit.

The situation didn't suit him, but twenty-two years ago, with his cash reserves gone and rival cartels baying, he'd been forced to sell out to the cabal to survive. The rescue package had come at a price. In return for financial backing Lopez had gotten his hands dirty brokering terrorism, transporting arms and, on occasion, personnel.

Unlike his father, Marco, he didn't have access to the highest echelon of the cabal, although over the past twenty years he had made it his business to identify a number of cabal personnel. His father had been content with the cabal calling the shots, because the resulting wealth from the association had been immense.

Marco had been content; Lopez was not.

This shipment was a turning point, the first time they had made a mistake. Organizations came and went, they peaked and bottomed out as corruption and dissatisfaction crept in. As the Americans said, every dog had its day, and he took the madness of this latest shipment as a clear signal that the day of the cabal as it presently existed was over. Once his plans were in place, the ultimatum he planned to deliver was simple: either they accepted him into the highest echelon, with its rarefied wealth and power and political influence, or he would expose them.

It was ironic that Thompson, a man who had been used as a scapegoat by the cabal in one of their early, cruder forays into the cocaine business, had fallen into his hands now and would be one of the instruments of their downfall.

Lopez packed the scope in its case, locked the apartment and took the private lift to the ground floor. His bodyguard, Earl Slater, was waiting in the car park, pale gaze alert despite the fact that it was after three in the morning.

After a brief conversation, Lopez climbed into his own vehicle and headed for home. Slater's Rodeo nosed in behind, following closely. In terms of security, traveling in separate vehicles wasn't ideal, but it was a provision Lopez insisted upon with all of his security staff. Despite the added risk, he was meticulous about preserving his personal space.

Minutes later he turned into his driveway and acknowledged the security guard as he opened the gates and lifted a phone to his ear to advise house security that he was home.

Lights glowed softly as Lopez accelerated up a small incline, illuminating the pleasing curve of the formal gravel drive and the fountain that took center stage outside the portico of the main house. Slater peeled off in the direction of his private quarters, headlights sweeping across a smooth expanse of lawn.

Seconds later, as Lopez exited the car, a faint sound registered over the hum of the garage door closing. He reached for the handgun that was secured beneath the driver's seat.

Cold metal touched the side of his neck. "Don't."

Lopez released his hold on the gun and slowly straightened. "Thompson."

"Your security's sloppy."

His security was very good. But for Thompson to have breached his perimeter defenses and the house security in the few minutes' head start he'd had meant it wasn't good enough.

Lopez turned his head and met Thompson's cool stare. If the younger man were going to shoot, he would have done it by now. "What do you want?"

Thompson stepped back from the car, methodically ejected the magazine from the handgun and placed both the gun and the magazine on the floor of the garage. His gaze was cold. "Promotion."

Twelve

Rina registered the growing heat of the morning sun beaming through the French doors that opened off the sitting room and the sound of a pen moving rapidly across paper as her therapist, Diane Eady, made notes.

A click signaled she had set the pen down. "The fact that you recovered some kind of visual ability, whether real or imagined, is interesting."

"Have you heard of that happening to anyone else?"

"No, but the mind is a powerful, complicated mechanism. People create all sorts of conditions that shouldn't exist. It's possible that because you want to see, your mind has created a 'safe' way for you to see."

"Safe" meaning a way that didn't include the risk of triggering the images and memories that were the cause of her psychosomatic blindness.

She settled back deeper into the armchair and pushed the dark glasses she habitually wore during the day a little higher on the bridge of her nose. "Just before I fell I can't remember feeling that I *wanted* to see. That's not something I consciously think about. I was hungry, I was on my way to the kitchen to get something to eat."

"Do you want to be blind?"

Rina's stomach contracted against the emotions the question evoked. The night she had hit her head she hadn't slept. Aside from worrying about a concussion, for those few hours she had lived on a knife's edge of hope and expectation, waiting to see if her vision *would* return. She had wanted to see with a fierceness that had shaken her. "No one wants to be blind."

And Rina knew she wasn't…entirely.

She couldn't see Diane, but she could make out a dim smudge of light where she was sitting. The predominant color was a cool, indistinct gray-blue, with tinges of green. After a visit to the local surgery for a checkup last week on the morning after her fall, she had noticed similar colors around the practice nurse and the doctor. "So what *am* I seeing?"

"Scientifically, I don't know. At a guess, what's popularly known as auric colors. Although don't quote me on that."

Rina noticed that an additional color, orange, flashed through the blue-gray, the flare as brief as Diane's spurt of amusement.

Over the past few days, the colors had sharpened and become stronger. She didn't know how it worked, but she was "seeing" more and more clearly.

Grasping Baby's harness, Rina rose to her feet, signaling the end of the session. Diane had a flight to catch and appointments in San Francisco that afternoon. In her busy schedule, this had been an unplanned consultation, fitted in because Diane had become increasingly concerned about the oddball results of Rina's head injury. "I figured it had to be something off-center."

"And how do you feel about it?"

The question was typically Diane, dry and no-nonsense, belying the affection that had spilled over the bounds of professionalism and formed the basis of a friendship that had long outlasted—in Rina's opinion—her need for therapy. "The way I see it—" her mouth twitched "—excuse the pun, no one can sneak up on me again. I just wish the furniture glowed in the dark."

"You know, it is possible the accident could spark memories about the car crash. Sometimes there's a delayed reaction, so be prepared. The injury doesn't seem to have affected you unduly, but it is a head injury and you are vulnerable. The colors you're seeing could be an indication of change. Sometimes even a small trauma can stimulate a reaction and shake things loose that we would rather not handle."

The statement ended on a subtle questioning note. Rina smiled and ignored the bait. She'd had years of therapy with a number of specialists. Most of it had been aimed at releasing her memories of the accident. In theory, if she remembered, the psychosomatic block would go and she would get her sight back, although there were no guarantees.

The chair scraped as Diane got to her feet. "Any more problems with the house?"

"Nothing I can't handle." Rina's fingers tightened on Baby's harness. She'd had a couple more unnerving experiences after her fall, all owing to workmen leaving equipment in unexpected places. Baby had kept her safe, but that didn't change the fact that she was quietly, furiously angry.

"I can have a word with Alex if you like."

"And expect to get through?" The past week Alex had been away more than he was home. When he was in he spent most of his time on the phone or in meetings. Rina had never known him to be this busy, or this unapproachable. But, whether they discussed the situation or not, Rina's decision was made: the marriage was over.

"Don't say I didn't tell you. He's a cold fish. Charming, but cold."

Rina controlled her expression as she negotiated the coffee table and directed Baby toward the door. She had made the decision to marry Alex for a number of reasons she had considered valid at the time. At the top of the list was the fact that she had been thirty and lonely, and there hadn't been anyone on her personal scope for more than three years. She had wanted the company and security of a committed relationship, and she had wanted to start a family. The fact that her father had supported the relationship had been an added bonus.

Big mistake.

The door popped open before she reached it.

"What's the prognosis?" a gravelly voice demanded.

Rina's surprise at her father's unexpected visit was buried in the brief bear hug Cesar Morell gave her, although the reason for his visit was self-evident. The stiffness of the jacket he was wearing on such a warm day meant he was here for a business meeting with Alex. "You didn't ring to say you were coming."

"I didn't know myself until a couple of hours ago. What's this I hear about you walking into walls?"

Rina hid her surprise at the question. She hadn't broadcast the fact that she'd had a fall, so the only person who could have told him was Alex, which, lately, was out of character. The fact that Cesar had walked in on her therapy session, however, *was* typical. Ever since she had been discharged from the hospital after the accident, he had smothered her with attention. In all that time he had never once questioned his right to check up on almost every detail of her life.

"Is that why she's having therapy?" The question was directed at Diane. "What's wrong with her?"

Rina's knee-jerk irritation at Cesar's habit of talking about her as if she wasn't there was canceled out by the sense of wonder that for the first time in twenty-two years she could see her father, even if it was only in shades of mahogany-brown tinged with touches of yellow and red.

The colors, Rina decided, matched his personality. Cesar was a forceful man, used to having his way. Among his business associates, his lack of tact and volcanic temper were legendary.

The snap as Diane closed her briefcase was louder than normal. "There's nothing 'wrong' with Rina. This was just a routine session."

Cesar's reply bordered on sarcastic; Diane's riposte was equally sharp.

Smothering a grin, Rina sidestepped Cesar, who was building up a full head of steam, and directed Baby out into the hall and toward the front door. Cesar and Diane had been dueling for years. Rina was certain they both secretly enjoyed the encounters.

The brisk tap of Diane's heels sounded behind her. "I see your father hasn't gained any charm with age." She paused at the door, the hug redolent of Chanel No.5. "I wish I could have stayed for a real visit. If you need to talk about *anything,* call me. I'm always willing to listen."

When the quiet purr of Diane's car receded, Rina turned in the direction of her studio. As she strolled around the house, the crunch of tires on gravel signaled that yet another business associate of Alex and her father's had arrived. Normally, aside from the inevitable phone calls, Alex didn't bring work home. He had an office in Winton and another in Vegas. If a meeting was required it usually happened on his business premises.

Frowning, Rina stepped into her studio, the frustration of trying to end a marriage to a man she had to make an appointment to see dissolving as she ran her fingers over her latest work. The table-size sculpture was the clay prototype for a bronze she'd been commissioned to produce through a gallery in San Francisco. The demand for the tactile sculpture she specialized in had grown, until she was now in the comfortable position of being able to pick and choose commissions. This one was destined to be the centerpiece of a water feature in the courtyard of a hotel in the Embarcadero district in San Francisco, where the changing shapes and textures could be highlighted by both water and sunlight. Once the clay work was complete, the piece would be carefully packed and trucked to the small specialist foundry she used just outside of Oakland. There a mold would be made and the casting done.

Sliding her fingers over the delicately ridged clay, Rina settled to work, but achieving any kind of flow was difficult. Now that she'd made up her mind to leave, she was itching to put her plans in motion. But first, she needed to have a conversation with Alex.

* * *

Cesar Morell sat back in his chair and surveyed the occupants of his son-in-law's study, uncomfortable with the exposure when anonymity was usually preserved. He knew Slater, but the rest of the men he'd been introduced to were strangers.

McDonnell and Johnson were cold fish. Santos looked like muscle, pure and simple. James Thompson was laid back, yet watchful. He hadn't said much, which made him even more of an unknown quantity than the other three.

Santos shrugged out of his jacket. As he hooked the jacket over the back of his seat, Cesar glimpsed a tattoo visible on one bicep just beneath the sleeve of his T-shirt. An Army Ranger's insignia.

That was what was wrong. They weren't businessmen, they were soldiers.

The cold sense of unease increased. He was tied to Lopez, but normally, he was excluded from the illegitimate side of the cartel business. In effect, he did what he had always done, made money through developing properties and trading stocks, shares and companies. The fact that in doing so he had become the largest cog in Lopez's money-laundering operation and that a large percentage of the profits he made flowed back to Lopez was a fact that he didn't dwell on any more than necessary. He had made his choice and struck a bargain. As long as Rina's safety was assured, he would do what he had to do.

McDonnell poured a glass of water, the tinkle of

ice cubes breaking the silence. "I think we need to slow this down. We're biting off too much, too fast. We need more time."

Alex's expression didn't change. "We either bite big, or we don't bite at all."

"McDonnell has a good point." The hint of Southern in Thompson's voice relaxed the tension. "But if we don't pull this off, I'm going to lose my shirt."

Alex lifted a brow. "And the Ferrari."

Soft laughter rippled around the room. The moment was further defused when a knock at the door signaled afternoon tea was about to be served.

Cesar accepted a cup of coffee, his mind running over a conversation that should have been mundane, but wasn't. Heavy trucks, a storage facility, shipping...they were discussing storage and delivery options, but the items concerned didn't sound like electrical products or furniture or even cocaine.

When the maid wheeled the trolley out and closed the door, he set his cup and saucer down on the coffee table and made direct eye contact with Lopez. "Just what is it that's being delivered?"

"Missile components. Let me complete the introductions. Johnson is an engineer and an expert on nuclear armaments, McDonnell is a chemist, Santos is in charge of security, and Thompson is taking care of the transport."

Missiles. The unease he always felt in Lopez's presence tightened into a pressurized band across

Cesar's chest. His heart was pounding; he could feel his blood pressure rocketing. Now he knew Lopez was insane. "What do I have to do with all this?"

Lopez settled back in his chair and steepled his fingers. "You're going to store them for me."

Rina closed the door of her studio and lifted her face to the sun, enjoying the warmth, her mind still pleasantly disengaged by the soothing ritual of turning clay into movement and form.

Baby waited patiently for her to give the command to walk on, more than happy to rest, his rapid pants signaling that he was feeling the heat despite sleeping beneath her workbench for most of the afternoon. Absently, she rubbed at his head, enjoying the rough texture of his fur after the damp smoothness of the clay.

For a Seeing Eye dog, Baby was a little on the large side. When Rina's name had finally come up as a guide dog recipient, she had had a choice of two dogs. But Baby hadn't allowed her a choice. He had staked his claim, planted himself at her side, and stayed there. In the monthlong training course the institute had provided, the usual growing pains of fitting a human with a guide dog hadn't happened; she and Baby had been a team from the first.

With a touch, she signaled they were moving on. Baby ambled quietly at her side as they moved through the grounds toward the house, taking a circuitous route so Baby could stretch his legs.

Rina was finishing earlier than usual. Normally she worked to a rigid routine, eating the cut lunch the housekeeper, Therese, supplied in a small shady gazebo that adjoined her studio, but after the discussion with Diane she'd felt too restless to keep to routine.

Auric colors.

Of course she had heard of them. Over the past week she had come to the same conclusion herself, because nothing else came close to explaining what she was seeing. But having a trained expert like Diane confirm the phenomenon had been unsettling. She would never in a million years have imagined that she was psychic in any way.

She paused by a rose and bent closer, taking pleasure in the rich perfume. Voices drifted from an open window. She didn't need to study the intonations to know that Alex was in the library with Slater. As she straightened, the words *coca* and *product* jumped out at her.

Her spine tightened as the conversation became clearer, as if the two men had moved closer to the window. Instinct, sharp and visceral, had her stepping quietly back beneath the shady overhang of a rhododendron. Her hand dropped onto Baby's head, staying him. Another phrase floated out of the window. Something about a shipment.

Cesar pushed to his feet, ignoring Lopez's warning glance. The second McDonnell, Johnson,

Santos and Thompson had left the room, the gloves had come off. Incredibly, Slater now had a gun in his hand. "What are you going to do? Shoot me if I don't agree?"

Lopez's gaze was flat. "It can be arranged."

"The way you arranged for Esther to die?"

"Your wife's death was regrettable but unavoidable. Sit down."

"I could go to the police."

"And arrange for your own indictment? Don't forget, I have written and taped evidence that you agreed to the partnership. There isn't a court in this country that wouldn't convict you."

"Indictment doesn't scare me."

"So long as your daughter is safe."

Cesar stared into Lopez's eyes and felt his blood run cold. One of the reasons he had been anxious to visit Lopez had been the now-rare opportunity to check on Rina. Ever since Lopez had moved her to Winton, he had been on edge. When she had been in San Francisco he had been able to keep an eye on her, protect her. Now Lopez had her isolated. "What are you doing to her?"

"She's my wife."

Cesar's stomach tightened. "If you harm her—"

Lopez smiled. "Why would I do that, when she could be so useful to me?"

Thirteen

Adrenaline shoved through Rina's veins. For a disoriented moment the heat and the scents of the garden, the intermittent sound of the voices, faded as another conversation played, similar, but different. She had been a child, sitting at the dinner table taping with her Walkman.

Alex had been there.

The memory was followed by a stark image: her mother staring at her, one hand gripping hers, the sensation so real she could feel the pressure of Esther's fingers tight around her own.

Blood. There was blood everywhere.

Rina's jaw clenched against the instant gag reflex.

Slater's voice registered, wanting to know if Rina suspected anything. Cesar replied in the negative.

Blind or not, she had the eerie sensation of staring down a long tunnel. The flashes of memory had been real. For a split second the blank wall that had closed off her memory had dissolved. She had heard Alex's voice. She had looked into Esther's eyes; she had smelled the blood. She had *been* there.

Twenty-two years ago her mother hadn't died in a car accident. She had been murdered. The man Rina had married had ordered her death.

It didn't make sense. She was supposed to have met Alex Lopez for the first time just over two years ago.

She pressed at her temples, pushing at the ache growing there as she tried to find an explanation for the fact that he had murdered her mother, then, twenty years later, married her.

Cocaine. Product. Shipments.

The motivation for murder was clear enough. Why Cesar and Esther, why *she* was involved, wasn't.

The scrape of a chair signaled the meeting was over. Numbly, Rina retreated, placing her feet with care to minimize the sound as she moved into the deep shade of the garden, pulling Baby in close beside her. She waited, listening, until she was certain Alex's study was empty. Then, just to be sure, got down on her hands and knees and crawled past the window. When she was past, she rose to her feet and walked to the corner of the house, just yards away from the graveled sweep of the drive at the front of the house.

Laying a hand on Baby's head, and cautioning

him to be quiet, she flattened herself against the warm brick of the house, felt for the edge of the building with one hand and peered around.

Her father left first, his colors and the sound of his Cadillac distinctive. Two more men she couldn't identify, then a third, climbed into a vehicle with Slater. Slater's colors were easy to pick, a brownish-gray tinged with a murky yellow. Two of the strangers had distinctly yellowish glows, while the third was more defined, gray tinged with dull red.

With a shudder, she retreated a step and crouched beside Baby. There was one last man, talking with Alex on the steps. His voice had a faint but distinctive Southern lilt. Minutes later he left in a truck. A click signaled the front door had finally closed. She hadn't seen what the man with the Southern accent had looked like, or picked up any more details about what was actually happening, but she no longer cared: she'd heard and seen enough.

Disbelief gripped her. The whole interlude was unreal. What she'd picked up initially had been disjointed. It was possible she had misheard or put the wrong construction on what had been said.

But Alex's statement—that her mother's death had been regrettable, but unavoidable—had been clear enough.

The fact that either Alex or Slater had been holding a gun on her father was even clearer.

Stroking Baby's head, she rose to her feet and started back in the direction of her studio. She needed to think, to decide what to do next. Her knee-jerk reaction was to call the police, but if Alex was what she thought he was, he would have the phones tapped.

A shudder went through her. If he had married her as some kind of insurance to keep Cesar in place in his organization, calling the police from any of the house phones would be dangerous for them both. She would have to use her cell phone.

There was one other option to calling the police. She could go directly to the FBI by calling Taylor Jones.

In the weeks after she had gotten out of hospital, Taylor's mother, Dana Jones, had moved in with them and taken over as housekeeper. They had only stayed a few months, but in that time Rina and Taylor had become firm friends. The friendship had continued despite the fact that they had both gone in different directions career-wise, Rina into the arts and Taylor into the FBI.

"What are you doing here?"

The light baritone, tinged with the slightest hint of humor, almost stopped her heart. Alex.

Rina turned to face Alex, her expression carefully blank. "Baby was dying of heat in the studio. We decided to go for a stroll."

She heard the rustle of suit fabric sliding against the sleeve of his shirt as Alex consulted his watch, and "saw" the movement. Unlike most of the auras of the people around her, there was nothing fuzzy or indistinct about Alex's aura. It was symmetrical, distinct and oddly bisected: one side red, the other black.

"I've got a meeting in town this evening. Why don't you join me for an early dinner instead?"

Forcing a smile, she agreed. Half an hour ago, if Alex had issued an invitation to dine with him, she would have leapt at it, if only to discuss the fact that she wanted a divorce. Now she was under no illusion that leaving would be that easy. Both she and her father were caught in some kind of trap. Added to that, she was almost certain Alex suspected she had overheard the conversation in his study and was testing her.

His hand cupped her elbow. She controlled the urge to wrench away. She didn't want him touching her; she didn't want him anywhere near her.

"Therese's serving gazpacho on the patio. I'll get her to set an extra place."

Her stomach rolled. Gazpacho wasn't blood, but it looked enough like it that she didn't want to eat it. Normally it was never on the menu.

Her husband's love of South American dishes registered, along with his ability to speak fluent Spanish. He sounded American and he had a business degree from Harvard. He had told her he had been born in Boston. His family was, apparently, American, but since the wedding they had melted away and hadn't bothered to visit.

"Watch the steps," Alex murmured.

Stiffly, she mounted the patio steps, waited for Alex to pull out her chair, then sat down. Baby settled close, lying across her feet and huddling against her legs, despite the heat, as if he had picked up on her fear and was trying to comfort her.

Alex made desultory conversation while Therese fussed around the table. The chink of china and cutlery punctuated the soothing flow of a small waterfall in the courtyard that adjoined the patio.

Therese was South American. So were most of the staff on the property.

The house was beautiful, so Rina had been told, more of a palazzo than a house. It was large and rambling, built for entertaining on a lavish scale, with extensive grounds and a complicated security system. There was a separate housing estate for the staff and security personnel. A helicopter pad, and a river bordered one edge of the property.

Not a house; a fortress.

Therese, aware of Rina's dislike of gazpacho, served her a salad and a bread roll. With slow, careful movements, Rina broke the bread and placed a piece in her mouth, suppressing her revulsion as Alex started on his soup.

The world she thought she had known so well, and in which she had comfortably existed for most of her life, was a sham. Cesar had always been wealthy. He ran a successful property development company, owned prime real estate and rental properties in a number of cities, casinos in Vegas and Reno, and a string of businesses in cities up and down the West Coast. She had never questioned the basis of his wealth, but she did now.

Her father's involvement with Alex wasn't the three years he had claimed when he had introduced him to Rina. The relationship went back more than *twenty* years.

Rina chewed and swallowed and started on her salad. Tomatoes, sweet red peppers and chunks of feta cheese. The white cheese would be stained pink by the juices.

Her stomach tensed. Think about the sculpture, the smooth whorls of damp clay, free flowing but ordered, disciplined. Controllable.

Her mother had been murdered and Cesar had known about it.

She swallowed, picked up her glass of water and sipped. The betrayal was numbing…incomprehensible. She was certain Cesar had loved Esther. She still believed that he did.

Grief and white-hot anger slammed into her, squeezing her chest and making her eyes burn. She reached for another small fragment of bread, slipped it into her mouth and gritted her teeth against the need to wrap her arms around her middle and rock like a baby.

Therese removed her salad and placed a bowl of homemade ice cream in front of her. Rina's nostrils flared and her throat closed up again. Strawberry. Not red, exactly, but close enough. With an effort of will, she lifted a tiny spoonful to her mouth and forced herself to swallow.

"Not hungry?"

The light tone in Alex's voice registered. The anger flashed again. She lifted her head and stared at Alex, grateful for the concealment of the dark glasses. Her husband was clever. He had destroyed her family and fooled her. *He had murdered her mother.* She didn't know how to stop him yet, but she would find a way. "Not very. Therese served morning tea while Diane was here, and I had a late lunch."

She stared at his aura and wondered that she had ever thought that he was charming, or even likable.

For the first time, she allowed herself to ackowledge that the red part of Alex's aura looked like blood.

Fourteen

Therese cleared the table. Alex's phone made a beeping sound. He excused himself and walked down the steps of the patio to take the call.

Rina rose to her feet and picked up Baby's harness. Her first instinct was to leave, to simply walk off the estate and keep walking until she could get help, but leaving when she was blind wasn't so easy. The estate was on the fringes of Winton, more in the country than in town, so walking out wasn't a sensible option. Besides, if Alex was suspicious, she wouldn't get past the security at the front gate.

To get out, she would need someone to drive her, and to avoid suspicion, she would need a legitimate excuse to leave.

She needed help, which meant she had to call someone.

To avoid passing anywhere near Alex, she

directed Baby through the house. Taking the back route through the kitchen, she crossed a paved area, strolled past a series of garages and implement sheds and out onto a shady path that meandered down to the river.

Baby stopped, the low hum in his throat gave her an instant of warning.

"Where are you going?"

The voice came from the left, about ten paces away. She hadn't heard Alex's step, which meant he was stationary, standing on the lawn, watching her.

She pressed a hand to her heart. "You gave me a fright."

"Would you like some company?"

Automatically, she stroked the top of Baby's head, soothing him as she struggled to adjust to Alex's deceptive casualness. If Baby thought he was a threat, then he was. "You're welcome to come if you want. We're just going down to the river so Baby can have a swim."

His phone beeped. Alex spoke briefly and paused. "Looks like I'll have to take a rain check on that walk."

"No problem."

Minutes later, she and Baby reached the river-bank. Hands shaking, Rina unfastened Baby's harness, shooed him into the water and sat down. For long minutes she listened. When she was certain she was alone, she slipped her cell phone from her pocket and keyed in Taylor's short dial.

Rina had several cousins, and an aunt and an uncle on her mother's side she could call, but Taylor was the only person she could trust for the simple reason that she was an FBI agent. Right now, more than family, she needed help from someone who had taken an oath to uphold the law.

Seconds later, Taylor picked up. Briefly, Rina outlined what had happened.

Taylor asked a few staccato questions, her voice low.

Rina listened while automatically staying attuned to the myriad of noises around her. It occurred to her that the sound of Baby splashing was enough to drown out footsteps if Alex had decided to take that walk after all. "I know the snatches of conversation I heard aren't exactly hard evidence, but I've decided to go to the police."

There was a brief moment of silence. "Don't do that. We need to get you out of there. There's just one hitch. I can't come and get you. Someone else will have to do it. What we need to do is work out a game plan."

We. That meant the FBI, not the Winton P.D. "It's got to be tonight, or tomorrow morning, otherwise I walk out on my own. I think he's suspicious."

"Honey, if Alex really was suspicious, you would know about it."

The flat tone of Taylor's voice and the distinct lack of surprise about everything Rina had said suddenly registered. "You're not in Washington, are you? You're already here. In Winton."

* * *

Within an hour, Rina had made arrangements to leave. She contacted the firm that shipped her work and left a message for them to call first thing in the morning, pack the almost-completed sculpture and express it to Oakland. She collected the file that contained all of her personal papers, tax records and bank accounts from her office and tucked it, along with the few personal possessions she refused to leave behind, in the knapsack she usually wore when she and Baby went walking.

Her phone buzzed. It was Taylor. She had organized an examination for Rina in San Francisco with a leading neurologist the following day. The flights and the appointment were real, so that if Alex checked on any of it, there wouldn't be a problem. The arrangements made sense in light of her recent head injury and also necessitated a night away, so she wouldn't be due back at the house until the evening of the next day. When Rina and Baby climbed into the taxicab Taylor had ordered to arrive at the house in the morning, they would be home free.

It was crucial to Rina's safety that Alex continued to believe that Rina was unaware of his double life or Esther's murder, and it gave the FBI the extra twenty-four hours they needed. If, at any point before that rendezvous time, she felt she was in danger all she had to do was dial Taylor's number and they would get her out.

The fact that the FBI needed twenty-four hours made the back of her neck crawl. If they were running to a schedule, that meant they were planning a bust. It made sense. Taylor was in Winton, undercover; they were surveilling Alex. They had to be close to moving.

The cold reality of her situation hit. If she hadn't phoned Taylor, wanting out, they would have raided the house while she was in it. She would have been rounded up and arrested along with Alex and Slater. "Did you think I was part of this?"

"*I* didn't, no."

But others had. She was the wife of an organized-crime boss, living off the proceeds of his illegal earnings. No matter what she did or said, she would be viewed as guilty by association. Her fingers tightened on the phone. "Dad needs protection."

There was a brief silence. "I can't guarantee that. Honey, Cesar's *involved.*"

It was Therese's evening off. Rina fed Baby, made herself a sandwich, then took her usual walk, letting Baby have a run before returning to the house and turning in for the night. Walking through to the sitting room, she released Baby's harness, picked up the stereo remote and flicked it on. Instantly the room filled with the strains of a Beethoven sonata. Carrying the remote with her, she circumnavigated the furniture, automatically counting paces as she walked toward her favorite armchair. The evening walk, followed by music, was a soothing evening pattern. Normally the ritual helped her to relax, but there was nothing normal about her present situation. A plan was in place to catch Alex and his organization cold. Arrangements had been made to get her out in just a few hours. According to Taylor, everything was running to schedule.

Something was wrong.

She didn't know what exactly, but something was. Despite all of their precautions, the hours she had spent going over every detail, she had missed something important.

A low-pitched rumbling emanated from Baby.

She jerked her head around at a faint sound off to the left. She had a moment to register the movement of cool air off the patio. Simultaneously something wrapped around her shins and she was falling.

Her hands shot out, the remote went flying. Something hard caught the side of her face, snapping her head back. Her hand shot out, tangled in what felt like a phone cord. She had a dazed split second to register that aside from Baby's glow there was another color in the room: red.

The insistent beep of the disconnect tone and the swipe of a wet tongue on her cheek registered. Beethoven's "Moonlight Sonata" played softly. Rina touched the left side of her head and winced at the swelling. There was another lump on her right temple.

Another lick, this time on her jaw, was followed

by an insistent nuzzle. She hooked her fingers into Baby's harness. He whined, nudged her jaw again, then began to back up, towing her into a sitting position. Rina gave Baby the command to stay, keeping a firm grip on his harness while she waited out a wave of dizziness.

She had lost consciousness, again. Her head felt thick and heavy, and prickled like cold fire—the cerebral equivalent of pins and needles. Her eyes felt achy and pressurized.

She tried to remember every detail of what had happened. She had made the mistake of dropping Baby's harness, confident that nothing could go wrong in the sitting room. Baby had growled, but the split second of warning hadn't made any difference.

Something warm trickled down her cheek. The thick, sweet scent of blood made her stomach turn.

Blood soaking the leather upholstery and the tangled mess of objects strewn across the seat…

The notepad…in the water, the ink smeared…

"Repeat the numbers I gave you to remember."

Numbers.

She frowned. The ache in her skull sharpened. Her blindness impaired her photographic memory because it was a visual talent. If she couldn't look at words or numbers or images, she couldn't remember them. But when she had been a child, she hadn't had that problem. Esther had trained her to use her memory. She had been able to glance at a sheet of numbers and guarantee total recall.

Reaction shuddered through her.

The hood of the car snapped up in the air, hanging at an odd angle....

Esther must have given her numbers to remember while they were in the car, which meant they had been important. She had no idea what the numbers had been. They could be anything: telephone numbers, safe codes, account numbers, locker numbers...

In a moment of clarity the wrongness she had been trying to pin down ever since she had overheard the conversation between Cesar and Alex clicked into place.

Esther's body had never been recovered. It was presumed that she had drowned, but Rina now knew that she had been murdered; in all likelihood because she had known about the drugs and had threatened to go to the police. For years Rina hadn't been able to remember the crash or any of the events around it, but that didn't change the fact that she had *been* there, and that she had quite possibly witnessed the murder.

Maybe her amnesia, or the fact that she was Cesar's only child, had saved her life, but she didn't think so. Cesar hadn't had the power to save Esther. If Rina was a witness to Alex's crimes, she should have died along with her mother.

Her survival and the fact that Alex had married her almost two decades later didn't make sense; she should have died.

Keeping one hand hooked into Baby's collar, Rina felt around until her fingers connected with the plush brocade of an armchair. Blinking to try to ease the pressure behind her eyes, she tried to orient herself. She had been on the south side of the room when she'd fallen. She could still feel sunlight across her legs, which meant only minutes had passed.

Relinquishing her hold on Baby, she lurched forward and gripped the arms of the chair, holding her breath against the throbbing in her head. Baby moved in close, using his weight to steady her, as if he was afraid she might slip back to the floor.

She blinked. The room looked gray.

She squeezed her eyes closed. The movement sent a flash of pain through her skull. When she opened her lids, the grayness was still there.

"What's wrong?"

Adrenaline pumped. As preoccupied as she had been, Rina was stunned that neither she nor Baby had reacted to the stranger. She caught a whiff of a faint, clean scent—not cologne, soap—as he crouched beside her. Relief made her dizzy. It wasn't Alex.

Keeping a firm grip on the chair, she pushed to her feet, gritting her teeth against a wave of nausea. A warm hand fastened around her upper arm, steadying her as she lowered herself into the seat. She tensed, noting that Baby had still failed to react. She couldn't pin down the voice. It was possible he was part of Alex's security team and had seen her through the French doors and realized she needed help. "I'm blind. I slipped and fell."

"Looks like you walked into the armoire."

For a blank moment Rina wondered if she was having trouble with her hearing. "What armoire?"

"The one pulled out from the wall. There are some tools behind it. Someone's been checking the wiring."

Cold congealed in her stomach. "Where, exactly, is it positioned?"

"It's pulled out at a forty-five-degree angle from the wall."

Right into the path she usually took to reach her chair. "I tripped over something before I hit the armoire. Are there any other obstacles?" She could clearly remember pressure against her shins, the sudden loss of balance.

"Just the armoire."

And Alex. She remembered seeing his colors just before she had passed out. He must have picked up the rope, or whatever it was he had used to trip her with, and left. The tools behind the armoire made it look as if work was in progress and she'd had the misfortune to have another "accident."

Suddenly the series of accidents, the reason for the gazpacho and strawberry ice cream, the red salad—all foods that Alex knew triggered her blood phobia—made sense. He wasn't trying to kill her; at least, not yet. The cold premeditation of what he was doing made her stomach hollow out. He was deliberately traumatizing her to re-create conditions that would stimulate her to remember.

The realization triggered a recollection. Twenty-two years ago, shortly after she had regained consciousness after the car accident, Cesar had spent an entire afternoon beside her bed. The first thing he had wanted to know wasn't how she felt, but what she remembered. For weeks she had been questioned, by Cesar and a number of therapists, but always with the slant that remembering would help her regain her sight.

The reason the tactic had failed was textbook. Traumatic amnesia was a little-understood but well-researched phenomenon. There were recorded instances of people who had shut down so completely after being traumatized that they had forgotten their identities, their families, even their careers—anything and everything that might open up a pathway to remembering what had traumatized them. In several documented cases, years later something had triggered the subjects to remember. In more than one case it had been the emergence of an unexplained ability or knowledge or a language or skill they had no memory of learning. In others it had been an event that in some way duplicated the trauma.

Rina registered faint scuffing sounds as the bureau was repositioned against the wall. "Who are you?"

"James Thompson. I had a meeting with your

husband, but apparently he's gone out. I thought the house was empty until I saw you through the French doors."

The voice was curt, nicely masculine with a hint of a Southern drawl. She realized she recognized it from earlier in the day. He had been the last of Alex's "business associates" to leave. For him to be here at all—even at night—meant he had to have an appointment. The security around the house was very tight. No one gained admittance, or left, without passing through gate security.

"Keep still and I'll clean that cut up." She felt the touch of a handkerchief on her cheek.

Blood. Her throat tightened. She had almost forgotten. She could feel it now, congealed on the side of her face and in her hair. It would be on the carpet as well.

Inconsequentially, she thought of Therese. The old Hispanic woman would go crazy. The carpet was an antique silk runner that Alex had paid a fortune for on one of his trips abroad. Once Rina had gotten her to describe it and had spent hours trying to remember exactly what claret-red, royal-blue and turquoise looked like.

"I'm going to apply some pressure. Tell me if it hurts."

He gripped her chin and tilted her head slightly. Rina winced as the handkerchief was pressed firmly against the side of her face. The bare skin of a forearm brushed the top of her arm as he worked.

She froze at the contact. She had expected him to be in a suit jacket, not a short-sleeved shirt or T-shirt.

His fingers closed around her wrist.

She tensed. "What are you doing?"

"Taking your pulse."

Heart pounding, she jerked free of his hold. She had taken his offer of first aid on trust, but she was over letting him help her. He was a stranger, in her house without her knowledge, and she couldn't forget he was tied up with Alex. "My pulse is fine. It's my head I'm worried about. My eyes are history, but I really would like to hang on to my brain."

She sensed his surprise at the humor, but she was more interested in the fact that he moved away a step and took the blood-soaked handkerchief with him.

"Your pupils look okay, but you could have a slight concussion."

"Just what I need to complete another perfect day."

"Looks like you've had your share of accidents. Stay there. I'm going to find some ice."

She heard him walking in the direction of the kitchen and turned her head enough that she caught a glimpse of deep blue tinged with bright turquoise around his head. She stared, for long seconds. Unlike any of the other auras she'd seen, the colors were bright and distinct and utterly clear.

When he came back he had ice cubes, which he'd wrapped in what felt like a kitchen towel. She set the ice against the side of her head, clenching her jaw against the shaft of pain the change in temperature caused.

"I've put a glass of water on the table to the right of you. Drink it all, the fluids will help ease off the shock. When was the last time you ate?"

"I'm not going to pass out again." Now that she had the ice, all she wanted was for him to leave.

Rina blinked, distracted by the blurry grayness. She felt distinctly shaky. The pain in her head had increased and her skin felt acutely sensitive.

"I've called an ambulance. Is there anyone else you want me to call?"

"No one…thank you. I've got a cell phone, I can make my own calls." She noticed Thompson hadn't offered to escort her to the hospital or call any of the security staff. Neither had he mentioned contacting the police, but then he wouldn't. Alex was involved with drugs and murder; by association, so was Thompson. He would be as averse to contact with the police as her husband.

And that brought her back to the appointment he had mentioned. Alex was meticulous about business. If he had arranged to meet Thompson, he would have been here, and it was highly unlikely he would have staged this "accident" with a business associate in the house. Which meant Thompson was lying.

As he left the room, Rina stared after him, transfixed, but the shimmer of color around James Thompson was eclipsed by something far brighter in the corner. The shape was regular and defined and nothing like the colors she saw around people: the light was clear and bright enough to hurt.

Her chest tightened, the pain in her head grew, and for a moment she thought she was going to pass out again.

She was looking at a window.

Fifteen

The curtains of the cubicle Rina was occupying in Winton General's ER twitched aside.

A woman stepped into the room. "Damn, you *are* hurt."

Baby whined in welcome. Rina dropped a hand on his head, where he lay beside her chair. His tail thumped the floor.

Taylor's gaze skimmed the cubicle. "I've had enough of this. I'm getting you out of Winton now."

Rina stared at Taylor through eyes that were painfully sensitive. She was tall, with long dark hair pulled back in a ponytail, smooth, tanned skin and dark eyes. She was dressed in black track pants and a plain white tank, and she was wearing running shoes. Despite the fact that Rina had been blind for most of her life, even she could recognize that Taylor made no concession to fashion or style. With Taylor, what you saw had always been what you got. "How did you find out?"

"JT called me."

Rina frowned at the unfamiliar name. "James Thompson?"

"That's him."

Comprehension dawned. Apart from the clear colors around Thompson, that was what had been different about him. "He's an agent."

"He's been in place for months. Thanks to JT, we're finally reeling in Lopez and a big chunk of his network. He broke cover because he was worried about you."

The fact that James Thompson was an agent explained why he had been in the house when Alex wasn't there.

Taylor's brows jerked together. "Something's happened. You're looking at me."

Rina lifted a hand to the bandage on the side of her face. She still felt wobbly, and now that the shock of what had happened had mostly worn off, she felt even sorer. It had taken a few minutes for the ambulance to arrive and, once it was established that she didn't have any serious injuries, a further half hour to see a doctor. She had examined the swollen areas and the butterfly dressing the medic had applied to the cut and checked her for concussion, of which Rina did have a mild case. One concussion was bad, two in as many weeks was evidently very bad. After trying to convince her to check into the hospital for the rest of the night as a precaution, she had reluctantly prescribed a few quiet days at home and had gone to get painkillers from the dispensary.

Rina stared at Taylor, and resisted the urge to close her eyes. Her head was on fire and her eyes were burning. She was having trouble with the light and focusing, and difficulty with perception and balance. On top of the pain and disorientation, the bewildering speed with which people and vehicles moved and the brashness of the colors was unnerving. After years of craving light and color, all she wanted to do was crawl back into the dark shell she'd lived in for so many years and hide. "I can see. When I hit my head, it must have done something."

Taylor's face lit up. She crouched down and pulled her into a brief, fierce hug. "I can hardly believe it. I'd almost given up hope."

Emotion pushed past Rina's rigid control. Until Taylor had hugged her she hadn't realized how much she needed the contact. "It wasn't an accident. Alex set it up. I saw him." She met Taylor's gaze. "Why am I still alive? What does he want?"

"My boss will have my badge if he finds out I've given you any details, but you're going to find out soon enough. Lopez wants money."

Finally, something that made sense.

"Esther stole from Lopez. He thinks that before she died she gave you an access code for an offshore account that contains a very large sum of money."

Taylor stated a figure. "Don't quote me on it. That's just in the ballpark."

The numbers on the notepad. Now it made sense. Esther had found out what Alex Lopez was and cut him off at the knees by taking his money. There was no other explanation. Her mother had had rigid principles and values; she wasn't a thief. Rina frowned. "If that was the case, why wasn't the theft, and Alex, investigated twenty-two years ago?"

Taylor checked the corridor. "Lopez used his influence to cover it up. No crime was ever reported. Indirectly, about a year ago, we received information through a South American source. The information fitted with Esther's death and a few other events that happened at the time. The FBI's been gathering the threads of Lopez's operation and chasing the money ever since."

She glanced at her wristwatch. "We don't have much time. You can't go back to the house. Let them keep you in for observation for the night. We'll put twenty-four-hour protection around you. That's as believable a way as any to take you out of the equation, with the added bonus that Alex won't be suspicious, since he was the one who put you here. Does the doctor know you can see?"

"I didn't tell her. I haven't told anyone."

At first she hadn't been able to believe it. Like the auric sight, she had waited for the vision to go. Then, when the ambulance had arrived and one of Alex's security staff had come in to see what was wrong, an innate caution had kicked in. Alex's attempts to stimulate her memory had been brutal. If he knew that she had regained her vision and that she was beginning to remember, he wouldn't let her out of his sight. It was even possible he would attempt to remove her to some place where Taylor and the FBI couldn't reach her.

Taylor checked her watch again. "Time to go."

"No. I'm going back to the house. I need one more day." Esther had entrusted her with the account numbers because she had known she wouldn't survive and she had wanted Lopez stopped. It was now the FBI's job to stop Alex, but making sure Alex never recovered the money was her responsibility. She was beginning to remember, bits and pieces—fragments. She knew what she needed to remember. With the right stimulus she could get it all back.

"You can't go back. It's not safe and, as a witness for the prosecution, we don't want you there. We can recover any physical evidence when we move on the house."

"It makes sense for me to go home. The concussion is minor and Alex knows I hate hospitals. If I elect to stay in, he will be suspicious. The second he finds out, he could insist on having me removed to a private clinic. Besides, I'm safe. He's not hitting me or pointing a gun at me."

Given the last interval between "accidents," the way she saw it, she had a week before he rigged another. By then, he would be behind bars.

"The answer's still no. You're not supposed to know this, and I wasn't going to tell you because it's damned scary. If Bayard finds out, I *will* lose my job. Lopez isn't Alex's real name. It's Chavez, Rina. *Alejandro Chavez.*"

The Chavez cartel.

Her stomach turned.

Colombia. Brutal killings. Mass graves.

The Chavez cartel was Colombia's preeminent drug operation. For years Marco Chavez had run the family business like a dictator. After his death his son, Alejandro, had been just as efficient, but much more secretive. A killer at age twelve and despised in his own country, Alejandro had been labeled a dangerous psychotic.

And she had married him.

The room spun, the sick feeling turning to raw panic. She had let him touch her, kiss her. She had let him inside her.

Revulsion shuddered through her. No wonder Esther had run, no wonder she had gone against the principles of a lifetime and stolen from Lopez. She had known *who* he was. She had been desperate to stop him, desperate to get them both away. "How long have you known?"

"Don't look at me like that." Taylor shook her head. "A few weeks. I wanted to tell you."

"I understand why you couldn't." Cesar had known all along. He had introduced her to Alex; he had agreed to the marriage. The betrayal was incomprehensible. "Cesar—" Her voice sounded thick, her head was pounding.

Taylor was crouching down again, gripping her arms. "Don't go there. I promise you, it doesn't look good. I've been studying reports and profiles for weeks, looking for an out. I couldn't believe it, either."

"Alex is blackmailing him."

"He gets a hold over everyone, but they still take his money, and they still commit the crimes. It's called selling out."

"To protect *me*." She had to hold on to that; no matter what, Cesar was her father. She understood him in a way no one else could. Cesar was brilliant, but only at business. Without Esther in the equation, the Chavez cartel would have swallowed him whole.

Alex had held her hostage for more than twenty years. He had formulated a plan to contain and control her and extract her memories. The scope of the deception and the passage of time that had passed were almost incomprehensible, but one thing was clear. He wanted the money. He would never stop until he had it. Once he had it, he would kill her.

Another salient fact registered. It was cartel money. Even if Alex were imprisoned or killed, the cartel would remain. The missing thirteen billion dollars couldn't be erased by a prison sentence or one death, no matter how significant; they would still want their money.

Esther had died trying to get free of the cartel. Regardless if Alex were caught or not, the only way out for Rina was to remember the account numbers and do what Esther had intended: turn the money over to the authorities.

She pushed to her feet and found her handbag. The movement sent stabbing pain through her skull. She needed to go back. She needed to remember the numbers and get rid of the money. It was the only way. Once she was safe the horror would recede; she would stop remembering. She needed to capitalize on the fear and adrenaline, keep pushing—

"What are you doing?"

"I have to go back. I've started to remember."

"Rina, *no*."

Rina gritted her teeth. Once she had pills she would feel better. A few more minutes, then she could leave. All she wanted was to sit somewhere quietly—in the dark. "I need to get into Alex's study. He has things, things that disappeared from the crash site. There's a tape. It could vindicate Cesar."

"It's too dangerous. He's a killer. His father was a mass murderer."

Weariness swept her. "I was safe enough before. I'm safe enough now, as long as he doesn't find out I've recovered my sight. Even then, Alex won't kill me. I'm no use to him dead. He's trying to make me remember. He wants the account numbers."

"Numbers. That's plural."

"Two accounts, and, no, I don't know what they are. Yet."

Taylor went still. "Oh, shoot. So that's what's been happening."

Baby was on his feet, aware they were leaving. Rina gripped his harness. The smooth leather, Baby's warmth against her leg was an anchor. "Taylor, he doesn't know I can see."

The possibilities inherent in the situation were huge, and Taylor was adding them up. No one was closer to Alex than Rina. She lived with him; she had free access to his study.

The curtain swished aside. The doctor stepped into the cubicle, a carton of painkillers in her hand. Her gaze zeroed in on Taylor. "Are you with Mrs. Lopez?"

"No," Rina cut in, before Taylor could reply. "She's not."

The doctor directed a cool glance at Taylor. "Then you shouldn't be in here."

Taylor held up her hands and backed out of the cubicle. Rina could see she wanted to argue, but she didn't want the scene Rina was threatening when she was supposed to be undercover.

"Tomorrow night," Taylor said flatly. "That's your deadline. Keep in touch."

Sixteen

Rina walked through the sunlit house with Baby, her movements stiff and slow, courtesy of the eggshell tenderness of her head, as she refamiliarized herself with the rooms.

Being able to see was powerful and overwhelming, the light almost too much for her eyes, even with dark glasses. She would find herself staring, her mind frozen, the sensory overload too much when for years she had been trained to use every sense but sight. Even the simple motion of walking felt strange. She was used to memorizing her routes and counting out steps, her movement through a space a three-dimensional calculation. When she reached for her toothbrush she knew exactly how far to extend her hand from her body, and the small downward motion required before she could grasp the handle of the toothbrush. Everything was placed where it always was, but she kept missing her objective, her mind caught between two systems.

This morning when she had made herself a hot drink, despite the fact that the jug was in its usual position and she could *see* it, she had somehow managed to miscalculate and burn her fingers. If she had closed her eyes, the accident wouldn't have happened.

She paused in the sitting room and stared at the bookshelves that lined one entire wall. She picked a book at random and opened it to a page. With an effort she could identify individual words, but it was like learning a foreign language; en masse the words were a jumble. The difficulty she was having with the written word posed an unexpected problem. She wanted visual stimulus and, if possible, evidence, but if she couldn't understand the written word, searching Alex's files was going to be that much more difficult.

Flipping the book closed, she slid it back into its place on the shelf. The gold lettering on the spine caught her eye, a date, 1500. Somehow, numbers were easier; her mind grabbed them, no questions asked. She concentrated on the writing above the date, Ferdinand of Aragon. It was a book on Spanish history. She checked books at random, and several more turned out to be history tomes: English, Spanish, French and South American. Some of the material appeared to be written in Latin. There were a large number of books on the Second World War and Nazi Germany. She frowned. The amount of historical reference material Alex owned was substantial and some of the subject matter was surprising. He had never once indicated he had any interest in history. If he talked about anything at all besides business, it was usually art or current events.

The sound of a door closing alerted her. Alex had been at home most of the day to keep an eye on her, he'd said. To make sure she didn't have any more accidents.

Rina had stayed in bed and pretended to rest. When Alex had left for a meeting, she had managed to search his private suite, but she hadn't yet got into his study.

Slipping into the soft easy chair closest to the bookshelves, she ordered Baby to lie down, then eased her head onto the rest and pretended to be dozing.

Alex paused at the door to the sitting room. Gaze concealed behind the lenses of her dark glasses, she stared at an empty space somewhere in the region of his left shoulder and repressed a shudder. She hadn't looked into his eyes. If she did that he would know.

Sometime during the afternoon he had changed from casual clothes into a suit. According to Therese, he had a meeting this evening, which meant he should be out of the house for at least an hour.

When he left just minutes later, Rina walked toward Alex's study. When she stepped through the door, she closed Baby out. "Sorry, boy, you can't come in here."

Letting Baby into Alex's personal space was the equivalent of leaving a calling card. If he smelled dog or found a dog hair, he would know she had been there.

Thirty minutes later she gave up on trying to access his computer. She was used to a voice-activated system with Braille keys. English type and the garish color pulsing from the screen were beyond her. She concentrated on searching his desk drawers. The top one was filled with pens and notepaper. As she slid the drawer closed, the light caught on an indentation in a notepad. Pulling the pad out, she stared at the blank page.

The notepad was in the water...ink smeared, numbers dissolving.

For a moment she hovered on the brink, then the wisp of memory slipped away.

Frowning, she slanted the pad so the light picked out the indentation. She sat down at the keyboard and entered the series of indented numbers and letters. The password wasn't accepted. Almost an hour later, after searching through every file she could find, she checked her watch. She was out of time. Apart from the moment with the notepad, nothing had stimulated her to remember anything more, and she hadn't found anything that looked remotely useful as evidence. If Alex kept details of his criminal activities, they were either in computer files, or kept elsewhere.

As she pushed to her feet, a tiny glowing light

caught her attention. Adrenaline pumped. A discreetly placed video camera was situated in the corner, aimed directly at her. Whether Alex found out she was snooping in his office or not was no longer the question, it was when; she had been on camera all along.

Tires crunched on gravel.

Ripping the top two sheets off the notepad, she shoved them in her pocket and replaced the pad in the drawer. She closed down the computer, positioned the chair where it had been, walked from the room and collected Baby.

Seconds later, Alex paused by her office door. "I thought you would be in bed."

Rina slipped off the earphones of her voice computer and swung around on her swivel chair as she normally would. Keeping her head up and her gaze straight ahead, she stared past his shoulder. "I get tired of lying down. My head aches just the same sitting up."

"If you need anything, buzz Therese. She's staying on late tonight to make sure you're okay. I've got one more meeting."

She forced a smile and tried to slip back into the groove of being the resigned half of a dysfunctional married couple. "Don't worry. When I'm finished here I'm going straight to bed. I didn't get much sleep last night—doctor's orders. Will you be late?"

Her skin crawled as he studied her face. He seemed fascinated by the cut on her temple. The butterfly plaster was still in place, but the split skin was visible on either side. Combined with the bruising, it wasn't a pretty picture, and it would scar. "Not tonight. It shouldn't take more than an hour."

She smothered a yawn and didn't have to manufacture a wince when the movement of her facial muscles pulled at the cut and the bruised areas. "Then I'll probably see you in the morning."

She listened to the sounds he made as he walked upstairs to his suite. Minutes later, the front door closed behind him. She waited until she heard the sound of his car leaving, then headed back to his study to see if the series of numbers that had been indented on the notepad would open his wall safe.

An hour later, after giving up on the safe combination, searching his trash can and even his adjoining bathroom, Rina walked back out to the sitting room looking for Baby. A cold prickling at her nape warned her. She spun, but not soon enough to avoid the blow.

Seventeen

Dully, Rina heard Baby growl. He was crouched low, his gaze fixed on Alex. Holding her nose, Rina pushed to her knees in time to see Alex lash out at Baby with one booted foot.

Moving a step back toward the open French doors, he lifted a gun and trained it on Rina. "You can see."

Baby growled, stalking forward. The barrel of the gun swung toward Baby's head. Movement out on the patio flickered. A large figure charged through the open French doors.

Cesar's gaze locked with Rina's. *"Get down."*

The first slug caught him square in the chest. Cesar attacked Alex with a grunting roar. The second shot sliced past Rina's ear, close enough that she felt the pressure wave.

The two men grappled and went down. The gun skidded across the floor.

Rina lunged at the weapon. The gun felt unexpectedly heavy and warm in her grip. A chill gripped her as Alex rose to his feet, the movement fluid.

Cesar wasn't moving. Grief clawed at her and her hands shook, but she kept the gun steady. She had never fired a weapon, she could only hope that the gun worked when she pulled the trigger, because there was no doubt in her mind that she was going to have to shoot Alex.

The smell of blood filled the room, some of it hers, most of it Cesar's, and it was having its effect on Baby. His muzzle was peeled back from his teeth, a low vibration issuing from his chest.

Baby crept closer to Alex. Alex glanced at the gun Rina held in her hands. For the split second he stared at the weapon, she had the uncanny notion that he didn't register the threat, that she herself was close to invisible, without substance: unimportant. He had gotten so used to walking all over her that he didn't believe she would have the guts to pull the trigger.

She kept the barrel of the gun trained steadily on his chest. Alex wasn't a tall, bulky man, but he had always kept in good shape, and that was never more in evidence than now. In a black T-shirt and black pants, his skin tanned, his hair cut neatly against his skull, he looked sinewy and powerful. Without the business suit and the persona that went with it, there was an animalistic quality about the man who stood in front of her, and she wondered that she could ever have missed it, no matter how "blind" she had been.

With a curious, flickering smile, Alex stepped over Cesar's sprawled form. In that moment Baby lunged, a streak of gold fur and muscle. With a ferocious baying he engaged, his teeth sinking into the arm Alex instinctively flung out.

With a muffled grunt, Alex attempted to physically pry Baby's mouth open with his free hand and break his grip. Blood flowed down his wrist and coated the back of his hand. With a short, vicious kick, he shook Baby off.

The thump of helicopter blades jerked Alex's head around. Lights strobed across the patio. In the distance, gunfire erupted. His gaze fastened on hers, cold, calculating. A split second later he was gone.

Rina kept the gun pointed at the open door. Baby crept toward the place Alex had been, teeth still bared, instinctively avoiding Cesar's body. Rina stared at Cesar. He was dead. There was no mistaking the complete lack of animation.

The whine of the helicopter reached a crescendo as it lifted off. Grief sliced through the stasis that gripped her. For a split second, when he'd come through the door, Cesar had been the father she had known as a child, big and rambunctious and protective. To intervene like that, he must have known what Alex had intended. If he hadn't charged in and knocked the gun out of Alex's hand, she wouldn't have had a chance. Alex would have shot Baby and dragged her onto the helicopter with him.

The sound of the helicopter faded. She let her

arms drop so that the gun was pointing at the floor. If Alex had taken her with him, she would have been dead. Not soon, perhaps not for weeks or even months, but eventually. He would have tortured her until her mind gave up what he wanted. Once he had the numbers, and the money, he would have killed her.

Baby growled. The gun swung back up as if it had a life of its own. Rina called Baby to heel. Baby ignored her and every hair at the base of her neck stood on end. Now that the helicopter had gone, it was pitch-black outside. She was acutely aware of a myriad of sensory details, the thick scent of blood, the breeze flowing through the open French doors, the distant cascade of water from the fountain at the front of the house.

Someone was on the patio.

A shadow flickered. Baby launched with a bloodcurdling baying. Glass shattered as his shoulder caught one of the partially open doors and flung it wide. A sharp oath was followed by high-pitched keening, the sound terminated by a dull thud, then a scuffling sound, which receded into the distance.

Silence closed in, thick and oddly muffled. She was having trouble retaining her focus. Her breathing was too rapid and her hands where they were wrapped around the gun were shaking.

She lowered the gun. Her nose felt swollen, she was unable to breath through it, and the back of her throat tasted of blood. A throb of black humor surfaced. She was beginning to get used to the blood.

A dark figure flowed through the open French doors. Rina froze. He was armed, a large, black handgun gripped in both hands and pointed directly at her.

For a moment she didn't recognize him, then the faint bluish glow around him registered. Something about his size and the smooth way he moved clicked into place. She hadn't seen James Thompson, or JT as Taylor had called him, up close with her physical sight before, but he was recognizable despite the flak jacket and the lip mike.

His gaze locked on hers, the impact faintly shocking. Thompson was a stranger, and male. It was an odd time for that fact to register.

"Put the gun down. On the floor."

His voice was cold, measured. She dragged her gaze from Thompson's and stared at the gun gripped loosely in one hand. She had forgotten she was holding it.

With slow movements, she complied.

"Kick the gun under the sofa."

The words were flat and very clear. He wanted the gun out of commission. Using the side of her foot, she nudged the gun so that it slid across the tiled floor and disappeared beneath the nearest sofa.

His gaze swept the room as he stepped around Cesar. His questions were curt. How many men had gotten on the chopper with Alex? Had Slater been one of them? Was there anyone else in the house? All while he held a separate conversation with someone on the other end of the lip mike.

His assessment of her injuries was lightning fast and clinical, but that didn't disguise the fact that he checked her out for more weapons. Dressed in sneakers, jeans and a clinging tank top, she didn't have many places to store one, although, in the world Thompson came from, maybe that was a defeatist attitude.

He checked the hallway. "Most of the security staff are concentrated at the front of the property, so we'll be going out through the kitchen. Are you okay to walk?"

"I'm fine." Her gaze touched on Cesar. Her throat closed up. "Just give me a moment."

Crouching beside Cesar, she touched his sleeve, brushed her fingers over the back of his hand and gripped his fingers. Abruptly, the memory she'd had of Esther holding her hand after the car accident was strong in her mind. The prayer flowed as clearly as if she was still ten years old and in church. A split second before she opened her eyes, she caught a glimpse of light floating, shimmering, then JT's hand closed around her upper arm and they were moving through the house.

JT paused at the entrance to the path that led to the garages, then pulled her to one side into a clump of shrubs. Seconds later, a shadowy form ghosted past. Rina recognized one of Alex's regular security staff.

The pressure on her arm increased, the signal to move on. As they moved behind the garages, lights flared in the house and a flat popping noise split the air.

Thompson changed direction, pulling her deeper into the shrubs and trees that bordered the river boundary.

When they reached the river, he released her. "We're going to cross. It's not deep here, but the stones are slippery. I can carry you if you can't make it."

"I can make it." She still couldn't breathe through her nose, but she would run if necessary.

He went first, stepping into the slow-moving water with barely a sound. Bracing herself against the chill of the water, Rina followed, taking care with her foot placement. She'd spent enough time wading on the fringes with Baby to know that the rocks were treacherous.

Baby.

Her heart almost stopped in her chest. She hadn't seen or heard Baby for a good ten minutes. She wanted to whistle, but doing that would give away their position and she wasn't about to jeopardize either herself or Thompson. Besides, after the episode with the gun, she was under no illusions that Thompson would tolerate interference of any kind.

A pale blur in the distance that could have been Baby distracted her and her foot slipped sideways on a rock. She went down on one knee, her hand shooting out, saving her from submerging completely.

Thompson's arm clamped her waist. He hauled her up and half carried her to the far bank where a chain-link fence formed the boundary of the property. Crouching down, he began clearing branches away from the wire.

Rina gripped a trailing shrub to keep from sliding down the bank. "The fence is electrified."

"I disconnected it when I came in."

If he'd done that the alarm should have gone off, which meant he had altered the security program at some previous point. The permutations required to bypass Alex's security so that none of the complicated series of checks and alarms had alerted the security staff was briefly mind-boggling. The "hole" in Alex's security explained how Thompson had come to be in the house the previous evening.

Peeling back a section of chain mesh, he motioned her through. Seconds later they were on the other side, the branches pulled back in place and the cut section of the fence fastened down.

The thin beam of a flashlight cut through the darkness. Thompson's hand closed around her arm and they were moving again. Long minutes later, they stepped out onto the street. A van was parked at the curb, its dark paint job making it almost invisible beneath the arching shelter of an oak.

She stopped short of the van. "Mr. Thompson— James—"

"Call me JT."

It suited him, short and direct, not one unnecessary frill. "I need to get Baby out. I can't leave without him."

A short dark man in an FBI jacket climbed out of the front of the van. "There's no time. We need to go."

Gunfire erupted in the vicinity of the house.

The side door of the van slid open. A second man, this one with blond hair, touched her arm. "Come on, Rina. It's just a dog."

Rina's jaw clenched. The blond agent was Mr. Nice Guy in the double act, unlike Attila with the cold eyes. "Baby isn't just a dog." He had been her eyes and her lifeline. He had saved her more than once. Without Baby she wouldn't have survived Alex.

JT spoke briefly into his lip mike. He checked his watch. "I'll look." His gaze shifted, fixing on Attila. "Wait."

Taylor clambered out of the van. "And that's an order," she said beneath her breath.

She wrapped a jacket around Rina's shoulders and hugged her quick and hard. "I heard about Cesar."

Grief surged. Rina's throat clamped tight. She was aware of Attila watching her and the fact that from this point on, everything she said, every reaction, every detail of her life, past and present, was under a microscope.

When Taylor released her, Rina huddled into the jacket. Despite the mild temperature, she was cold, probably because her jeans and her sneakers were soaked.

Taylor tried to coax her into the van, where it would be warmer. Attila sent her a cold glance when she refused to get into the van until JT came back with Baby.

Moments later, JT melted out of the darkness. "I can't locate him. I've been feeding him for weeks. Unless he's with you, he comes when I call. He didn't come this time, which means he's not within hearing distance."

And for dogs, "within hearing distance" was a long way, which meant Baby had either been forcibly removed or he was unconscious. There was a third option, but she stubbornly refused to acknowledge it. She would *know* if Baby was dead.

"Right, that's it." Attila started the van.

Rina allowed herself to be hustled into a seat. Mr. Nice Guy, who she noticed had a not-so-nice gun jutting out of a shoulder holster, slid the door closed. Taylor fastened a safety belt across her lap as the van pulled smoothly away.

Rina glanced back. JT was no longer on the sidewalk. Since he hadn't gotten into the van that meant he must have gone back to the estate.

"Don't worry about JT, he's got other fish to fry." Taylor settled beside her and fastened her own seat belt. "Besides, he was never coming with us. He's not FBI."

Rina stared out of the tinted windows, scanning the streets. Baby was out there somewhere. Minutes later, as they left the outskirts of Winton, she abandoned the search and sat back in her seat. Her head was aching, her eyes hurt and her nose was sore.

An image of JT, calmly giving Attila the order to wait—and it had been an order—before he merged back into the trees to search for Baby, popped into her mind. He had gone back to look, despite the risk. "What is he, then? An undercover cop?"

"He's a contract agent for the CIA. With Lopez's connections outside of the country, they wanted in on the action."

Rina studied the shadowy landscape flashing by, fewer and fewer houses now and longer stretches of farmland interspersed by glimpses of the sea on the right, which indicated they were headed south. The prospect of having to cope with a murder inquiry, retelling the past few days and hashing over her relationship with Alex, wasn't a pleasant one, no matter how necessary. The unpleasantness was highlighted by the fact that she wasn't just a key witness. For years, she had also been a suspect in the case. "What happens now?"

"We're taking you to a safe house for tonight. Translate that as meaning we're checking into a motel until Genius—" she jerked her head at "Attila" "—can get the interviews done."

"Then what?"

Taylor's hand gripped hers. "WitSec. Witness

Security. I'm sorry, Rina, but there's no other option. You need to disappear at least until the trial, and probably for a lot longer."

Part 3

Eighteen

Beaumont, Texas, three months later

A divorce, a new identity, a new town.

Rina, now known as Rina Mathews, should have been happy she had escaped Alex's tight grip with her life, but she couldn't settle. Stepping back from her easel, she studied the still life she was working on. The moment she had picked up a brush and started painting, she had known this was what she was meant to be doing. Sculpture had satisfied a creative need, but now that she could see color, *light,* the urge to sculpt, powerful as it had been, had faded.

Out of curiosity, she had walked into the foyer of the building that had commissioned her last piece, which she had finished in the weeks following the bust. Even though she had created it, the sculpture had been subtly unfamiliar. She was used to relating to it by touch, not sight, and picturing it in her mind in a three-dimensional, spatial way, not glinting in sunlight with water pouring over the delicate rills.

Rina continued to study the canvas, her gaze slightly out of focus, letting the swimming light register so she could reproduce the glowing bowl of peaches she had set on a small table beneath the dappled shade of an oak.

The FBI debrief and the slow, painstaking dissection of her life from the time of the accident through to the present day had been intrusive and unsettling. It hadn't taken hours, it had taken days, and had involved repeated questioning until the evidence was as clear as "Attila," otherwise known as Paul Hennessey, an agent from the Portland field office, and Marc Bayard, the special agent from D.C. who was heading up the investigation, could get it.

On top of the evidential work, they had requested that she undergo various forms of therapy, including hypnosis, to try to unlock her memory and retrieve the account numbers. Rina had been more than happy to agree, despite the fact that she had been in and out of various clinics for years trying to achieve the exact same result. If wanting to remember made a difference, then she should remember. She had seen what Alex was firsthand; she knew what had driven Esther, and what she had been fighting to avoid. Esther had died and Alex had destroyed their family, but if the money could be salvaged and used in some way to capture Alex, that would be a victory of sorts.

The sessions had been interesting, and at times harrowing, but apart from clarifying what she had already remembered, they hadn't been able to unlock anything new.

Bayard's distinct lack of humor at her inability to remember wasn't improved by the fact that his investigation, which had taken months and cost millions of dollars in man-hours and federal resources, had been compromised. Despite the tight security, Alex had been tipped off. Bayard had closed in on his cocaine operation, making significant arrests, but Alex and Slater had escaped and Cesar had died, taking a mountain of evidence with him.

JT had penetrated Alex's organization, following a trail of stolen armaments, in this case missile components destined for the Middle East, but the shipment hadn't materialized. To further complicate matters, a military nuclear arms specialist, a chemist and two administrative officials from separate military bases had died, reducing the suspect pool to almost zero. The executions had all been carried out in different parts of the country, but they had occurred on the same night and in the same way—two shots to the chest, one to the head.

With most of the players dead and Alex gone to ground, JT and Bayard's investigations were stalled. But on the plus side, he was now wanted on a number of counts, including illegal entry into the country, grievous bodily harm, murder and conspiracy charges. Rina's testimony would put him away on the murder charge alone.

Once her statements had been made and the legalities of her participation in the case as a witness for the prosecution had been finalized, Rina had met with Ed Marlow of WitSec.

Ed was a U.S. Marshal in his mid-fifties, lean and clean cut, with a precise way of speaking that cut out any possibility of gray areas. He had given her two options: the East Coast or the South.

Her knee-jerk reaction against going anywhere near Boston, where Alex had supposedly gone to school, was enough to make her settle for the South. Moving so far away from Winton made sense, and it was in line with WitSec's policy that, with the risk that Alex would find her, she cut ties with her old life. Relieved as she was at the promise of safety and anonymity while she waited out the months before Alex was found and put on trial, Rina couldn't dismiss the nagging worry that putting all those thousands of miles between her and her past also made it less likely she would ever locate Baby.

Taylor had searched for Baby in the days following the bust, but he hadn't been sighted on any of the neighboring properties and he hadn't turned up in the local pound or the animal shelter. She had handed Rina the photo she had used for her inquiries, a snap of Baby she had taken just months previously. In a last-ditch effort, Rina had circulated the photo in Wiston's local paper for several weeks, but seemingly, Baby had disappeared from the face of the earth.

Touching her brush to her palette she delicately smudged the outline of a peach so that the shape appeared to shimmer on the page.

Three letters, followed by four numbers, popped into her mind.

She blinked at the sudden intrusion. The numbers, clear as day—black on white—winked out. Suddenly cold, she painted the letters and numbers onto the canvas before she could forget them.

Heart pounding, she studied what she had written. For a split second, knowledge hovered at the edge of her mind. Then it slid away, leaving her mind blank.

She stared at the figures, trying to recapture the relaxed looseness of mind that had allowed the memory to surface, but her mind was once more locked down. It was entirely possible that this was just some kind of short circuit, a random wisp of memory left over from her childhood and, like the indented numbers she had found on the notepaper in Alex's desk, another dead end.

From the configuration, the numbers could be a vehicle license plate. She would pass the information on to Ed Marlow, to give to Bayard to check out.

After lunch, Rina walked to her local shopping center. As wonderful as it was to be able to see and to have the freedom to go wherever she wanted without assistance, she couldn't get used to not having Baby by her side.

She stopped at the newsagent and picked up a number of newspapers, including the local one. Reading the written word wasn't her strength, but she was improving. WitSec had helped rehabilitate her. For two months she had been enrolled in the same kind of intensive language lessons and training program that a foreign refugee was granted, with one difference—she had been the only pupil in the class. Marlow had personally overseen the program. He knew how important her testimony was, and he was as interested as Rina in making sure she could blend comfortably into Beaumont.

With the papers and a glossy magazine tucked under her arm, Rina began the slow trek home, enjoying the afternoon breeze and the warmth of the sun. So far she had resisted buying a car, for the simple reason that she didn't have a driver's license and the walk to the shopping center only took a few minutes. She had started driving lessons a few weeks ago, and was booked in to take her test, but, like reading, managing a vehicle wasn't her best skill.

A kid with a golden retriever on a leash walked out of a gate and crossed the road to a park. Rina's chest squeezed tight as she watched the boy unlatch the lead and let the dog streak across the grass.

As happy as she was in Beaumont she couldn't forget Baby, and she hadn't given up on him. Marlow would have a fit if he knew, but she had kept her contact with Taylor, and through her was continuing to try to locate him.

Fifteen minutes later, she collected a glass of water and a dictionary from the sitting room and carried them, along with the papers, out to the picnic table she'd set up beneath the oak. Anchoring the papers with the bowl of peaches and the glass of water, she began to read the first paper, stopping to check words as she went. After twenty years of reading selected information through Braille publications or listening to what was served up on television or radio, access to the huge variety of information available in newspapers was like a drug; her mind soaked it up like a sponge.

Her photographic memory was still intact. She had tested herself, curious to see if after years of zero visual stimuli she could still do her childhood trick, and had found to her surprise that the odd quirk was still there.

Turning to the classifieds, she reanchored the pages. Automatically, her gaze ran down the lost-and-found column and snagged on a snapshot of a dog in the pet's section.

She studied the picture, frustrated at the grainy texture of the newsprint. Frowning, she bent closer. Her elbow connected with the glass, water splashed across the table. Jumping to her feet, she grabbed the paper, pulling it away from the moisture and letting the wet part of the page drip onto the grass. The breeze gusted, tugging at the rest of the newspaper and sending it tumbling over the lawn until it caught in the thick tangle of shrubs at the far end of the yard.

It was Baby.

Rina stared at the photo. The caption said the dog was called Baby, and it *looked* like Baby, but, after months of searching, she was well aware that there were plenty of pets that carried the same name.

She was almost certain it *was* Baby, but the fact that whoever had put the ad in the paper had gone to the extra expense of paying for a photo made her cautious. Just the name and the description would have been enough to catch her attention, but the photograph had drawn her like a magnet. It occurred to her that if whoever had placed the ad knew she had been recently blind and that she would have difficulty reading the written word, then inserting a photograph to make sure she saw it made a lot of sense. There was also the chilling fact that no one outside of the FBI team that had rescued her, and her contacts in WitSec, knew she could see—other than Alex.

Carrying the papers and the dictionary inside, she began systematically searching the other classifieds. The local paper didn't have the ad or the photo, but the other major tabloid did.

Rina stared at the second grainy print of Baby. Anyone finding a missing dog would naturally advertise in the area the dog was found. It didn't make sense to conduct a nationwide campaign. The cost would be prohibitive. It set the seal on her suspicions.

Alex was trying to find her, and he was using Baby as bait.

Cold congealed in her stomach. Alex had controlled and manipulated her life in an effort to extract the account information from her. Now he was actively hunting her. He would throw every resource he had at trying to find her.

The fact that an advertisement hadn't been placed in any of the local papers was a reassurance that, as yet, he had no idea where she was. The FBI had been compromised, but WitSec was secure.

She studied the phone number listed in the ad, and any doubts that she might be paranoid, or flat-out wrong, died.

The area code was for Winton.

Rina dialed Taylor and got put through to her answering service. A frustrating two hours later, Taylor returned the call.

"I'll check it out," she said crisply. "Don't, whatever you do, ring that number."

"Don't worry." As badly as Rina wanted Baby back, she wasn't stupid enough to jeopardize her life, or the case against Alex.

Within hours Taylor rang back. "We've got a line on the guy who's keeping Baby. His name's Gomez. Apparently, he's related to one of the security staff. According to Gomez, his cousin was picked up after the bust and the dog was left in his garage."

"He's lying. Alex is behind this."

"That's what Bayard is hoping."

"When can you get Baby?"

There was a brief silence. "First of all, Bayard's not letting me take part in the op. Second, you have to understand that retrieving Baby is not Bayard's priority. He'll retrieve him if he can, but it's Slater and Lopez he wants. Everything else comes second. He's organizing an agent who looks like you to meet with him, then they'll move in. The bust is timed for four-thirty tomorrow afternoon. That gives Bayard time to get in place and it's a believable time scale, since Lopez is aware that you'll probably have to fly in."

Rina's fingers tightened on the phone. She had already done the logic; she knew the way Bayard would have to play it. She wanted Alex and Slater caught, too, but she also wanted Baby safe. "You'll call when it's over?"

"Nobody else." Taylor's intonation was dry. In theory she wasn't supposed to know where Rina was, or have any contact with her. To cover up Rina's involvement, Taylor had told Bayard that she was the one who had seen the advertisement. "Which brings up another point. Don't use your landline to call me. Buy a new cell phone and use that. If Marlow finds out you've broken security, he'll go crazy. I'm wiping your details off my phone, just in case."

The precaution made sense. If Rina had been thinking straight she would never have used the landline.

Hanging up, she stared through the kitchen window at the backyard, barely registering the purple splash of shade on the lawn or the heat shimmering off a neighbor's tin roof. Shoving a loose tendril of hair behind her ear, she began to pace. The thought that Alex had Baby sent a shudder through her. He had shot Cesar as coldly as if he was shooting at a target on a range. She knew from the reading she had done that it was suspected that Alex had shot his own father—at point-blank range.

Before she had seen the ad in the paper she had been able to imagine that some family had found Baby and taken him in, that he was a much-loved pet. The thought that he had been chained and probably abused made her clench her jaw. Baby had been adored and cared for from the moment of his birth. He was a gentle, intelligent animal; he wouldn't understand abusive behavior.

Blankly, Rina stared at her bedroom, with its queen-size bed, regulation dressing table and reading lamp, and the small silver frame with Baby's photo in it. She had been pacing the house and had somehow ended up there. It was an old habit—when she got upset, she walked, and Baby had used to walk with her. The rhythmic action of putting one foot in front of the other had always had a soothing effect, but now it was just one more reminder. Rina had escaped, protected by all of the considerable resources of the United States government, but Baby had been left behind.

Turning on her heel, she strode out to the sitting room. She checked her watch. Fifteen minutes had passed since she'd hung up the phone. She had another twenty-four hours to wait before she could hope to hear anything. It was going to be a long night. Tomorrow was going to be an even longer day.

Nineteen

Rina jammed her foot on the brake. The vehicle, a small SUV that belonged to the driving school she was enrolled at, jolted to a stop at an intersection. A horn blared.

She checked the rearview mirror. A truck was stopped behind her, the hood so close it was evident that whoever was driving had almost rear-ended the SUV. A single finger appeared in the window, jerking upward for emphasis.

Rina's jaw tightened. Learning to drive was a necessity. She was doing her best, but everyone drove too fast and some people were rude. This guy was downright intimidating.

The lights changed. Taking her time, she remembered to flick the indicator on, took a left and bunny-hopped sedately into a parking area. The truck, which had followed her around the corner, roared past, peeling rubber. Rina risked a glance at the disappearing streak of red, but she was too late to get his license plate. Not that she wouldn't know him again—fire-engine red was distinctive.

As she slotted the car into a space, she noticed the driving instructor's knuckles had gone white and both his feet were jammed against the firewall.

She forced her jaw to loosen up. *Join the club.* She hated driving with a passion, but she was determined to learn. With a sleepless night behind her, and most of the day to fill before she heard any news, she had to occupy herself with something. Denny Klimek's driving school had been the obvious answer; nothing was guaranteed to absorb and irritate her more than the constant battle on the road, and with her test just two days away, she needed the practice.

Denny unhitched his seat belt. "I need a drink."

Rina watched as he climbed out of the car and repressed the urge to say, "Make mine a double." Denny was middle-aged with a paunch, and graying hair at the temples. His wife did the paperwork and manned the reception desk, and Denny did the driving lessons. The first time she had walked into his office he'd had an amused twinkle in his eye and a "no sweat" attitude. Lately there had been no sign of the famous humor and he'd done plenty of sweating.

Letting out a breath, she wound all the windows down and forced herself to relax as she watched Denny walk across the car park and into a small café adjacent to the mall entrance. A family group strolled along the sidewalk and walked into the mall. A man strolled from behind a delivery truck and disappeared into the shaded entrance.

She frowned. She couldn't see his face, but something about the back of his head was familiar.

Her pulse kicked. There was always the possibility that, new life or not, she would bump into someone from the past.

Reaching for the bottle of water that was sitting in the drink holder, she continued to watch the mall entrance to see if the man would walk out so she could get a look at his face. Bayard and Marlow had both drummed into her the importance of completely disassociating herself from that previous life. If she thought that someone had recognized her, or was showing any undue interest in her, all she had to do was pick up the phone and they would be there.

Long minutes passed. When the water bottle was empty, she slotted it back into the drink holder, then reached into the backseat, found her handbag and extracted a tissue to blot perspiration from her face. She noticed a truck, similar to the red one that had almost rammed her at the lights, parked in the row behind her, although that wasn't surprising. In Beaumont, lots of people drove trucks and four-wheel-drive vehicles. This particular beast was black.

She checked her watch. She could see Denny standing talking to a woman on the sidewalk outside the café. Plenty of people had entered and exited the mall, but none of them looked anything like the man she'd glimpsed. When Denny finally ambled across the car park, she was more than ready to leave, and the idea that Alex had dispatched someone to find her had wilted in the heat.

Instead of climbing directly into his seat, Denny walked around the hood and hovered by the driver's-side window. "Maybe it's not a good idea to continue if you don't feel up to it."

"I've paid for the afternoon. Have you got a problem with continuing?"

He forced a grin. "Me? No way. You know our motto."

Drive 'Til You Die. She could see where he might be regretting that. The driving school's ad promised to get her licensed and on the road, period. Age, infirmity and disability, according to the fine print, were no barrier. As far as she was concerned, the sooner she got her license, the sooner they would both be put out of their misery. "Then, let's get going."

She waited until Denny had fastened his seat belt, turned the key in the ignition, checked the rearview mirror and prepared to reverse.

As she pulled out of the space a horn blared. Her foot jammed on the brake. A strangled oath was cut off as Denny was propelled forward, then jerked back by his seat belt. Rina's fingers tightened on the wheel. The truck that had been parked directly behind her had just reversed out. She had almost backed into him.

Muttering an apology, Rina shoved the gear shift into Drive. As the SUV eased forward, she checked the rearview mirror again, but the tinted windows of the truck made it difficult to make out anything beyond the fact that the driver was male. Seconds later the truck cruised past and pulled out onto the highway. Automatically she noted the registration plate.

He hadn't done anything wrong, it had been her fault. She had taken too long from the time she had checked behind her until she had started backing out, and in the interval, he had pulled out, but it was becoming second nature to check numbers. Taking a deep breath, Rina started the process of backing out again.

Two hours later, she exited the driving school building and strolled along one of Beaumont's pretty side streets. She still had an hour to spare before it was likely that Taylor would ring. On the way home, she stopped by a variety store and bought a cheap pre-pay phone.

Deliberately, she made herself stop at the supermarket and buy groceries, then the newsagent, where she picked up another load of papers. As she strolled out of the newsagent, she noticed the back bumper of a black truck.

The door of the store banged softly behind her as she studied the vehicle. A car obscured her view of the license plate, but she could make out two numbers. They matched with the license plate of the truck she had almost backed into earlier on.

Shaking off the unsettled feeling as just one more dose of paranoia, she began the walk home.

When she reached her kitchen, she laid the groceries and the papers on the counter, spread the first paper out and turned to the classifieds. The skin at the base of her neck crawled. There was another photo of Baby.

She slipped the cell phone she'd bought out of its bag, inserted the battery and plugged it in to charge. The urge to ring Taylor was so strong she almost gave in to it, but she couldn't use the cell phone yet and she couldn't risk using a landline again. In any case, Taylor wasn't part of the bust. Like her, she would be waiting it out.

Taylor pulled up outside a small block of condominiums in an exclusive seaside estate south of Winton. Slater's ex-wife had not only changed her address, she had changed back to her maiden name after her marriage had ended and was now known as Elaine Pierce. Officially, Taylor wasn't supposed to be within a mile of her. Bayard had taken care of this part of the investigation weeks ago and signed it off as just one more dead end in an investigation that was full of blind alleys.

Taylor wasn't so sure. She didn't know exactly why Elaine Pierce could be any more interesting than a dozen other leads that had gone nowhere, but for some reason her mind had latched on to the idea, and when that happened Taylor paid attention. As minds went, she didn't have genius status or a special talent, like Rina. What she had was focus and a reputation for never giving up. That tenacity, coupled with the fact that she was female, had caused her a lot of grief over the years and some name-calling, but that was all water off the proverbial duck's back for Taylor. The way she saw it, if she had wanted to be a sheep instead of a bulldog, she would have been one.

Pulling the rearview mirror down, she checked her wig, which was a sleek honey-blond.

It didn't quite go with the aforementioned personality, but the disguise was workable. Elaine Pierce's house could still be under surveillance, and if Bayard heard that a tall brunette had knocked on Slater's ex-wife's door, he would railroad her out of the FBI so fast she'd be spinning. No way was Taylor finished with her law-enforcement career yet. She'd worked hard to get where she was. She'd aced her class at Quantico and had consistently graded so highly she'd had her pick of field assignments. Once she was in, she hadn't rested on her laurels. She had worked her way through the ranks, and without the brownnosing, thank you.

After qualifying, she hadn't let herself hover around the "just fit enough" range like some of the agents. Fitness had always been as natural to Taylor as breathing. Maybe it was masochistic, but she liked training. She had done athletics at school and won a few medals. She also had a black belt in karate and judo, and she regularly worked out with weights and ropes. A few years ago when she'd been dating a Navy SEAL, she had even gone to the trouble of finding out how they trained and she had found that nothing got you fitter in the upper body than training with ropes.

A couple of months post-"the SEAL" she had hooked up with a mountaineering guy for a while and done some rock climbing. That had been fun, and he'd been amazed at how strong she was, not to mention a little condescending. Romantically, he hadn't lasted long, either. Taylor could only close her mind to so much.

Slinging her handbag over her shoulder, she locked the car and strolled toward the walled estate, enjoying the heat of the sun, and the mouthwatering views out over the bay.

Elaine Pierce wasn't happy to see her.

Taylor smiled. "I'm a debt collector. According to our records your husband failed to pay a number of bills relating to an address on Brady Street where you both had an interest in a condominium." The condominium part, at least, was true.

Elaine Pierce was middle-aged and petite, with steely-blue eyes and short, dark hair. The untouched gray at the temples told Taylor that the ex-Mrs. Slater was of the "no frills" variety of ex-wife—which was interesting. Earl Slater had a reputation for liking the ladies.

She crossed her arms over her chest. "If you're a debt collector, I'm Santa Claus."

Okay, so acting wasn't her best skill. "You're right, I'm not a debt collector. I'm Earl's girlfriend."

The statement dropped into blank silence.

Elaine blinked, her gaze settling on the blond wig. Her cheekbones went a dull red. "You've got a nerve coming here."

The door—solid teak, if Taylor was any judge— swung to, the movement so fast it took her by surprise. She jammed her foot in the gap, wincing when her instep got crushed. Elaine had just gone up about a hundred points in her estimation. Not many people suckered her like that.

Using her shoulder, she leveraged the door open enough that her foot didn't sustain any further damage. She liked her feet, and she liked them to be in good condition so she could run. In Taylor's opinion, running was one of the enduring pleasures of life; it frequently beat eating, conversation and, lately, company of the male kind.

Elaine's face, viewed through the hard-won six-inch gap, went scarlet. Tiny beads of sweat stood out on her upper lip. "I'm not paying you money. Haven't you gotten enough?"

She added a few unladylike and precisely worded phrases. But the most interesting part by far was that Slater *did* have a girlfriend.

Nothing in any of the surveillance records had mentioned anything about a romantic relationship, which meant he had been extra sneaky about it.

Taylor kept up the pressure. "Not yet. He left me. I need the money."

The whining phrases, ground out while she pushed against Slater's ex-wife's door didn't quite carry the selling power she intended, but Taylor wasn't giving up until she got something she could use.

Abruptly, Elaine let the door go. Taylor clutched at the door frame to prevent herself from overbalancing and sprawling on the tiled floor of the hallway.

Elaine's hand landed in the center of Taylor's chest. She shoved, her expression livid. "Then earn it on your back at Tony's. You're not getting a cent out of me."

The door slammed a bare inch from Taylor's nose.

She let out a breath. Life was good.

Slater had been dating a hooker. Which was why he had hidden the relationship—he hadn't wanted Lopez to know. As head of security, and an insider on cartel discussions, Slater was in a privileged and delicate position. Dating a hooker was a definite no-no. If Lopez had ever found out, Slater would have been wearing a concrete jacket at the bottom of the Pacific Ocean.

Tony's was a discreet bar and massage parlor at the edge of town. The wig now lying on the backseat,

Taylor sat back and watched the entrance, sipping a coffee she'd picked up from a drive-through.

At this time of the day, late afternoon, nothing much was happening, which was predictable. After another fruitless half hour, where only a handful of men strolled in and out of the premises, she locked the car and walked across the road and into the bar. There were half a dozen guys just off work seated at tables and at the counter, and a couple of girls, trolling the crowd. Taylor ignored everyone but the bartender.

After ordering a glass of wine she barely sipped, she picked up her bag and walked through to the bathroom, which she really needed to use. When she was finished, instead of walking back into the bar, she slipped through a back door into the massage parlor. An attractive dark-haired woman seated behind a desk stopped flipping through a magazine and lifted a brow. Taylor could tell from the look that they didn't often get women in.

Taylor plucked a name out of the air. "Excuse me, maybe I'm in the wrong place, but I'm looking for a friend. She said she worked here. Her name's Miriam Butler." In a place like this, she was pretty certain there couldn't possibly be anyone by that name.

"I'm sorry, we don't have a Miriam here."

Taylor manufactured a frown. "I'm sure this is the place. I was really looking forward to seeing her. We were at school together."

The woman closed the magazine. "Just a minute, I'll check." She shrugged. "Sometimes the girls do change their names."

When she pushed a curtain aside, Taylor followed her into a small lounge. There were four girls seated watching TV. A redhead, a delicate Asian girl and two blondes—one platinum, the other honey-blond. Elaine had reacted to Taylor's honey-blond wig, so she was betting she was the one.

The receptionist spun around when she realized Taylor was behind her. "I'm sorry, you do have the wrong place. There's no one called Miriam here."

Taylor pulled out her badge and flashed it. The effect was instantaneous. "If you do hear of her, let me know. I'll be in town for a while. I'm staying at the Winton Court Motel, so I'm easy to find."

When she reached for a pen the woman said, "Don't bother, we know where the Court is."

No one would ever ring, but that didn't matter, because the charade had achieved exactly what she wanted. The honey-blonde had gone as white as a sheet.

Smiling and apologizing for the disturbance, Taylor backed out of the tiny room, turned on her heel and strode out of the bar. Ignoring a catcall, she strolled across the road, climbed into her car, drove around the block and found another place to park where she could see the staff exit.

Five minutes later, she watched the honey-blonde get into a small, sporty car and glide into rush-hour traffic. Evidently, she had decided not to work tonight.

Taylor followed, keeping a discreet distance. Half an hour later, the sports car took a steep incline that ended in a cliff-top coastal settlement dotted with huge homes and walled estates. Taylor had hung back all the way, using the homebound commuter traffic as cover, and she was certain the woman hadn't spotted her. Slowing even further, Taylor watched as the car rolled through a set of electronically controlled wrought-iron gates.

A dog barked as she cruised past the entrance, making all the hairs at the back of her neck stand on end. Maybe it was a coincidence that there was a dog here, but then again, maybe not. It could have been a guard dog she had just heard. But if that *was* Baby, then, right at this moment, Bayard was raiding the wrong address.

Rounding a corner, out of sight of the estate, Taylor pulled over onto the verge, reached for her cell phone and thumbed in a short dial. The smart thing to do now that she had Slater's probable address was leave, but Slater's girlfriend had left Tony's in a panic. If Slater did live here, he could react by packing up the dog and leaving immediately.

Bayard's phone rang once, twice. Glass exploded, showering her face and hands as the windscreen vaporized. A split second too late, her foot stamped on the accelerator. The car lunged forward, straight into the back of a reversing truck. She was flung forward, then back, her forehead connecting with the steering wheel hard enough that she saw stars. When her vision cleared, the barrel of a businesslike Glock positioned in the driver's-side window froze her in place. Somewhere, distantly, she could hear Bayard's answering service asking if she wanted to leave a message.

Twenty

Rina checked her watch. The time for the bust had come and gone. A restless hour later, she dialed Taylor's cell phone. After the predetermined number of rings, she was transferred through to Taylor's voice mail. She hung up without leaving a message.

At eight o'clock the phone beeped. She checked the screen. Not a call, but a text message from Taylor, asking her to ring her at a Winton number because the battery on her cell phone was low.

Rina set the phone down on the kitchen table. She was tempted to call, and she would in a microsecond, except for one problem: whoever had sent the message, it wasn't Taylor. If Taylor had taken the time to text, why hadn't she simply rung? The conversation would have been a brief "Yes, they had Baby" or "No, they didn't." Alternatively, she could have texted the information. No call was necessary.

Pulling out a chair, Rina sat down and stared at the message, her skin crawling. She had to figure out what to do. Whoever had sent the message had Taylor's phone and now her cell phone number. It was possible Taylor had simply lost the phone and that someone had gotten hold of it and was playing a prank.

It was also possible that the message was a setup, designed to locate her.

The third option was that Taylor was in trouble, but that didn't make sense. Taylor hadn't been a part of the bust. In theory, she was doing exactly what Rina had spent the day doing, kicking her heels, waiting.

She wasn't going to reply to the text. If it was Taylor, she would make contact again. If she hadn't heard from Taylor by the morning, she would assume the worst and get hold of Bayard. She had his cell phone number in her old address book, which was stored with her passport and the other personal papers that belonged to her previous life. Even if she couldn't get through to him straight off, she would reach him eventually. He wouldn't ignore a call from her.

Another hour ticked past while Rina waited for Taylor to call. She switched on the television and flicked through the news channels, half dreading to see something about the bust or Taylor, but nothing even remotely close to Winton was making headlines.

At ten she made herself a sandwich and sat nursing a glass of iced lemonade, keeping an eye on the news. At midnight, she switched the television off, checked her security alarm was set, had a shower and went to bed. Fifteen minutes of tossing and turning later, she deactivated the alarm, pushed open the French doors leading off her bedroom and stepped out onto the long, narrow deck that ran the length of the back of the house. The temperature was cooler outside, but it was still hot, the moon full enough to throw a pale silvery glow over the back lawn.

Settling down on the swing seat just outside her bedroom, she plumped cushions and tried to make herself comfortable. The silence should have been soothing, but tonight it grated. A mosquito whined. Absently, she slapped at it. Another zeroed in and she began to rethink her plan of cooling off outside.

A shadow moved at the edge of the lawn.

The paranoia that had gripped her that afternoon flooded back. The movement could have been made by an animal, maybe a large cat or a dog, but definitely not a breeze, because there wasn't one. Aside from an animal, that left a human prowler. Not for the first time, she decided it was time she got herself a gun and learned to use it.

A shadow detached itself from the outline of a rhododendron and something clicked into place in her mind, a brief flash of the way the man at the mall had merged into the shadows.

Sitting bolt upright, she stared at the dark figure strolling across the lawn as casually as if it was daylight and he was invited.

"Don't tell me you can see in the dark."

"You wouldn't believe me if I did."

JT stepped up onto the deck. "I've read your file. I don't think you could surprise me."

Ridiculously, considering that he had just broken into her property, Rina was suddenly aware that she wasn't wearing nearly enough—a camisole and a pair of light cotton drawstring pants. Neither the top nor the pants were see-through, but they were definitely meant for bed. "Don't you ever knock?"

She caught the flash of a grin, quickly gone, and her stomach lurched ever so slightly.

"I've gotten out of the habit."

The voice was the same—deep, mild, with that slight Southern accent. Nothing that should make her stomach do somersaults. Despite that, she definitely had butterflies. The only thing she could put it down to was the odd sense of camaraderie she'd felt toward him the night he'd helped her escape. Or maybe it was out-and-out loneliness. For weeks now she hadn't seen anyone who knew who she was or cared. She wouldn't say that JT cared, exactly—he was just doing his job—but he was a familiar face and a link to her past.

It was the "link to her past" bit that worried her now. She studied the black T-shirt and jeans he was wearing. They weren't exactly a uniform and a flak jacket, but the dark clothing was definitely useful for sneaking around in the dark. "How did you find me?"

"I've got working agreements across the board. One of them is with the U.S. Marshals. I'm not supposed to be anywhere near you, but the fact is, you spotted me in town, so I'm touching base. If Marlow finds out I'm in Beaumont, he won't be happy."

That was an understatement. Marlow had been categorical about the parameters of the WitSec program. In order to secure her safety, she wasn't to have contact with *anyone* from her past, and no one from her past could contact her. To bypass Marlow, JT must have gotten some kind of high-level permission.

She was now certain that the man she'd glimpsed walking into the mall had been JT. She was also willing to bet he was the owner of the black truck. For her to have missed seeing his face as he had walked back to his truck meant he must have exited the mall by a side entrance and worked his way around the perimeter of the car park to stay out of her line of vision. Later on, the same truck had been parked just across from the newsagent, which meant he had been following her most of the day, including the three hours of driving lessons.

Her cheeks warmed when she thought about all the mistakes she'd made. Denny had nearly had a heart attack a couple of times. "Just how long, exactly, have you been in Beaumont?"

"Three months, give or take a day."

A sharp tingle went down her spine. That was exactly how long she had been here.

She wasn't happy that she was under surveillance of any kind. She hadn't expected it, and for JT to have been surveilling her for *weeks,* not days, made her feel distinctly uneasy.

She trusted him; in a weird way, she trusted him more than anyone, except Taylor. He had risked himself for her back in Winton, then, against the odds, for Baby, but she didn't trust his agenda. JT's focus had always been Alex. The only reason for him to be in Beaumont now was that he thought there was a good chance Alex would find her.

He propped himself against one of the veranda supports, arms folded over his chest. The stance was nonthreatening, although after her initial shock that there was someone sneaking around her house, Rina hadn't felt any real anxiety. Once she'd realized it was JT, apart from her reaction to seeing a familiar face, she had felt okay. One of the things she had noticed about JT was that he had the facility to seem neutral, so that even though he was definitely male and tough, he wasn't threatening. "I thought you would have been in on the bust in Winton."

The statement was probing, but he didn't show any surprise that she knew about the operation. More alarm bells rang. Taylor had been worried about her phone being tapped. Rina was now certain that it was: by JT.

"Lopez wants you, not the dog. He's a smart operator. Bayard won't find it easy to nail either him or Slater. That's the other reason I'm here. Bayard rang me a couple of hours ago. The operation went bad. Taylor's gone missing."

She had known something was wrong. "Taylor was supposed to ring me when they got Baby." Pushing to her feet, she stepped into her bedroom. "I've got something you should see."

As she reached for the light switch, JT's soft "Don't switch that on" stopped her.

The need for darkness reinforced the message that she wasn't living a normal life, no matter how much she tried to pretend otherwise, and JT's visit wasn't anywhere near as casual as he was making out. Feeling her way in the darkness, she found the cell phone, which was sitting on her bedside table. When she stepped back out onto the deck, she flicked through to the message she'd received and passed it to JT. "That came through. It's Taylor's number. I didn't answer it, because I didn't think the message was sent by Taylor."

He studied the message, took his own cell phone out of his pocket and made a brief call, relaying the number. "We can try to get a fix on it, but the chances are whoever's got the phone won't use it now for that reason."

"What about Taylor?"

"Bayard's doing what he can, but there's no news yet."

"And Baby?"

"They did find dog hairs that they think belong to Baby, and signs that a dog was kept at the house they raided."

So now Alex had both Baby and Taylor.

Her jaw tightened. She was thousands of miles away and powerless to help, but JT could. He had contacts and resources. The possibility that he could do anything now was slim, but she had to try. "Will *you* look for Taylor?"

The hesitation before he answered underlined that Taylor wasn't his priority. "I'll see what I can do, but you've got to leave it with me. Whatever you do, don't call Bayard or anyone else connected with the FBI. Bayard's got a mole. He's been working to identify him, but he hasn't found him yet."

The warning was softly spoken and, she realized, the motivation behind this visit. Today she had noticed the back of a man's head and a truck, but she'd had no idea the two were connected, or that it was JT. If he had changed his vehicle, he could have continued to watch her and she wouldn't have been any the wiser.

The reason he had followed her was now also clear. He knew she had made contact with Taylor and that it was highly likely she was compromised. Whether he had been staying close to her as a protective measure or to get a line on Alex was a moot point.

A chill ran down her spine. She had been going

to ring Bayard in the morning, but if he had a mole that would have been tantamount to serving herself up on a plate to Alex.

JT handed back her cell phone. "I've entered my cell number. Try not to use it unless there's an emergency."

Heart pounding a little too fast, she watched until he disappeared over the back fence.

An engine started up in the distance: definitely a truck.

Another vehicle drove past, although this one sounded more low-key—a sedan, not a four-wheel-drive.

Walking back into her room, she locked up, set the alarm and went back to bed. Tired as she was, though, she was too keyed up to sleep. Her mind kept running over her last conversation with Taylor and a raft of unsettling possibilities. She refused to dwell on the fact that her friend could be dead. If Alex did have Taylor, he needed her alive; there was no point in killing her.

JT had stated that he didn't think either Alex or Slater were in Winton, which let in a small ray of hope. If one of Alex's other men had gotten hold of Taylor, then maybe there was a chance that JT, or even Bayard, could get to her in time.

As for Baby, she couldn't bear to think what had happened to him. The only positive was that if he had survived three months because Alex thought he was useful, there was no reason to kill him now. The same logic applied to Taylor. She had to believe that they were safe, so long as Alex thought there was a chance he could use them to get to her.

Knowing that JT was on the job relieved some of her tension, although she had to remember that he was working on his own investigation; he wasn't here to protect her. Even though he had broken the no-contact rule to warn her against contacting Bayard, JT viewed her in exactly the same way that Alex viewed Taylor and Baby: as bait.

Twenty-One

When Rina woke the sun was fully up and it was closer to afternoon than morning. She hadn't fallen asleep until after three. The fact that she had slept at all, let alone slept in, surprised her.

She checked her cell phone, but there were no new messages or missed calls. She hadn't expected to find any. If either of the phones had rung she would have been awake instantly. The lack of contact from Taylor confirmed that something had gone badly wrong.

Feeling physically sick, she picked up her cell phone, sat on the edge of the bed and dialed JT.

He picked up on the second ring.

"I want to help. I could be bait."

"Marlow won't allow it, and if Bayard tries anything like that he'll lose his job."

"What about you?"

"Honey, don't push it—"

Her jaw tightened. "That's why you're here, isn't it? To catch Alex."

A small silence stretched out. "I've got leeway, but I'm not endangering you. And don't forget, Lopez knows I'm working for the government. That's narrowed my options."

That made sense. He couldn't take part in any of Bayard's operations for that reason, and he'd lost his own line on the cartel. "I'd forgotten Alex knows what you look like."

"Now you're getting it. If he could put a hole in me, he would."

"So what now?"

"Just stay quiet and sit tight. I've got a guy in Winton who's looking, and Bayard's a good operator. He doesn't take kindly to losing one of his own. If anyone can get Taylor back, he'll do it."

Her fingers tightened on the phone. "Will you let me know when something happens?"

"I'll call as soon as I get news." He paused. "And don't worry about the fact that I'm here. Think of me as a little extra insurance. If Lopez, or any of his people, turn up in Beaumont, you'll be moved out and a look-alike moved in. There's no way you'll be put on the front line."

Rina tried to paint, but from the first stroke she knew she was wasting her time. An hour later, with a throbbing headache and her stomach rumbling because she hadn't eaten or had anything to drink since the previous evening, she cleaned her brush and went to the kitchen to make coffee and breakfast.

She switched on the TV, tuned into the news and paged through yesterday's newspapers, incapable of concentrating on either medium but desperate for distraction.

Putting her mug of coffee down, she turned a page. A blurred photo of a bank robber wielding a gun dominated the page. For long seconds the emotionless way Alex had lifted the gun and trained it on Cesar replayed itself.

Unclenching her teeth, she forced herself to relax, to look at the sunlight beaming across the pine floor, the glimpse of the front yard and the peaked roof of the house directly across the street visible through the sitting room window. Normal everyday sights.

Dwelling on what had happened was a waste of time. Yes, she had been blind in a much worse way than physically. Yes, she had been manipulated and abused, but she had gotten through it. More important, she had gotten away. Now Alex didn't have any power over her unless she chose to hand it to him.

But he had power over Taylor and Baby.

Anger stirred. But there was no outlet for the anger or the powerlessness, and no practical way she could do anything to change the situation. She couldn't even share her outrage and her grief with anyone, because she had no one. They were all gone. Alex had taken them away.

With slow, deliberate movements, she opened the local paper and forced herself to read. A story about the community center's difficulty getting funding to have their roof fixed was barely able to hold her attention, but eventually her pulse rate slowed and her stomach settled. Directly after the sports page she ran into the classifieds. These ones were safe to read, because the photos of Baby were only in the papers that had national distribution. As she skimmed down the page, bypassing the "lost and found pets" section, her gaze caught on an ad in the "employment wanted" column.

Private Investigations.

She went still inside, the grief and fear that had threatened to overwhelm her momentarily suspended. The advertisement stated that inquiries were effective and discreet with a high rate of success, and that contacts could be anonymous.

She studied the phone number, memorizing it. She wasn't allowed to do anything. She was watched and contained, but a private eye was a free agent.

If Bayard's organization was compromised, then the likelihood that they would be able to rescue either Taylor or Baby was remote until they weeded out the mole. Rina had no idea how long that would take, but if the mole had remained undetected for this amount of time, she didn't imagine it would be an overnight job.

Rina continued to study the advertisement. She couldn't go to Winton herself, but a P.I. could.

Walking through to the kitchen, she picked up the phone, the action automatic. She dropped the receiver back in its cradle almost immediately. She couldn't afford to use a landline at any time.

Picking up her cell phone, she dialed the number in the ad.

Harold Sayer, one of the partners of Wendell Sayer Investigations, picked up the call. After running through a checklist of questions, she broached the subject of money.

"I'm going to need some money up front to pay for the travel and accommodation expenses."

She had already thought about that, but the sum Sayer mentioned was at least double what she had calculated.

"Winton's quite a distance, and sometimes there's a lot more legwork in these investigations than people anticipate. Anything left over gets credited off the final account and, remember, I don't bill you for the travel time, just the standard investigative fee. That's what makes my agency competitive. Most firms charge by the hour, or the day. Plus, I'm free to travel right now, which fits in with the urgency of the case."

Wary as she was at paying such a large lump sum up front, Sayer's immediate availability was exactly what she needed. "How do I get the money to you?"

Sayer gave her his account number, with instructions to pay the amount in immediately. That way he could get an afternoon flight out and have something to report by midmorning the next day. As she had said, time was of the essence.

Twenty-four hours later, Rina stared at the neat exterior of Wendell Sayer Investigations. The door was locked, the office, viewed through a venetian blind, was empty.

It had taken her an hour of ducking through shops and changing her clothes in a public restroom to finally make it to her destination without a tail, only to find that what she had suspected was true. She had been duped.

Harold Sayer hadn't responded to any of her calls, and neither had anyone at Wendell Sayer Investigations. At first she'd been afraid he had fallen into the same trap Taylor had, and that it was possible that Sayer was either in grave danger or dead, until she had begun making inquiries. Sayer hadn't flown to the West Coast. His ticket had been for another destination entirely—Florida. He had taken her money and run.

A small, dapper man halted beside her and stared at the empty office. "I take it Sayer was carrying out an investigation for you."

"He was supposed to be." Rina hooked the strap of her bag more firmly over her shoulder. Now that it was established that Sayer really had left town, all she wanted to do was move on. Time was ticking away and she was back to square one. She had to find someone else to do the inquiry.

"Took the money and ran, huh?"

"Something like that."

"You must be Rina Mathews. I've just been reading through the notes Harold made." He fitted a key in the lock and pushed the door open. "Let me introduce myself. I'm Robert E. Wendell, the other half of Wendell Sayer Investigations. When Harold left town yesterday, he also emptied the company account. I've just come back from the police station. I've been trying to locate you, but Harold didn't leave a record of either your telephone number or your address."

"That's because I didn't give him one."

Wendell's expression was thoughtful. "Then I'm glad I caught you. I have the details of the inquiries you want made and I believe I can help you—at no further cost, of course. You've contracted Wendell Sayer to do the work. Just because Harold's absconded that doesn't mean the job won't get done. Believe it or not, I used to work for Pinkerton. Before that I was a cop."

Rina stared at Wendell. After being taken for a ride by Sayer, she was, to put it mildly, suspicious, but the lure of the name Pinkerton was both wacky and irresistible. Wendell himself was unimposing, of medium height and build, balding, and sixty if he was a day. If he had been a cop, it had been a long time ago.

"You can check my qualifications if you want. I have them all on file."

Ten minutes later, a cup of tea steaming gently at her side, Rina finished examining Wendell's impressive credentials. Her only reservation was that Wendell, lean and spry as he looked, was on the wrong side of sixty. "I'm trying to locate a missing pet and a missing person. I have to warn you there is an element of danger connected with the inquiry."

"It's been some years since I've had occasion to fire a weapon, but you can trust me, Ms. Mathews, I still know how to use a gun."

Twenty-Two

After repeating the information she had given Sayer, Rina strolled out of Wendell's office, checked that the street was empty, and walked through the mall until she reached the ladies' room.

Locking herself in a stall, she changed out of the tan pants and dark shirt she'd been wearing and into an uncrushable pink halter dress she'd had folded in her bag. Slipping on a pair of strappy heels that matched the dress, she uncoiled her hair from the tight knot she'd had it in and finger combed it into loose curls. She studied the effect in the mirror, then slipped dark glasses on the bridge of her nose, satisfied that she looked a lot different from the woman who had walked into the restroom.

Folding her clothes neatly and stowing them in her bag, she strolled to the DPS office where she had an appointment to take the written test for her license and, if she passed, do the practical. She had arranged to use one of Denny's cars. After a little judicious horse-trading, Denny had agreed to her offer: once she got her license, that was the last Denny saw of her, and if she didn't pass, she didn't qualify to get her money back. That way his motto stayed intact, his wife was happy with the bank balance, and he got to escape bypass surgery.

Requesting a copy of the learner's manual, she sat down and started to read, letting her gaze flow down the pages, not allowing herself to become attached to any particular piece of information.

Ten minutes later she replaced the manual on the counter. "Thank you."

The receptionist, an elegant black woman with a name tag that identified her as Denise, looked stunned. "Don't you need it? Your test isn't until three."

"I've read it."

Twenty minutes later, she walked back into the testing station, sat down and did the test. When she was finished, she waited in the reception area for the paper to be marked.

A bespectacled man came to the counter with her application and signed it off. "One hundred percent. Not often we get one of those."

Half an hour later, after hesitating twice at intersections, Rina pulled into a parking space directly outside the testing station.

Officer Doucet studied his clipboard. "It's borderline."

Rina's stomach sank. Despite the hours she'd spent with Denny, she just hadn't had time to build up confidence or the automatic reflexes that seemed to make driving go smoothly.

A huge SUV cruised through a red light just ahead. A delivery truck braked and the driver leaned on the horn, giving the SUV a one-fingered salute. "I'm better than that."

He stared at his clipboard and flipped the page. She caught a glimpse of her test paper and the one hundred percent mark. "At least you know the rules. Okay. You're passed, but promise me you'll get some more coaching." He signed off on the test, detached a sheet and handed it to her, smothering a grin. "Denny, huh? He's a killer."

In light of Denny's Drive 'Til You Die motto, she wasn't sure that was a compliment.

The tension increased as she waited for Doucet to exit the car, but now that he'd passed her, he didn't seem to be in any hurry. He studied his clipboard some more, and it finally registered that the reason he was still sitting in the car was that he was attracted to her. She had been aware of his interest in the pink dress and more probably the length of leg the dress revealed as she had driven. For a woman who had gone through puberty and adolescence in hospitals and special-needs schools, the concept was life changing.

He turned slightly in his seat. "You're new in town."

"That's right." Rina noticed his cheeks were slightly flushed and that his gaze kept settling on her legs. She cast around for something else to say, but small talk had never been her area. Since her new life had officially begun a little over three months ago, her pool of conversational topics had shrunk to close on zero. She couldn't even talk about her struggle to teach herself to read again, or why she was so late getting her driver's license, because that would mean explaining she had been blind for most of her life. Marlow had impressed on her that that was a key piece of information that would stick in people's minds. The last thing she wanted to do was stand out as "different" in the community. She shrugged. "I've been here around three months."

He slipped his pen onto a little holder attached to his clipboard. "You sound like you're from the northern states. I guess, like a lot of people, you moved down here for the climate. It's certainly hot today."

And getting hotter. In terms of dipping her toe in the water, sexually, she should be interested in Doucet. He was tall, dark and good-looking in a slightly rough-hewn way, and he was making no bones about the fact that he was interested in her. Unfortunately, as handsome and charming as Doucet was, she didn't want to spend one more second with him than was necessary.

"So, what do you do in your spare time?"

You wouldn't believe me if I told you. "I'm a little tied up with research at the moment."

"If you're interested, there's a new movie at the multiplex tomorrow night—"

A black truck pulled into a space just in front of the vehicle. A door slammed. Rina watched as JT strolled toward the car.

Doucet's expression turned rueful. He unlatched his seat belt. "Boyfriend, huh? I should have known."

Her first thought as she stepped out of the car was that for JT to break cover, he must have news about Taylor, but when he shook his head, her confusion mounted. If this wasn't about Taylor, he shouldn't be here.

JT's gaze fixed on Doucet and the temperature dropped by a few degrees. JT crossed his arms over his chest. The movement stretched the T-shirt he was wearing across his shoulders. She caught a glimpse of a small tattoo, high on one muscled bicep, and something tightened low in her stomach. In the faded T-shirt, the sleeves cut off, he was a lot bigger and more muscular than she'd first thought, and the tattoo added a primitive edge.

Rina collected her handbag, locked the car and took time to thank Doucet. He looked over her head at JT, then disappeared into the testing station. She noted the male body language. Doucet hadn't cringed, but it had been close. Whatever JT was doing, it had been enough to intimidate the cop.

Abruptly, she felt the same awareness of herself as an attractive, available female she had experienced when Doucet had glanced at her legs. Even more ridiculous, she felt like JT was her boyfriend and that she had been caught cheating. "What *are* you doing here?"

His gaze was cool. "I decided to take some time out."

The fact that he wasn't working on official business threw her even more off balance. "If you'll excuse me, I have to leave the keys at the front desk so Denny can collect his car, and get my license."

He leaned against the truck. "I'll wait."

When she strolled out of the testing station, JT was still leaning against the truck.

"If you need a lift home, I can drop you."

"I'm not going home just yet. I need to buy a car." Cancel that—she was getting herself a giant SUV or a truck.

"Then get in. I'm helping you."

She stalled, suddenly wary. She might be slow on the uptake with female things, but she knew that if she got into JT's truck that meant something. "I'm capable of buying my own vehicle."

His expression was grim. "That outfit might have worked on the cop, but if a car salesman sees you dressed like that, you don't have a chance." He opened the passenger-side door. "It'll be like taking candy from a baby."

The invitation wasn't exactly irresistible. She noticed the tattoo again, registering the symbol. Reluctantly, she walked toward his truck. Most of the larger car dealerships were situated in places that weren't easy to reach on foot. It was a fact that she could look around more of them if JT gave her a lift. "If Marlow hears about this, we'll both be fried."

His hand landed in the small of her back as he helped her climb in. The heat from his palm burned through the fabric of her dress into her skin.

"Today, that's a risk I'm prepared to take."

His offer to take her around the car yards was practical, but sitting just inches from JT in the confines of his truck cab didn't feel practical. For months she had been "the job" for JT, but suddenly she didn't feel remotely like a key witness for the prosecution or a link to an international crime syndicate.

She studied the laptop set up on a console, and a compact fax mounted where the glove compartment had once been. The dread that Taylor was now enduring the situation she had most feared—being caught in Alex's power—surged back. "What have you heard about Taylor? There has to be something."

JT signaled and turned into traffic. "Bayard's information is that Taylor went out on a limb, paid a visit to Slater's ex-wife, found Slater and got isolated. The last reported sighting of Taylor was at a bar in Winton. Lopez was seen in Bogotá this morning, which means Slater has her. At a guess, Slater's waiting for Lopez's return before he acts." JT slid his cell phone out of his jeans pocket and studied the screen. "If anything had happened I would have been informed. Every agency on the West Coast is looking, but so far no news has broken."

"Thank you." The fact that Alex wasn't in the equation yet meant there was hope, although the clock was ticking. If he had been seen in Bogotá this morning, he could easily be back in Winton by this evening.

JT stopped at an intersection. While he waited for the lights to turn green, he passed her a bottle of water. She drank, watched as he took a long swallow from his, then looked away, feeling distinctly on edge. In a subtle way, JT was different. It took her a while to figure out what exactly the difference was, but she decided it came down to her awareness of him. Until last night she had seen him only as a controlled, committed agent, but the tattoo underlined everything she didn't know about him. Today was the first time she had seen it, but it had been there all along, distinctly male, faintly subversive. The mark provided her with one of the few solid pieces of information she had about him; that whatever JT was now, he had once been a Navy SEAL.

They cruised past several dealerships and finally pulled into a large gaudy entranceway lined with flags.

Rina stared at the glittering sea of vehicles. "Why this one?"

"It's the biggest in town and it's got the most choice."

"As simple as that?"

"Some things don't need a lot of science."

JT's tone wasn't lost on her. "I didn't use sex to get my license." She examined the gaudy office of the dealership as JT pulled into a parking space. "You were tailing me again."

"For most of the day. You got away from me for about an hour."

He had obviously seen her go into the mall, but she had managed to elude him when she'd gone to check on Wendall Sayer's office. "I was shopping."

Hooking the strap of her purse over her shoulder, she reached for the door handle. JT's "Wait there" stopped her.

Her stomach tightened as he walked around the truck, opened the door and helped her down. The touch was brief, the eye contact that went with it even briefer, but the effect of both made her heart pound.

The car salesman, apart from an appreciative but ultimately dismissive glance at her, concentrated solely on JT, despite the fact that she was the buyer. The lesson was salutary. It was clear that some things worked for females, but JT had been right; some situations were definitely male territory.

She interrupted Brad's impressive sales pitch, all aimed at trying to sell her a small Japanese import or maybe a sports car. "I don't want a car. I want a truck."

Surprise flickered over JT's usually impassive features.

The salesman made the mistake of laughing. "Honey, which color?"

And just like that, they were back in female territory. She smiled sweetly. "It isn't one that you've got."

JT put a hand to his mouth. It took her a few seconds to realize he was laughing.

He coughed. "Uh, I think we'd like to look around for ourselves for a few minutes."

When the salesman backed off, JT lowered his hand. "What kind of truck?"

"Don't dare laugh, but I like yours."

"I use mine for rough country and carrying equipment. That's the only reason I have it. Otherwise I'd probably get something more comfortable, like an SUV."

"I'd still like a truck." She cast her gaze over the ranks of cars. "And, actually, color *is* important. I don't want a red one. People who drive red trucks have psychological problems."

His hand moved over his mouth again. She deduced that he had seen the red truck that had almost rear-ended her the previous day.

"For driving around town, a car makes sense. It's easier to handle, plus you'd have a secure trunk."

She had a brief flash of tumbling in a car. Her fingers tightened on the strap of her handbag. "I don't want a car."

His gaze sharpened, all trace of humor gone. "What is it?"

She shifted her gaze to the sea of vehicles, uncomfortable with the impression that JT had somehow locked into her thoughts. And that, attractive male or not, like Alex, JT had a vested interest in her recovering her memory. "I remembered a couple of good reasons not to buy one."

"I'd forgotten about the accident. Sorry."

She met his gaze. The moment of focused awareness also told her that JT probably knew more about her and her past than she did.

Time for a change of subject.

He had told her he needed the truck for rough country and carrying equipment, but he hadn't said why. Aside from his job as an agent, she had no idea what JT did with his spare time. "Why do you need a truck?"

He shrugged. "I own a ranch."

Open spaces, the wholesome smell of grass and wind, and contented animals.

The car yard and the smell of hot asphalt faded. She was seven and on horseback for the first time, Esther coaxing her around the dusty pen, hair loose, eyes smiling, looking as at home in jeans and a shirt as she had in glamorous evening gowns. They had only ever visited a family friend's ranch, never owned one, but Rina had lived for those holidays. Esther had had to drag her away every time.

A car engine revved. The smell of car fumes filled her nostrils. Rina swallowed against a sudden tightness in her throat. Despite the fact that JT was an agent, the ranch fitted. She couldn't imagine him in an office.

After an hour of browsing and test-driving a couple of trucks, in the end she decided she wanted an SUV. She still liked the idea of a truck; she just wasn't up to driving one yet.

The salesman, Brad, kept a low profile. The SUV she finally chose was silvery beige—not exactly a he-man vehicle, but not a girly one, either, and it had the compensation of a powerful engine.

JT checked beneath the hood, then requested the keys so they could take it for a test drive.

Climbing behind the wheel was an unexpected thrill. At first she stuck to residential streets, then moved onto busier roads. As she relaxed, she finally got what Denny had been talking about when he said she had to "feel" the car and the road. She wouldn't say she was ready for heavy traffic, but for the first time she felt confident.

Half an hour later she had signed a check, completed the paperwork and was the owner of the SUV.

As she slid behind the wheel, JT ducked down at the driver's-side window. "Follow me and I'll make sure you get home safely."

That was a good point. Apart from her driving lessons with Denny, she had walked everywhere she needed to go in Beaumont. She had absolutely no idea where the dealership was in relation to her home suburb. First thing tomorrow, she would have to buy a road map.

She let JT turn out onto the highway first, then fell in behind him. The late afternoon was fading into evening, and the roads were crammed with rush-hour traffic. When she finally turned into her driveway, JT cruised on ahead. As she locked the vehicle and found the keys for the front door she pondered what she would have done if JT had pulled into her driveway. She hadn't issued any invitations. Apart from helping her buy the SUV, neither had he, but something had changed between them.

Twenty-Three

Two days later, at six in the morning, Rina's cell phone rang. She had half expected to hear JT's voice, but it was Wendell. He had found Baby.

Jackknifing into a sitting position, she listened as Wendell gave her a rundown on what had happened.

He had made some discreet inquiries about the man who had put the ads in the paper, Pedro Gomez. Gomez had disappeared and the house had since been rented out to new tenants. Wendell had abandoned that line of inquiry as a dead end, and had checked with the dog pound and the local vets. He had finally struck gold when he had investigated police complaints about barking dogs. A couple in an outlying suburb had been keeping a dog in their garage and the barking was upsetting the neighbors.

Wendell had called on the address. A woman had answered the door but she had denied having

a dog, saying her husband had gotten rid of it
because of the trouble neighbors had caused. Suspicious, Wendell had waited until after dark, then
had investigated the rear of the property. The
garage had had blacked-out windows and heavy
locks on the door. He'd used bolt cutters and a set
of lock picks to get in and had found a muzzled
dog matching Baby's description. Now he was
about to board a flight to Denver, then he was
picking up a connection to Dallas. He had
managed to get Baby on both flights at short
notice, but he would have to hire a rental and drive
to Beaumont.

Rina listened while Wendell outlined the precautions he had taken, and the fact that he was certain
he had gotten away without the owners of the
property being aware that anything was amiss. She
wanted to believe it was Baby. She wanted to believe
everything was as straightforward and uncomplicated as it seemed. The blacked-out window, the
locks and the muzzle didn't point to the behavior of
normal pet owners, but she had difficulty believing
that Wendell had succeeded where JT, Bayard and a
number of law-enforcement agencies, including the
local police, had failed. "Are you sure it's Baby?"

"As sure as I can be. Winton isn't that big a place.
There's a good chance that this is your dog."

"What about Taylor?"

"I found the last place she stayed, the Winton
Court Motel, and the license plate of her rental. Ac-

cording to the rental firm, the car hasn't been returned. I'm sorry I couldn't be of more help."

With having to drive the last leg, Wendell wouldn't get to Beaumont until close to nightfall. Rina arranged to meet him in Liberty, a town just over half an hour west of Beaumont. She had broken the rules in getting Wendell to act for her and retrieve Baby. She had entrusted him with her cell phone number, based on the logic that whoever was holding Baby already knew it, but that didn't mean she had to behave stupidly. If the dog was Baby, she couldn't allow herself to believe his retrieval was as straight-forward and easy as it seemed. If there was a nasty string attached, she wanted to be prepared. Arrang-ing to meet in Liberty was a start. It would put Wendell in unfamiliar territory, and it would protect her address.

She considered calling JT, but dismissed the idea. Her reasons for getting Wendell to do a little digging for her hadn't changed. Until either Slater or Alex made contact with some kind of demand, it was the only way she could reach out to try and help Baby and Taylor and preserve her anonymity. If JT found out she had contracted a private investigator, he would close her down and she wouldn't get another chance. He would contact Marlow. Once that happened, she would be moved out of Beaumont and put under twenty-four-hour security until the threat from Alex and Slater was neutralized.

Rina showered and dressed and tried to keep a lid

on the growing hope that the dog Wendell had *was* Baby, but despite that she couldn't stop smiling. Getting Baby back was like reclaiming a part of her family, and a piece of her old life.

After breakfast, she forced herself to do some chores and follow her routine, only this time she didn't walk to the shops to get papers and groceries, she drove.

Getting into her own vehicle was a heady thrill, if a little nerve-racking, but she needed the practice if she was going to drive to Liberty then back in the dark. After finding a parking space she strolled around the shops and bought papers, magazines and a road map, then called into the local supermarket and bought a small bag of dog biscuits. Whether or not the dog was Baby, he would still need feeding. She asked the checkout operator to double-bag the biscuits so the distinctive wrapper wouldn't be visible. If JT saw the dog biscuits, he would know something was up.

When she got home, Rina took a couple of pain-killers and forced herself to lie down for a couple of hours, but she was too wound up to sleep. When five o'clock finally approached, she got up, showered and dressed, choosing tan cotton pants and a mid-blue shirt, muted colors that would cut down her visibility. At eight o'clock, the time she had agreed to meet Wendell, it would still be light for a good hour, so dark clothing would make her stand out. Rummaging through her drawers, she unearthed a blue baseball cap. As a disguise, it wasn't much, but with JT watching her so closely, she'd had to abandon her plan to make another trip into town and buy a wig.

Standing in front of the mirror, she experimented with winding her hair on top of her head, then flattening it out so the cap would fit, but her hair was too bulky, and the cap kept sliding off. As a compromise, she pulled her hair back in a tight French braid, so that it lay flat against the back of her skull, and tucked the tail beneath the collar of her shirt. With her hair compressed, the hat came down a lot lower, shading her eyes.

Studying herself, she decided it wasn't a disguise that would net her more than a few seconds of confusion from someone who knew her, but it did make her blend in. The shapeless shirt hid her figure, and with her hair pulled back and half of her face in shadow, she looked like a lot of kids who hung out at the mall.

There was no easy way to get out of the house without being seen. All she could do was bank on the fact that JT had to eat sometime. If he followed any kind of routine she was willing to bet he ate at the same time she had dinner, which was around six.

Checking her watch, she collected her bag and her cell phone, and packed a grocery sack with the road map, a peanut butter sandwich, a bottle of water, the bag of dog biscuits, and Baby's food bowls and a spare lead and collar, which she'd kept along with the rest of his stuff. After glancing out at the road and the backyard, which were both empty, she stepped out of the kitchen door and walked quickly to the SUV. Slinging her purse and the bag on the passenger seat, she climbed behind the wheel. Adrenaline pumping, she slid the key into the ignition. The engine turned over smoothly.

Checking the rearview mirror, half expecting to see JT's truck gliding in to block her, she put the SUV in reverse and depressed the accelerator. The SUV shot back, almost scraping the block wall to one side of the drive. Stamping on the brake, she jerked to a halt, drove forward a few feet, took a deep breath and started to back up again, this time taking it more slowly.

By the time she got out on the road, she was drenched with sweat and her heart was pounding. Putting the gearshift in Drive, she accelerated down to the first intersection, then took a left, heading for the highway, her gaze darting to the rearview mirror every few seconds. So far, so good. If JT had seen her, he should be behind her now.

Five minutes of nervous tension later, she turned onto the Beaumont Highway. A patrol car shot past in the opposite lane, lights flashing, siren wailing, and she remembered she hadn't put her seat belt on. The last thing she needed was to get pulled over for an infringement. Dragging at the belt, she eventually got it fastened, then settled down to drive. According to her road map, Liberty was only a half-hour drive away. She had plenty of time to get there and get herself in place before her meeting with Wendell.

Thirty-five minutes later, she pulled over to the side of the road and checked her street map, looking for the popular chain motel Wendell had suggested. It was near the center of town, just a couple of blocks away. The map showed a residential area with a small park, which meant she should be able to find a place where she could watch the motel while remaining unobserved.

Putting the SUV back in gear, she waited for a gap, then pulled out into traffic. She drove a block, saw a shopping center and mall complex, and on impulse pulled in, braking hard as a truck filled with teenagers and pounding music accelerated toward the exit, cutting her off as she was about to turn into the parking area. When a second vehicle, a sports car also filled with teenagers, cruised past, she remembered that it was Friday night, which would explain why the town was so busy this late.

She made her turn, cruised slowly between ranks of parked vehicles and slotted into a space. The parking lot was more than three-quarters full. Several of the vehicles were silvery gray and beige, which made her SUV blend in nicely. Putting the drink bottle and the sandwich in her handbag, she locked the vehicle and proceeded on foot, walking past shops and cafés. A woman strolled out of the entrance of a supermarket just ahead, carrying a bag of groceries. On impulse Rina walked inside, grabbed a basket and walked down the aisles to the bakery. She loaded three loaves of bread into her basket, walked briskly to the checkout and paid for her purchases. She didn't want or need the bread, but they would add to her disguise. If anyone were watching for her, they would be looking for a woman with long dark hair, not an androgynous kid carrying groceries.

Purse slung over one shoulder and carrying the sack of groceries, she walked through the car park. The sign for the motel glowed ahead. Slowing her pace, she studied the layout of the street, looking for possible places to conceal herself. The motel was on the other side of the road, which meant she didn't have to expose herself by crossing the road. Checking her watch, she noted there was a good thirty minutes before Wendell was supposed to meet her there.

When she reached the edge of the small park that bordered this end of the mall, she strolled across the grass, as if she were taking a shortcut. When she reached the cover of a clump of trees, she dropped the sack of groceries on the ground and began working her way closer to the motel, taking up a position behind a clump of shrubs that gave her a clear view of the entrance. Making herself comfortable on the ground, she sipped some water and ate the sandwich she'd packed. If Wendell did bring Baby, when she got him she would have to move, and move fast.

Ten minutes later, a dark blue sedan turned into the motel complex. She studied the vehicle as it turned, frustrated that she couldn't quite see the driver, although he was definitely male. The car had been a rental, but there had been no sign of a dog. It was possible that Baby could be lying asleep on the backseat.

She checked her watch. If the driver of the sedan was Wendell, he was early. A further five minutes ticked by. No one else went into the motel or came out. Another few minutes passed, and she decided the dark blue sedan must have been Wendell's.

Rina packed the wrapping of her sandwich and the half-filled water bottle away, took out her cell phone and dialed Wendell's number. He picked up immediately. The blue sedan was his and he was waiting in the parking lot.

"I didn't see Baby."

"He's in the trunk."

Her temper flashed. Wendell had just crossed a line. He hadn't struck her as callous when she had talked to him in his shop, but as far as Rina was concerned, anyone who put a dog in the trunk, especially in this heat, deserved to be shot. "Get him out. Walk him to the nearest streetlamp and tie him up so I can see him, then drive away."

He wasn't happy. They had a contract. He had retrieved Baby, and he'd made sure he wasn't followed. He had gone out on a limb for her and it had cost him.

Rina stuck to her guns. Wendell could bill her for any extra costs, but she needed to know he'd gotten the right dog, and that her ex-husband hadn't followed him.

She watched as Wendell appeared with a big, light-colored dog on a leash. Her chest squeezed tight. It *looked* like Baby.

As Wendell stooped to fasten the leash to the streetlamp she placed her fingers in her mouth and whistled. The dog's head shot up. A split second later, he jerked free of Wendell's hold and lunged across the road, leash trailing.

A car braked, horn blaring. Baby ignored the traffic, blatantly disobeying years of careful training, as he threw himself across the road, his gaze zeroing in on the clump of bushes Rina was hiding behind. A split second later, he barreled through the garden, scattering bark and snapping branches. Rina crouched down as he skidded to a halt. Her eyes blurred as her arms clamped around his neck. A rope, not a leash, hung from his neck. He was thin, close to emaciated, his coat rough. Scars encircled his neck, where the rope had bitten in, but Baby was *alive.*

A wet tongue swiped across her cheek and she pulled him closer, her chest squeezing tight as she buried her face against his coat. He was quivering, his eyes dilated as if had been permanently stuck in fight-or-flight mode, which he probably had. She couldn't believe she had gotten him back, that against all the odds Wendell had retrieved him.

The snap of a twig sent a shock of adrenaline through her. Grabbing the rope around Baby's neck, she urged him to be quiet. Slinging the strap of her handbag over her head so that it hung securely beneath one arm, she backed into the dense shade of the trees. Baby slunk beside her, sticking close, as if he understood there was danger. As they moved behind the trunk of a tree, she straightened. Simultaneously a gunshot split the air and she was knocked to the ground.

Twenty-Four

Panic exploded. Rina had a confused impression of a dark T-shirt, a muscled bicep, the sharp scent of sweat. Baby leaped sideways, to avoid the tangle of limbs. The toes of her sneakers gouged the thick layer of leaf mold and soft dirt as she lunged forward, trying to scramble free of the man's hold. An arm snaked around her waist, a hand clamped her mouth, stopping her forward momentum. He shifted, pinning her more firmly.

Instinctively, she bit down, fastening on the pad of his palm and an index finger. He swore, and pressed his hand more tightly into her mouth, nullifying the bite.

"Don't move."

JT.

The heat of his body burned through the cotton of her shirt. The familiar smell of him registered; her heart rate began to slow. Jaw aching, she eased the pressure of the bite. He withdrew his hand and she gulped in oxygen. She'd bitten him hard enough to draw blood, but for once, she didn't have a reaction.

"Are you all right?"

Another shot cut off any reply she might have made, this one more distant now, and recognizable as a souped-up vehicle backfiring.

JT's weight shifted. "Stay down."

Rina grabbed Baby, commanded him to lie down and watched as JT began working his way toward a spot where he could get a clear view of the motel, a large black gun in his hand. It was the first time since he'd gotten her out of the estate at Winton that she had seen him with a weapon, and it was a blunt reminder of exactly what he did for a living.

Seconds later, he joined them, put a finger to his lips and indicated they start falling back, keeping to the cover of the trees until they reached the nearest boundary, a chain-link fence that separated the rear of the shopping center from the park.

Placing the gun on the ground, he gripped the bottom of the aging chain-link fence and lifted it so she and Baby could shimmy beneath, then retrieved the gun and followed. When they pushed through the belt of trees and shrubs running along the fence line they found themselves in a loading bay at the rear of a supermarket.

Slipping the gun in the waistband of his jeans at the small of his back, he adjusted the fall of his

T-shirt so it would hide the bulge of the weapon and led the way down a side alley and out onto a street. His truck was parked directly across the road, which meant he must have entered the park from this end. That was how he had taken her by surprise. She hadn't thought to look behind her. Her attention had been on the motel and Wendell.

The truck beeped as the door locks disengaged. JT opened the passenger-side door. Baby jumped in and settled on the floor. JT's hand landed in the small of her back. This time there was nothing remotely sexy about the pressure as he boosted her into the seat. He was in work mode, retrieving her like a cop rounding up a runaway kid.

Bending forward she ruffled Baby's ears. A rough tongue swiped across the back of one hand and her eyes burned again. She had taken a risk, but she would do it all again.

JT swung behind the wheel and she fastened her seat belt. Seconds later they were in traffic.

"My car is back in the shopping center car park."

"I know where it is. I'll arrange to have it picked up."

Rina's jaw tightened. She understood why JT had followed her, and why he was taking such elaborate precautions, but she and Baby hadn't been in danger; she had had it covered.

His gaze fastened briefly on hers, the chill enough to take the heat out of the evening. "Tell me exactly what's been going on."

In clipped sentences, she filled him in on Wendell

and how he had retrieved Baby. Technically, what she had done had contravened her agreement with WitSec, but she wasn't about to apologize for doing it. No one had been hurt, she had maintained her anonymity and her security, and she had saved Baby.

He picked up his cell phone and began making calls as he drove, to someone named Kurt, a CIA agent who evidently worked with JT, the Beaumont P.D. and, finally, Bayard.

Rina listened in silence to the long list of information JT wanted, and the checks he requested on Wendell. "Wendell isn't a criminal." Unless you counted locking Baby in the trunk of his car, she amended silently. "He's a P.I."

"If Wendell found Baby, he's a bona fide lead to either Slater or Lopez."

"Slater and Alex didn't have Baby, someone else did."

"According to Wendell."

"That's right." She stared at the thinning houses. They had just left Liberty. "If he had broken into a property controlled by either Alex or Slater or any of his people, he wouldn't be here now."

"Unless he's working for Slater and his aim is to locate you."

She shook her head. "He's a P.I. and an ex-cop. I met him for the first time two days ago. He took over the case when Sayer ran off with my money."

The gaze that pinned her was remote. "Who is *Sayer?*"

"His full name is Harold Sayer. He runs the investigation business with Wendell."

"So that's what you were doing when you disappeared in the mall."

The flat comment flicked her on the raw. "Last I heard, I'm not allowed much, but Marlow said I *can* have a life. I didn't sign up to be babysat 24/7."

"Honey, I don't usually babysit."

She stared at his profile and had the satisfaction of seeing a small muscle pulsing along the side of his jaw. "Just remember, I didn't ask you to."

She sat in stony silence while he made more calls, this time about Sayer. Rina couldn't argue with that. If they found Sayer, Wendell had a chance at getting his money back.

He drove in silence. It was a while before Rina realized that they weren't driving in the direction of Beaumont. "Where are we going?"

He took his gaze off the road. "We're not going back to Beaumont until I get Wendell and Sayer checked out."

"Wendell's got to be in his sixties."

"For what it's worth, so far the cops think he's harmless, but he did get Baby back when Bayard and our people failed. Now, that's interesting. They're pulling him in for questioning."

She stared straight ahead. "If Bayard's got a mole, maybe that's the reason *he* hasn't been able to find either Baby or Taylor."

"It's a possibility."

She was silent for a while. She listened while he phoned Kurt again and gave him the registration and description of her car. The sun finally sank below the horizon. As night fell they were still driving. They'd been through three towns and counting, and most of those in dead silence. If JT hadn't interfered, she and Baby would be safe and sound at home by now.

JT flicked his lights on, and she made herself comfortable, leaning her head into the curve of the seat and closing her eyes.

When he pulled into a service station she roused herself. "Baby needs a drink and some food." She rummaged in her knapsack and pulled out the half-filled bottle of water.

JT walked into the service station, then came back with a small bag of dog biscuits and a plastic bowl. She watched as he filled the bowl with water and tipped a small pile of biscuits beside it.

He whistled. Baby glanced at her. When she said "go," he scrambled out of the car and immediately began lapping at the water. She noticed he had a limp. Tomorrow she would have to take him to a vet to get him checked out. He also needed a flea treatment and vitamins. If he'd been around Slater or Alex, he probably needed a shot for rabies, as well.

Baby wolfed down a pile of biscuits, moved back to the water bowl and emptied it while JT filled the truck with gas, then walked across the forecourt to pay. When JT returned, he walked Baby out onto the grass verge to one side of the garage. When Baby had finished his business, JT produced a plastic bag he must have gotten from inside the shop and cleaned up the mess. Baby followed him, tail wagging, as he deposited the tied-off bag in a trash can.

JT disappeared inside once more, presumably to wash his hands. When he reappeared, Baby scrambled over the driver's seat and settled at Rina's feet. JT handed her the rinsed-out dog bowl and the biscuits, a new bottle of water and an ice-cold can of soda. He flipped the top on his own can as he started the truck.

An hour later, he pulled into a motel, checked in then moved the truck to a unit at the rear that wasn't visible from the road.

The motel unit was standard, a bedroom with a double bed, a couple of couches in the main room, a tiny kitchenette and a large TV. Baby followed her as she checked out the rooms, then waited outside the locked door while she used the bathroom. When Rina went back out to the sitting room, he settled on the carpet, keeping her in sight.

JT walked in with an extra pillow and a blanket. He dropped them on one of the couches. "You can take the bed. The next hurdle is getting something to eat. I can order takeout, or there's a late-night café down the road."

She settled for takeout. She was hungry, but after everything that had happened, she didn't care what she ate, and she didn't want to leave Baby. He'd been through enough of an ordeal. Every time she moved, she was aware that he was watching her with a haunted look in his eyes.

JT picked up the phone, ordered burgers and fries, then dug the truck keys out of his pocket and headed for the door. While he was gone, Rina adjusted the setting on the air-conditioning unit and found that the reason the room was so warm was that the unit didn't work, period. She compensated by opening windows as wide as she could and still keep them latched, but even so, the amount of air circulating was close to zero.

Fifteen minutes later, JT was back with a sack of food and foam cups of coffee.

Rina dug in, sharing tidbits with Baby. Normally, he wasn't allowed, but after what he'd been through he needed the extra pampering, and she wasn't about to say no.

She watched as JT ate, observing idly the controlled way he demolished his burger and the sheer volume of food he put away. When his gaze caught hers, she turned her attention to her own burger. "I guess you get tired of takeout."

"I usually cook my own food. This stuff's okay at a pinch, but you can't operate on it all the time."

It was the most civilized conversation they'd had since he'd thrown her to the ground in the park.

When she'd eaten all she could of the burger, she handed the rest to Baby and reached for her coffee. The quietness of the small town and the room, with its neutral walls and bland furnishings, sank in as she sipped, a stark contrast to the hours of nervous tension and adrenaline. At her feet, Baby whimpered and twitched. He had finally fallen asleep, his muzzle heavy on her foot, as if even in sleep he wanted to make sure he wouldn't lose her again.

She watched as JT cleaned up the wrappers and put them in the small stainless-steel trash can in the kitchen. After the tension and drama of the early evening, the only sign that anything out of the ordinary had happened were faint stains on his T-shirt, and the wounds on his hand where she'd bitten him.

He examined the air-conditioning unit and punched in a new setting.

"I already tried, it doesn't work." And that reminded her of something else that hadn't worked. "How did you find me?" She was certain she had gotten away clean. At no point had she seen JT's truck following her. "Did Marlow have me followed?"

"If Marlow knew I was within a hundred miles of you he'd break out in a rash."

She went still inside. "I thought you were working with WitSec."

"I have a working agreement with the U.S. Marshals, not WitSec. Maybe when hell freezes over Marlow would give me his list of most-wanted witnesses."

"Then how did you find me?" If JT had broken the

Witness Security Program, that meant she *wasn't* safe. If he could locate her, chances were, so could Alex.

"Give me your watch and I'll show you."

Reluctantly, Rina set her empty coffee cup down, peeled her watch off her wrist and handed it to him. JT dug in a pocket of his jeans and extracted a small multipurpose tool that sported a tiny screwdriver and levered the back of the bezel off. Once the bezel was off, he used the screwdriver to indicate a tiny metallic device attached to the watch mechanism by a small spot of clear glue. "I put a transmitter in your watch in Winton. It's a miniature global positioning device, designed for military use. The signal gets picked up by military satellites, which means I can track you."

Rina stared at the small metal dome. It was so simple it defied belief. "I don't believe you did that and got away with it."

"I knew you were going into WitSec. It was the only way I could break the protection program." He seated the bezel back into place and handed the watch to her. "You can leave the transmitter in, or take it out. It's up to you. You can tell Marlow if you want, although he won't take it well. He doesn't strike me as having any kind of a tolerance level for interference."

She put the watch on the coffee table. "Who else knows about the transmitter?"

"Kurt knows I'm tracking you. He has clearance to use the system, but he doesn't know the code."

He checked the lock on the door and pulled the drapes more securely, closing out the narrow slit that allowed a view into the motel unit from the small, lit area outside. She noticed the gun was still lodged in the waistband at the small of his back. She hadn't seen him do it, but at some point, probably when he had gone to get takeout, he must have taken the gun out of the glove compartment of the truck.

The gun, the calm way he secured the unit and the ease with which he had sidestepped WitSec to continue with his own investigation put him firmly in context. As attractive as JT was to her, she couldn't afford to trust him. He had fooled Alex and Slater, he had negated Marlow's security and he had run rings around her. He had his own agenda, his own reasons for watching her, and they had nothing to do with either her personality or her legs.

She could pick up the phone, call Marlow and be out of here within an hour, but the plain fact was, despite everything, in a bone-deep, instinctive way, she *did* trust him.

When Alex had tripped her and set the scene to make it look like she'd walked into a piece of furniture, JT had given her first aid and made sure she got to the hospital. He had gotten her out of the Winton estate alive then, and once she was safe, he had gone back to look for Baby. Both times he had risked himself and his investigation. Ambiguous or not, there was one thing she was clear on about JT: he might be working to his own agenda, but she couldn't ask for a better protector.

She picked up the watch and refastened it.

JT didn't make any comment, but she was aware that he had noticed as he settled down with the remote and began flicking through channels, finally selecting a game of basketball. "I'm not going to tell Marlow. Yet."

Not until she knew she was in the clear from Wendell and any possible connection with Alex. She wanted to avoid being shunted out of Beaumont and the life she was slowly building, and the second Marlow knew JT was in the picture, she would be gone.

He grunted and picked up his coffee, not taking his gaze off the ball game.

Feeling distinctly on edge, she watched as he swallowed and was reminded of the few minutes she had spent in the cab of his truck yesterday. It felt like a week ago. A strange thing had happened to her perception of time. Maybe it was the stress and the danger, the fact that after years of slow, quiet retreat, her life had gone crazy. In the past few months she'd packed in enough action to last a lifetime, and JT had put himself in the midst every time.

His gaze didn't move from the screen. "Don't do that. I'm trying to keep my perspective."

"Don't do what?" She picked up her empty foam cup, carried it through to the kitchen and dropped it in the trash. She was trying to figure out what emotion was uppermost in her mind—betrayal, irritation, confusion or the tension that just being this close to JT engendered. When she spun around, she walked into his chest.

His fingers curled around her arms, that first instant of physical contact electrifying. His gaze fixed on her mouth. "Don't watch me like that."

"Maybe I like watching you."

For long seconds he didn't move, didn't give in to the invitation, even though he was the one who had instigated this, and suddenly the reason she had fallen for JT was crystal clear.

He was fiercely committed to his cause. That focused, unshakeable dedication drew her like nothing else. He was a rock, and for years she had been swimming in quicksand with alligators. The fact that he wanted her, despite who she was, and enough that he could push aside his work and his goals, took her breath.

His fingers tightened, and she knew he was as blindsided as she was. "I don't want to take advantage."

"I'm almost thirty-three. I think I know how to make a decision."

Something flashed in his gaze. After a brief hesitation his mouth landed on hers.

The kiss was short and soft and the intimacy of it rocked her. "Is that another rule you just broke?"

"About the twentieth."

His mouth came down on hers again and her head

spun. Long, dizzying minutes passed while they kissed, an achingly slow dance. She slipped her arms around his waist and leaned in closer, breathing in his scent, adjusting to the feel of being held against a male, definitely aroused body. "I don't have any contraceptives."

"I do."

A hard jolt went through her. He couldn't have made it plainer that, while he hadn't exactly planned this, he had been prepared.

The bedroom was small, with a standard double bed. With all the windows closed, it was like an oven, and with JT in the room, it seemed smaller and hotter.

She slid her palms up over the firm muscles of his belly, peeling his T-shirt as she went. He shrugged out of the shirt and let it drop to the floor and they were back to slow dancing.

She felt the wall at her back, the rush of cooler air as her shirt slid off her shoulders, the sudden release as he unhooked her bra. He pulled her close, the skin-on-skin contact searing. As she lifted up into his kiss she had a moment to wonder at the single-minded simplicity of what she needed; a split second later she was lost. Being this close to JT was like being hit by a wave and rolled under. Sex was no mystery to her. She knew what it felt like to want, and the mechanics of the act itself. She knew what it was to touch and enjoy, but she had never felt like this.

Rina slipped out of her jeans and lifted a hand to her hair.

"Let me do that."

She stood still as he unfastened her braid, his fingers faintly clumsy as he sifted through the strands. She pulled back the covers and slipped into bed and watched as JT set his gun on the bedside table, peeled out of his jeans, sheathed himself and climbed in with her. Winding her arms around his neck, Rina pulled him close, holding her breath as his weight pressed her down. His forehead touched hers, the moment intense as he slid into her.

For long seconds they simply held each other. Like her, JT seemed loath to move, as if he, too, wanted to hold the moment. In the close heat of the room she felt like she was drowning, but there was an odd sense of peace.

Gray dawn light filtered through the curtains directly behind the bed, giving a glow to the walls and picking out the rumpled covers piled on the floor.

They were out on a limb. No one knew where they were, or what they were doing. For the first time in years, Rina wasn't being manipulated and corralled, led into choices that seemed all she had left because her options had been taken away.

From the moment JT had kissed her, he hadn't stopped touching her, keeping her close even when they slept. The few times she had moved to adjust her position, his arm had tightened around her. The contact was basic and primitive and it reassured her as nothing else could.

She'd had two relationships before she had married Alex, but they had dissolved before they had come to anything momentous. Killed, she now knew, by Alex the instant she had shown signs of getting serious. When Alex had made his carefully timed entrance into her life, she had been charmed by the attention and the sense of old-fashioned courtship. After years of virtually no male attention at all, she had been lonely enough to drift into the marriage with him.

JT stirred. She slid the palm of her hand across his belly, enjoying the feel of firm muscle tightening beneath her fingers and warm, slightly damp skin. She turned her attention to the small tattoo she'd noticed on one arm. She realized that while he knew every intimate detail of her life, she still knew very little about him. She didn't even know his full name. For all she knew he could be married, with children, although in his line of work that had to be doubtful.

His lids lifted. "What's wrong?"

She traced the tattoo. "Aside from the fact that I can't stop thinking about Taylor, I don't even know if JT is your real name."

He propped himself up on one elbow. "My full name's James Thompson Wyatt. I'm thirty-six and I was born in Louisiana. Before I started working as a contract agent for the CIA I was a Navy SEAL. My mother died a couple of years back—cancer—but my dad's still going strong. He was a naval engineer. He's retired now and based on a small farm just outside of Albuquerque, which is where my mother's people come from. The family's not big. I've got one sister, Claire, who also lives in Albuquerque. Other than that, I've got a couple of uncles and a whole rash of cousins."

"Any other family members in the navy?"

"Both of my uncles are ex-navy. One cousin is a marine, another's working in Naval Intelligence."

The reply was mild and matter-of-fact and it outlined the differences between them. JT came from a family with a military background. Sons had followed in their father's footsteps, their lives ordered and supported by a solid backbone of tradition, while Rina came from a background that, to put it kindly, was suspect.

She dropped her head on his shoulder. "I don't see how this can work." Apart from the fact that he wasn't supposed to be within a hundred miles of her, he had a job that was going to take him away, sooner rather than later. Once Taylor was found, he could be gone within hours.

His arm tightened around her. "Don't look too far ahead. Let's just enjoy what we have."

They got back into Beaumont late that afternoon. Before they had left the motel, JT had spent time on the phone and working online. After the sighting in Bogotá, Alex had disappeared. There was no news about either Slater or Taylor.

Baby had been checked over by the local veterinary service and found to be suffering from nothing more than mild malnutrition and an infection around the collar area. The vet had administered antibiotic and vitamin shots and prescribed a course of antibiotic pills.

JT made a call to Kurt a few minutes before they turned into her drive. Kurt had delivered her SUV and checked out the house. Everything appeared to be normal, including Wendell, who had been under surveillance since he had hit Liberty. Apart from a girlfriend who came and went, Wendell's movements were routine. The girlfriend was in her fifties, had lived in Beaumont for most of her life, and worked at the county offices. Apparently they didn't live together, just dated, and she stayed over occasionally. She had an apartment in town, in one of several apartment blocks built adjacent to the mall where Wendell had his premises.

JT stopped for a set of lights. "You're going to have to notify Marlow. If you don't do it, I will. Whether Wendell's on the level or not, you need to get out of Beaumont. Wendell left a trail a school-kid could follow. All Lopez has to do is check the flights Baby was booked onto, find out who bought the tickets, then trace Wendell's rental. It might take him a few days, but he'll get here."

"I've got Marlow's number. I'll call him."

"I've arranged for Kurt and Hal, another agent, to protect you until Marlow gets someone here. It shouldn't take more than a few minutes to get a response."

If that. There was a district court in Beaumont and a sizable presence. Her local contact, Dan Maloney, had assured her that if she needed help they could get an officer to her house in ten minutes, maybe even sooner. All she had to do was make the call.

JT turned onto her street. Seconds later he lifted a hand to a car parked just across the road and pulled into her driveway, braking directly behind her SUV.

Rina studied the man just visible behind the tinted windows of the sedan. "Is that Kurt, or Hal?"

"Hal's parked one street over, watching the back of your place. Neither of them will leave until your WitSec contact arrives." JT walked around to open her door. Rina roused a sleepy Baby, waited for him to scramble out, then joined JT, who was collecting Baby's biscuits and lead from the truck.

The smooth organization of the past half hour had signaled that her time with JT was well and truly over. They hadn't talked about their relationship— JT had specifically avoided that discussion, and suddenly that wasn't good enough for Rina. She knew exactly where she was. Maybe she was old-fashioned, but she didn't sleep with anyone unless she was committed. "Where are you going?"

"To see Wendell." He pulled her close. The kiss

was hard and brief. "I don't know when I'll be back. I'll call you."

Rina watched as JT backed out, then drove away. The weather had closed in, the clouds thickening and blocking out the sun. The air was filled with the scent of rain and the temperature had dropped.

She had wanted to ask more, but as promises went, that was more than she had expected.

Twenty-Five

After feeding Baby, she turned on the television to catch the news. An advertisement for one of the major banks was playing. The bank's logo flashed up on the screen, familiar to her because it was the bank she used. She stared at the lettering. The number she had remembered while she'd been painting had had those initials in front of it. A chill of excitement gripped her. The connection hadn't occurred to her before. It wasn't a license plate number: it was a safe-deposit box.

Leaving the television on so that Kurt would think she was happily employed watching the news, she systematically began searching through her possessions.

Years had passed since Esther had died, but she remembered her mother clearly. If one person had been stamped on her childhood, it had been Esther.

She'd been sharp and fiercely loving, and always there. She had also been the cleverest person Rina had ever known. With her photographic memory and bent for figures, Esther had never forgotten a fact or neglected a detail. If Esther had given her the safe-deposit box number, she would also have made sure she had the key.

She emptied her jewelry box onto the bed and began examining the pieces. There wasn't much, a few pendants and bracelets from her childhood, slender gold bangles Esther had used to wear, a set of long, dangly diamond earrings that Cesar had given to Rina one day, not long after the accident.

She lifted an earring to the light.

"...Red suits you, but you need different earrings. Those long dangly ones with the diamonds."

Esther lifted a brow. "I'll tell you what, you go and get changed, then we'll discuss earrings. Don't forget we've got guests."

Excitement gripped her. The memory had flowed out of the past, clear enough to send a tingle down her spine, but it hadn't provided her with any useful information.

She laid the earrings back in their case. She couldn't even be certain that the memory related to the period of time surrounding the accident. Esther had worn the red dress and the earrings on a number of occasions, and she had looked spectacular every time. It had been Rina's favorite outfit, and she had always insisted Esther wear these particular earrings with that dress.

When she'd finished examining her jewelry, she started on the few other personal items in her bedroom. She didn't have much, just the few things she'd had at Alex's house in Winton that the FBI had packed up and sent to her: a baby photo; an antique wooden music box with her name and the date of her first birthday engraved on it; some of Baby's toys and his harness; a few other family photos. Like Cesar's properties, everything Alex had owned had been impounded until the investigations into both men's affairs had been concluded. With the criminal charges pending, it was highly unlikely any of the properties or chattels would ever be released.

The music box, exquisite in rosewood with marble inlays, no longer worked. At some stage the musical mechanism had been damaged. Rina could have had it repaired, but for years she hadn't wanted to listen to the sweetly evocative Für Elise.

Lifting the lid, she examined the empty interior, with its finely crafted small drawers and compartments. The box was Victorian, made when expensive mechanical toys were in vogue. The red velvet lining was faded and a little tattered, the tiny ballerina that had used to pirouette in the center of the case long gone.

Holding her breath, she triggered the secret compartment. Victorians had loved secret compartments and had included them in all sorts of pieces of furniture and objects. The drawer sprang open, empty.

Rina replaced the box on the dresser. The only

key she had been able to find was the one that wound
the mechanism. She removed the key and examined
it, just in case there was something unusual about it,
but the tiny key with its simple tubular design was
definitely made for winding the mechanism, not
opening a safe-deposit box.

As she set the box down again a faint memory
surfaced. She had almost forgotten, because it hadn't
interested her as a child, but the music box didn't
have one secret compartment—it had two. The
second wasn't contained in the box itself, it was in
the lid. Rina had used the obvious one, because it
was easy to get at. All she'd had to do was depress
the side of the case and it sprang open. The lid had
to be unscrewed to gain access to the second secret
cavity, and the screws, masquerading as the centers
of tiny carved flowers, were tiny and notoriously
hard to see.

Taking the box out to the kitchen counter, where
the light was better, she rummaged in the cutlery
drawer. She needed a tiny screwdriver so she didn't
damage the box or the delicate screws. She didn't
have one small enough, so she compromised by
using the tip of a small, sharp vegetable knife.

With delicate movements, she unwound the screws
and placed them on the kitchen counter. There were
four in all. When she was finished, she lifted off the
lid. Heart thumping, she stared at the folded parchment
that filled most of the space. Alongside it, taped to the
wood so it wouldn't rattle, was a key.

* * *

JT parked on the street outside Wendell's house. Everson Crescent was a typical suburban backwater. Number thirty-nine was an older weatherboard house, surrounded by large trees and overgrown shrubs and hemmed in with a white picket fence.

Collecting the Glock from the glove compartment, he chambered a round, climbed out of the cab and slipped the weapon into the waistband at the small of his back.

He locked the truck, checking the cars parked along the street as he did so. Nothing looked out of place. Like Kurt had said, Wendell didn't have a record and there didn't appear to be anything out of the ordinary about him, apart from the fact that he had managed to retrieve Baby. The address he had supplied the police, and which he claimed he had retrieved Baby from, had checked out. The couple who lived there had been taken in for questioning. So far nothing had shaken loose. They claimed they had kept the dog for a relative and hadn't known it was stolen. They were lying, but unless Bayard could pin something else on them, there was nothing he could do but watch them.

Pocketing the keys, he strolled up the path. Wendell was home. His car was parked just outside the garage, but otherwise the house looked deserted.

He knocked on the front door. When he didn't get a response, he knocked again. Wendell appeared, his outline visible through a glass panel in the door as he unlocked.

JT moved back a half step, automatically checking over Wendell's shoulder to see if he had company and making sure he had plenty of room to go for the gun if he needed to, but nothing about Wendell looked threatening.

JT produced a badge. "I need to ask you a few questions. You retrieved a dog. I want to know who you had to deal with to get it."

Wendell examined the badge, then stared past JT's shoulder, checking out the street. "Like I told the police, I found the dog locked up in a garage in Winton. I took the dog because I believed it had been stolen."

He supplied the address and the name of the couple who had been living there. It was the same information he had given to the Winton P.D. and the FBI.

JT asked a few more questions. Wendell repeated the answers he had given to the police.

Minutes later, JT unlocked his truck and pulled away from the curb. As plausible as Wendell seemed, he still couldn't buy into it. It was *too* plausible, too perfect. As seamlessly as Wendell's story held together, he still couldn't dismiss the possibility that Baby was bait.

The evening news continued to provide background noise as Rina studied the number on the key. It was the same number she had painted on her canvas.

With fingers that weren't quite steady, she

removed the parchment and unfolded it. Her gaze skimmed the legalese. It was a simple document, appointing her executor of Esther's will and granting her power of attorney. Whatever else Esther had been doing twenty-two years ago, she had also been preparing for her death.

She lifted the brittle tape off the key. There was now no doubt in her mind that Esther had gotten her to memorize the number. Whatever was stored in the safe-deposit box, it had been important enough that she had wanted to make sure that Rina would be the one to open it. She had hidden the power of attorney and the key so well that even though Alex must have searched the box along with all of her other possessions, he had failed to find them.

A loud advertisement finished. The much quieter perfectly pitched voice of a reporter filled the room, followed by the precise cadences of a voice that was startlingly familiar. Distracted, Rina stared at the interview that was in progress.

Until she had been able to distinguish people by their auric colors, voice had been her best means of identification. She had never known who that particular voice had belonged to, but it was singular enough for her to be certain that it was the same person.

She had never been introduced to him, despite being newly married to Alex. The fact that she had overheard a portion of the conversation at all had been a matter of pure chance. It had been late and she had been looking for Alex, to see what was keeping him. When she had heard the discussion and realized he was talking business, she had turned around and padded back to bed.

The next morning, when she had asked Alex about the visitor, he had shrugged it off. It had been no big deal, a meeting with a client who had flown in late and who had to catch an early flight out.

Except that it had happened twice more. Both times, the same visitor had come to the house late, after Rina had gone to bed. Like the first time, though irritated that Alex was forced to work so late, she had dismissed the nocturnal visits as part of Alex's wide-ranging business empire and his client's different time zones.

The camera panned to the reporter as he asked Senator Radcliff for his views on the recent bomb blast in Colombia.

Radcliff. She hadn't expected the name to be familiar, but it was, because Radcliff was newly elected to the Senate and she had recently seen both his picture and his name in the papers. Another reason his name stood out was that she had read that he had a coastal retreat midway between Winton and Eureka. At the time, the mention of Winton had caught her attention more than Radcliff's election success, but that was all changed now. Not one connection with Alex, but two; Radcliff had a house that was only minutes away from Alex's Winton estate.

The cold tingling at her nape that had started when she had heard his voice increased. Crazy or not, the more she thought about it, the more certain she grew. The property Wendell had taken Baby from hadn't sounded like the kind of high-security estate Radcliff would own, but even so, she couldn't dismiss the idea that Taylor could be at Radcliff's estate.

The name "Chavez" jerked her attention back to the screen. A bomb blast, with buildings reduced to rubble and people picking through the ruins looking for survivors.

The actual content of the news story involving Radcliff registered: *Colombia...Chavez cartel...Rumors that this had been a clandestine military strike by the U.S. and not revenge by a warring cartel.*

"Would Senator Radcliff, a former Army Ranger who had fought in the South American theater, and a previous military adviser to the Pentagon, care to comment on the situation?"

Radcliff's answer was smooth and dismissive. He had been out of the military too long to make any kind of assessment on the attack.

The interview ended, and the local segment of the news began, headed up with the lead story, breaking news that a body had just been recovered from the Neches River. The dead man had been identified as Harold Sayer.

Wendell watched as JT pulled away from the curb. He walked back into the living room just as the hall door opened. A tall, balding man stepped out, followed by a woman. Slater was a hard-ass, and up until now it had been Slater he had been dealing with, but it was the woman who really frightened him. She was blond, well dressed and slim, with a pleasant face and a businesslike Walther in her hand. Slater exited by a side door, leaving him alone with the woman.

She stared at Wendell, making him feel about as important as an insect. "Now, I wonder if you can still be of any use to us?"

She raised the handgun and motioned him toward the back bedroom he used as a home office. Before the interruption, Wendell had been searching for every piece of information he had managed to unearth about Rina, which wasn't much. The details she had given Sayer had been scanty, but the combination of the missing dog and Winton had been enough to set off alarm bells.

Sayer, who hadn't had any connections with the criminal underworld, had had no understanding of who their client really was or the opportunity that had been presented, but Wendell had. With the seven-figure bounty Slater had posted for Rina Morell's capture—alive—every hit man, snatch artist and two-bit criminal in the country was searching for her. Once he had realized who she was, it had been a simple matter to make contact via a third party with Slater and set up a deal. Slater had supplied the dog; his job was to supply Rina's address.

So far he hadn't been able to trace her physical address. He had her cell phone number, but Slater already had that. After she had left his shop the previous day, he had followed her as far as the DPS office. He hadn't been able to get any details right then, because he hadn't wanted to alert her to the fact that she was being followed, but he had been content to wait. It had been obvious that she was applying for a driver's license, so finding her real address once it went into the system would be a cinch.

After she had caught him flat-footed and gotten away with the dog, she'd left him with a six-figure part payment in his account and still no address. He had e-mailed a contact in the police department and requested the information, offering the usual monetary reward. Rina had both a license and a vehicle, so he had her on two counts now.

Wendell booted up his computer. The woman perched on the edge of his desk. "How long before you can give me a physical address?"

He would have supplied it to Slater and have left town already, if his uninvited guests hadn't arrived.

Wendell's fingers moved rapidly over the keyboard. His mail program opened up. "Here it is now."

He opened up the e-mail, read the contents and hit the print button. Swiveling around in his chair to collect the sheet that was feeding out, he stared blankly into the thickened barrel of the Walther and a small, inane fact dropped into his mind.

While he had been busy online she had fitted a silencer to the weapon.

JT thumbed in a short dial on his cell phone while he waited in traffic. While he had been talking to Wendell, the weather had closed in, dark clouds blocking out the last yellowish glare of the setting sun.

Kurt picked up. "The surveillance team on Wendell reported in. A woman just left the house. She fits the description of his girlfriend, but they don't think she is."

The niggling unease JT felt about Wendell took on a sharper edge. He hadn't heard anyone else in the house, and he had been listening. "What does she look like?"

"Blond, about five-four, one hundred and ten pounds, and wearing a classy suit. She's a little younger than Wendell. Maybe early fifties."

The lights changed, JT inched across the intersection, then braked as traffic backed up. He was en route to Rina's house, but rush-hour traffic was doubling the time it should take him to get there. "If it's who I think it might be, that means Slater's in town. Did they get a tail on her?"

"McElroy's on it, but the traffic is tough."

"Rina?"

"Don't worry, she's fine. I can see her from here. Before you go, I did a little more digging on Wendell."

"And Wendell isn't his real name."

"Not for the past ten years. The real Wendell died in Detroit in the nineties, and for the record, *he* was a Pinkerton man. And get this, the Winton P.D. have just pulled in a couple of very interesting tourists— two hitters from L.A. They're not talking, but the word is out that Slater has put a bounty on Rina. Although, he wants her alive, not dead."

JT's hands tightened on the wheel. Now it all made sense. Slater had been working to a plan. The combination of the advertisement about Baby, circulated nationwide, and the bounty, had created an environment for Rina to be caught. Slater had wanted to make her visible, and it had worked. She had taken the bait, and Wendell had recognized who she was.

Wendell had been nervous, but he hadn't panicked when JT had produced the CIA badge. He had fielded JT's questions like a pro, because that was exactly what he was.

Rina had been careful, and he had made sure she couldn't be followed after she had picked up Baby, but Wendell would find her. It was possible that he already had.

JT calculated how long it would take him to get across town to Rina's place. Fifteen minutes if he ran every red light.

"There's one more piece of news you need to know. Harold Sayer's body has just been pulled out of the Neches River. If you want to talk to Wendell now, you'll have to line up behind the Beaumont P.D."

JT terminated the call and accelerated as traffic began to move more freely, courtesy of extra lanes and a major intersection just ahead. As he picked up speed a van cruised up next to him. The side door slid open a few inches. He glimpsed the familiar features of one of Slater's security goons as he sighted down the barrel of a high-powered rifle.

The first bullet exploded the windshield. The second slammed into the headrest just inches from JT's head. He swerved. Car horns filled the air, along with the sound of squealing tires. A truck-and-trailer unit appeared out of nowhere, filling the road. JT wrenched on the wheel and felt the rear of the truck fishtail out of control.

Twenty-Six

Taylor stumbled as the stony-faced security guard who was assigned to take her to the kitchen for her evening meal stood back and indicated she precede him through the door. It wasn't politeness. All the guards knew she was an agent. So far, Stavros hadn't taken any risks, despite Taylor's attempts at appearing sick.

Using her cuffed hands to steady herself against the kitchen wall, she straightened, her gaze automatically sweeping the large kitchen with its heavy stone pillars and stainless-steel catering fittings, glimpsing an empty hallway. Apart from the staff bathroom, which she had just used, this was all she had seen of the house.

Despite being locked in a shed with one tiny barred window, and only being able to use the bathroom twice a day, she was physically well. She didn't like the dark room or the captivity, but she hadn't been starved, and apart from the initial struggle, she hadn't been hurt. During the day, she occupied herself by exercising and mentally running through combat-training drills so that if an opportunity to escape fell in her lap, she didn't freeze up.

She was pale. That was easy, because she was genuinely frightened. She knew better than anyone what Lopez and Slater were capable of doing to people who were no longer important to them. So far, she had only seen Slater once—the day she had been caught—and she hadn't seen Lopez at all. The fact that neither Slater nor Lopez appeared to be in residence was both a relief and a cause for concern. It had given Bayard time to find her when she hadn't counted on any, but there could only be one reason they hadn't used her to reach Rina. The ruse with Baby had worked.

The absence of the second guard who usually accompanied Stavros registered. She had thought the lack of a second escort was a momentary lapse and that Tony would be waiting in the kitchen, but the kitchen was empty. Her interest sharpened. Normally when they let her out, there were two security guards with her at all times.

She let her head droop. "Where's your friend?"

Stavros looked mildly surprised that she had spoken. He smiled, without humor. "Texas."

They had found Rina.

Stavros jerked his head at the plate of food on the

table. As usual, it was a plastic plate and there was a plastic fork with it—no knife. The food was good, because they simply served her up whatever they were having.

Taylor sat down and picked up the fork. She stared at the steaming pasta swimming in a rich red tomato sauce, and one important difference from all of her previous meals registered. The fact that there were fewer personnel in residence meant she had gotten served sooner, and this meal was *hot*.

She let the fork drop, then got to her feet as if she was going to be sick. When Stavros stepped toward her she slumped forward slightly, bracing herself on the table, letting her hair slide forward, masking the movement as she picked up the plate. As soon as she gauged he was close enough, she straightened and flung the hot pasta at his face.

Dropping the plate, Taylor launched herself, driving him back against one of the arty stone pillars. The second he hit the stonework, she swung her fisted hands in a doublehanded punch, snapping his head back.

His head bounced, his eyes rolled, and he crumpled to the floor. She searched Stavros's pockets for a cell phone, her cuffed hands awkward. There was no phone in the kitchen. Slater had ordered it removed so long as she was a "guest," so she was banking on the fact that Stavros would have a cell phone on him.

She located the phone in his jacket pocket. She

would only have a few seconds at most. Someone would have heard the noise Stavros had made when she'd flung the pasta at him.

She stabbed the menu button. The key lock symbol glowed on the screen. Gritting her teeth, she tried the standard codes for unlocking, none of which worked. Seconds later, she gave up trying to break his lock code. Neither Lopez nor Slater were stupid. She doubted there would be a cell phone on the property that didn't have a security-coded lock. She was going to have to go looking for a landline.

Seconds later, she stepped into a small sitting room just off the kitchen that looked like it was used by the kitchen staff, and picked up the handset of a phone.

Rina shoved items into a knapsack: a change of clothing; the few personal possessions she couldn't risk leaving behind; the documents and the key from the music box; and food and water for Baby. Stuffing her handbag on top, she fastened the top flap.

Wendell had murdered Sayer and sold her out.

She walked through to the bathroom, grabbed her toothbrush and deodorant and shoved them into a side pocket of the knapsack.

She couldn't stop shaking, but her mind was clear. She hadn't given Wendell her address, and JT had made sure he hadn't followed her once she had col-

lected Baby. Despite that, she had to assume that if
Wendell was clever enough to connect with either
Alex or Slater and find Baby, he would find her.

She reached for her cell phone and tried JT's
number again. She was put through to his voice mail.
Hanging up, she tried again and was once more
shunted through to voice mail. Either he was too
busy to answer, or he couldn't.

She placed the cell phone on the bed beside the
knapsack. Almost immediately, it beeped.

She checked the screen. The number wasn't JT's.
She pressed the call button, put the phone to her ear
and waited for someone to speak.

"Rina?"

Adrenaline flooded her system. "*Taylor?* Where
are—"

"Eureka. Listen, I don't have much time. One of
Slater's men has been holding Baby. Whoever it is
you're dealing with to get Baby back, don't trust
him. He contac—"

A dull thud was followed by a series of sharp
clicks, as if the receiver had been dropped and was
swinging against something hard.

Heart pounding, Rina strained to listen. She heard
the faint but definite rhythm of breathing; someone
had picked up the receiver. Her stomach constricted.
There was no way she could be sure, but she was
abruptly certain the person on the other end of the
phone was Alex.

Filled with fear, Rina disconnected the call.

* * *

Alex Lopez studied the unconscious form of Taylor Jones where she lay sprawled on the floor of the sitting room, just yards away from the security guard she had knocked out.

The viability of keeping her as a hostage had always been in question. If the ploy involving the dog and Wendell had been successful, she would already be dead, but as it was, they had to keep her just a little while longer.

Reaching into his jacket pocket, he pulled out a plastic case which contained a syringe, prepped the needle and injected the full dosage into a vein in her arm.

The sharp sting brought her around. Lopez withdrew the needle and stepped back.

Taylor clutched at her arm, her gaze fastened on the syringe. "What did you inject me with?"

Lopez smiled. "Ketamine."

Raw terror registered. Street name "K" or "Special K." An anaesthetic and powerful hallucinogenic drug. A split second later, her eyes glazed over.

Rina rapped on the driver's-side window of Kurt's car. The window slid down.

Kurt had the driver's seat pushed back as far as it would go and was working on a laptop. When she relayed the news about Sayer, he looked grim but unperturbed.

"It's all right, JT knows. We got the information

through to him a few minutes ago. We've arranged to have Wendell picked up."

Kurt checked his wristwatch. "How far away are WitSec?"

Rina looked at her own watch and pretended to gauge the time, still reeling from the fact that both Kurt and JT already knew about Wendell and neither of them had bothered to inform her. She was beginning to understand what had driven Esther. When she spoke the lie was smooth. "Fifteen minutes."

Kurt nodded and picked up a cell phone. "I'll let Hal know."

The howl of a siren cut through the dull ache in JT's skull as he searched for his phone and the remains of his laptop, which had both, evidently, gone through his windshield. The truck was canted at an angle, stopped from being flipped completely on its side by the power pole that had punched in the left side of the vehicle, bending it like a pretzel.

"Are you all right?" The question came from a well-dressed man in his late forties.

"Never better."

"I'm a doctor. I can treat you if you need it."

He touched his nose, which was still bleeding after the impact from the air bag. Apart from that and a few minor cuts and bruises, he was uninjured. "I don't."

The intersection was a mess. JT couldn't see any sign of Slater's men. They must have made it through unscathed, but the truck that had clipped him had smashed into the median barrier. The trailer had jack-knifed, broken its coupling and slid on its side for about fifty yards, spilling a mountain of grain. Four lanes were blocked and traffic was backed up both ways.

The siren got louder. He couldn't find any sign of his phone. At a guess, it was also smashed and had probably slid beneath one of the vehicles littering the intersection. Limping around the truck, he picked up what was left of the hard drive against the possibility that some geek would get hold of it and actually manage to extract classified data, and threaded his way between traffic to a nearby shopping mall. The neon sign of a popular rental car agency glowed. He needed transport and he needed a phone, but most of all he needed to disappear before the highway patrol cruiser made it through the traffic jam. He had his CIA badge on him, but even with that, they would want to verify it, and that would take time he didn't have.

Keeping his gaze glued to the rental car sign, he crossed the car park, found a phone booth and placed a call. Kurt picked up on the second ring. McElroy had just reported in: he had lost the blond woman.

"Slater's in town. Two of his men picked me up just after I left Wendell's place. They fired on me and ran me off the road." He didn't have a license plate number, but he passed on a description of the van. "Pull Wendell in, and get Rina out of the house. *Now.*"

A woman with a shopping trolley stared at him as he hung up the phone. One glance at his reflection in a shop window told him he needed to clean up before he stepped into the rental firm's premises. Veering into the mall, he headed for the nearest public convenience.

His nose was bruised and swollen, and blood trailed down one side of his face and throat, staining the front of his T-shirt. Splashing himself with water, he sponged off the blood and walked through the mall to the rental car agency.

Rina closed the front door behind her, locked it and walked through to her bedroom, cold congealing in her stomach as she relived those few moments on the phone and the eerie sensation that Alex was on the end of the line.

She was certain he had enjoyed that moment of intimidation, just as he'd enjoyed the cat-and-mouse game he'd played with her over the years. Esther had died trying to stop him. In the end, so had Cesar.

Walking through to her bedroom, she collected the knapsack and her phone. Outwitting Alex might be impossible, but she had to try. For Taylor's sake, she couldn't afford to be stopped now.

The biggest problem was going to be getting Baby out. It was almost completely dark, but even in the dark, his light coat would glow. Still, there was no way she would leave Baby behind again. If she checked him into boarding kennels, Alex or Slater would find him.

Moving quickly, she changed clothes, pulling on black jeans and a thin, dark sweater. She retrieved the document folder that contained her personal papers from her closet, including her old birth certificate and passport. She slipped the folder into the knapsack, then walked out to the hall cupboard and took down a storage box that was filled with Baby's things. She no longer needed the Seeing Eye dog harness, but at the time she hadn't been able to bear throwing it away. Aside from the photo Taylor had given her, it had been her last link to Baby.

Calling Baby, she fitted the harness and the muzzle, which she used on flights. She wasn't sure how they were going to travel. Her first destination would be the bus station. If she had missed the last bus, she would try the airport, although that was riskier and she would be more likely to be seen. Either way, she was going to need all of her blind paraphernalia. There was no other way to keep Baby with her on a bus trip.

Checking her phone one last time, she switched it off and slipped it into her pocket. JT hadn't returned her call, but that couldn't concern her now. He was a tough, experienced agent and he knew about Wendell. Leaving him was a wrench she hadn't expected to have to cope with, but she couldn't allow personal feelings to distract her. The phone call from Taylor had frightened her to the bone and cleared her mind. *Alex had Taylor.* Every time she thought about the moments of silence following Taylor's choked-off statement, her blood ran cold. Taylor's safe release had to be her first priority.

Yesterday, she would have handed the information about Taylor's possible whereabouts and Senator Radcliff's involvement to JT and Bayard and let them deal with it. Today, she had a different perspective. She trusted both men as individuals, but she couldn't trust the organizations they worked for. Alex had a line into the FBI and possibly other law-enforcement agencies. The fact that he also had Radcliff, a former military adviser to the Pentagon and now a United States senator, in his pocket, was even more frightening.

If Taylor was being held in Radcliff's house, revealing that information could place Taylor in even more jeopardy. She had thought it through, going over and over the facts, and every time she had come to the same conclusion. If she followed the logic—that she was Alex's goal, that it was the money Esther had stolen that he wanted—then until he had her, Taylor was safe.

Once Alex realized that using Baby had failed, he would employ his backup plan and offer a deal— Taylor's release in exchange for her. The thought of handing herself over to Alex filled her with dread, but if she had to, she would do it.

Striking out on her own was a risk, maybe a stupid one. It was possible that Taylor's best chance at survival lay with the authorities, who were trained to deal with hostage situations. But with the FBI mole still in place and undetected, she didn't think so. The way she saw it, as long as she was on her own, she could control the way events unfolded.

She unfastened her wristwatch, then left it on the kitchen counter. She was tempted to take it, tempted to cling to the safety the watch and JT represented, but if she kept it then JT would follow and she couldn't afford the connection. If he knew what she was going to attempt, he would stop her.

A sharp rap at the front door almost stopped her heart as she led Baby down the hall to her bedroom, and she quickened her step. The caller was probably Kurt, although there was a remote possibility it could be JT.

Keeping Baby close, she slipped out of the French doors in her bedroom and onto the back deck. Baby's claws clicked on the bleached hardwood, the sound distinct, although it wouldn't be discernible to anyone standing on the front porch of the house. Seconds later, they stepped into the thick cover of a creeper that grew on the veranda and spilled over into the adjacent border of shrubs and trees. Rina urged Baby through the shadowed tangle, staying close to the fence line.

The fence was going to be a problem. There was no way she could get Baby over the six-foot-high wooden palings that bordered the rear of the yard. She was going to have to find a way under the chain link they were presently following, and walk out through the neighbor's property. The only blessing was that the nearest dog lived four doors away, which meant she and Baby should be able to make it to the street without a major ruckus.

Keeping a firm grip on Baby's harness, she began working her way closer to the mesh. It was overgrown by shrubs, and in places trees overhung it, but aside from the hazard of dodging low branches, Rina counted that as a positive. The trees were old and so was the fence. In places it was damaged and sagging.

Her fingers trailed across a section of bare mesh. A sharp rapping froze her in place. A soft drizzle had started, muffling sound, but the tinkle of glass breaking was clear enough. Whoever had been knocking on the door had just broken into her house.

Whispering a command for Baby to sit, she crouched down and felt around the thick layer of leaves at the base of the fence. Scraping the leaves away, she managed to get her fingers underneath the wire and lift it, but the gap was narrow. She would have to go down on her belly. Getting Baby through was going to be more difficult.

She shrugged out of the knapsack, pushed it under the fence, then snaked under the wire. It wasn't graceful, and it wasn't quiet, because leaves rustled and the fence made a jingling noise, but she was through.

Pulse racing, she hauled the fence as high as it would go, no longer worrying about the noise. Only seconds had passed since she'd heard the sound of breaking glass. Whoever had broken in would search the house before they would think to check the backyard. She softly commanded Baby to come and pulled on the harness, reinforcing the message that she wanted him to go under the fence. With a faint grunting sound, Baby shimmied under and surged to his feet.

Shrugging into the knapsack, Rina took a moment to listen. Apart from the distant hum of traffic, the faint sound of a television show playing in the Spur-locks' house just yards away, and the slow drip of moisture off leaves, the night was silent.

Gripping the harness, Rina stepped out from behind a neatly shaped shrub onto bare lawn and began to walk, Baby padding silently beside her.

The lawn was as flat as a bowling green and empty of all cover, apart from a row of trees placed with military precision down the side of the house and a tidy clipped hedge that ran parallel with the trees along the boundary. Blue light flickered through a gap in the drapes of the Spurlocks' sitting room window and the sweep of light from the kitchen lit up the neighbor's backyard, which bordered the rear of Rina's property.

A footfall made her freeze. Pulse thudding, she stepped into the deep shadow of a tree and held Baby in check. A flicker of movement beneath the ancient magnolia that hung over her back fence drew her eye. Someone was in the Spurlocks' neighbor's backyard.

Another movement registered, this time higher. Whoever it was, they were climbing the tree. The figure became briefly visible as he stepped across a thick tree limb and onto the rim of the fence and was caught in the wash of light flowing from the Spurlocks' sitting room directly behind her. As he turned to let himself down into her backyard, Rina caught a brief flash of a face and blond hair and froze.

Not a he. *She.*

Diane Eady was climbing into her backyard.

The second Diane disappeared over the fence, Rina moved. A twig snapped beneath her shoe just as she caught a second flicker of movement by the magnolia. She held her breath, certain she had been both seen and heard. Long seconds ticked by while she remained rigidly still. The figure moved, swiveling as he examined the line of trees, and she realized that even though he *had* looked directly at her, he hadn't registered that she was there, because the deep shadow of the tree trunk and the glaring light behind her had made her invisible. The line of the clipped hedge hid Baby from sight.

Something metallic gleamed. A gun.

The moment Alex had shot Cesar replayed itself. Her chest squeezed tight, a raw sound rasped from her throat.

A heavy droplet of rain exploded on her forehead, a second hitting her shoulder. All around she could hear the sharp rapping as the rain came down in huge droplets, spasmodic and tropically heavy. Still, the figure didn't move. She could feel his intensity as he continued to search. The rain increased in intensity, falling like a thick gray curtain, thundering on the roof of the house behind her and blotting out the night.

Still frozen, she stared in the direction of the tree, but she had lost him in the murk. He could have moved; he could be just feet away. She wasn't sure.

A flash of light reflecting off pale, wet skin jerked her gaze to the left. With a lithe, fluid movement, he dropped over the fence into her backyard.

Earl Slater.

A shudder worked its way down her spine. Diane and Slater, together.

Diane had been working for Alex all along.

Don't think. Move.

Numbly, she urged Baby to walk on. She didn't know how long Diane and Slater would be, but it could only be a matter of minutes before they discovered that she wasn't in the house. She needed to be gone before that happened. They would likely leave the property the same way they had entered it, and she couldn't count on the sheer luck that had kept them both invisible a second time.

She stepped from shadow into glaring light. Rain pounded on her head and soaked through her sweater and jeans as she strode beneath the wet rank of trees. She could feel Baby's warmth against her right leg. Canned laughter erupted from the Spurlocks' sitting room, the sound disembodied, and suddenly the abyss that separated her from that kind of normalcy registered, starker and more distinct than usual. The

Spurlocks would have had their dinner and would now be comfortably ensconced in front of one of their favorite game shows. She knew Audrey worked part-time at an insurance office, and that Walt ran his own marine-engines repair business in town. She had heard the sound of a lawn mower earlier, which meant Walt must have cut the lawns when he'd gotten home from work.

Audrey and Walt were inside their house, warm and dry and secure. No one was hunting them, or was ever likely to. No one wanted to dissect the contents of their heads. No one wanted them dead.

Slater had had a gun.

Water squelched in her sneakers as she made it past the sitting room to the front yard. Cast into shadow by a thick front hedge, the pretty formal borders and bricked paths looked grim and monochromatic.

For long seconds she hunched beneath a dripping rose arbor that curved gracefully over a white picket gate and surveyed the street. The yellowish glare of the streetlamps glimmered off slick sidewalks. There were two vehicles, a truck and a sedan, parked on the opposite side of the asphalt. Steam rose in tendrils off the road, as she studied the vehicles. One should have contained Hal, but both appeared to be empty.

One of the vehicles had to belong to Slater. The fact that they were parked close together didn't bode well. It was possible Hal wasn't in his vehicle because he had concealed himself on one of the neighboring properties to keep a watch over her backyard. If that was the case, there was no way he wouldn't have spotted her sneaking through the Spurlocks' place, or Diane and Slater going over the back fence into hers.

Pushing the gate open, Rina stepped out onto the sidewalk with Baby and broke into a run.

The rain eased to a thin drizzle as the intersection loomed. To reach the bus station, they would have to cross the road. Heart pounding, lungs aching, expecting at any moment to hear Slater call out, she launched off the curb. Now that the rain had almost stopped, apart from the mist, the night was clear. She and Baby were glaringly visible.

Seconds later, she paused in the deep gloom of an overhanging tree and studied the empty street. The only movement she could detect was the rustling of tree branches as a faint breeze sprang up, and the shadowy silhouette of someone in the house directly across the intersection as they walked past a lighted window. Apart from the two vehicles parked across from the Spurlocks' place, nothing was out of the ordinary. The street looked like it did most evenings when she had walked around the block: pretty, pleasant and utterly normal.

Tightening her grip on Baby's harness, she backed into the shadows, turned on her heel and, once more, broke into a run.

Twenty-Seven

Lights blazed in every room of Rina's house when JT pulled into the drive. It took him less than thirty seconds to conduct his own search and establish for himself that Rina and Baby weren't there. There were no signs of blood or a scuffle. The fact that she had left her SUV in the garage meant that either someone had gotten to her, or she had sneaked out.

He was going with the latter theory.

He studied the wristwatch sitting on the kitchen counter. She had left in a hurry—closet doors and drawers had been left open, a box of Baby's dog toys was abandoned in the hall—but she had taken the time to leave her watch in a place where it was instantly visible. The message was clear. She had left on her own and she didn't want to be followed.

Kurt joined him at the counter. "There's been some traffic out back. At least two came over the

back fence. From the footprints, either two men—
one large and one small—or else the small guy is a
woman. I'm betting on the blonde. And, no, the shoe
size wasn't Rina's." He jerked his head at the neighboring property. "She and the dog went out that way.
I've already talked to the Spurlocks, and they didn't
see or hear a thing."

"What about Hal?"

Kurt looked grim. "We found him in the trunk of
his car. The coroner's doing the paperwork now."

JT stared at the activity on the back lawn. With
three local, linked homicides now on the books,
complicating the ongoing federal case, the issue of
jurisdiction was sticky. Latham, a heavy hitter from
the U.S. Marshal's office in Beaumont, was here,
along with Maloney, Rina's WitSec contact. So was
Lawrence Atkins, one of Bayard's FBI agents who
just happened to be in town. He was willing to bet
Ed Marlow wouldn't be far behind, and neither
would the press. Time to leave. "I need your car."

Kurt dug in his pants pocket and handed him a set
of keys. JT swapped him the keys to the rental he'd
hired. No explanation was needed. JT had lost his
vehicle and all of his equipment, including his laptop
and his satellite phone. He needed the communications system. Kurt, who would be stuck in Beaumont
for the foreseeable future dealing with the for-
malities surrounding Hal's murder and the investigation into Wendell and Sayer's deaths, could get by
with a phone until replacement equipment arrived.

Kurt walked with him to the car, leaned in and retrieved his briefcase and files. "Where are you going?" His gaze slid to a car that had just pulled in against the curb, and to Bayard's distinctive profile. "No, wait, don't tell me. I don't want to know." Being squeezed by Bayard wasn't his favorite pastime.

JT slid behind the wheel. "I'll be in touch."

Kurt had already checked the flights out, and the bus and taxi companies. There had been a report of a blind woman with a Seeing Eye dog on one of the short, regular bus routes, but after that, nothing. Her name hadn't registered on any flight manifests yet, which could mean she had rented a car.

Something had happened, something big. It was possible that she had been frightened by Sayer's death and the implication that Wendell had led Lopez to her, but he didn't think that in itself was enough to scare a woman who had chosen to stay in Lopez's house, pretending to be blind so she could force herself to remember the account numbers and recover evidence that her father had been coerced.

The only reason Rina had to strike out on her own was Taylor. According to Kurt, she hadn't received any calls on her landline, but that still left her cell phone.

Somehow, she had managed to give Kurt the slip.

When he'd initially read Rina's file, like the other agents involved, he had wondered just how innocent she could be when she was married to Lopez. For a while the surveillance team had run a book on whether she was innocent or guilty, but after watching her for a few weeks, the joking attitude had begun to bug him. He'd come to the conclusion that she might be living with Lopez, but nothing about Rina Morell was cut and dried. For a while he had wondered if her detachment was caused by some kind of medication, but after checking her medical files and finding that the only medication she took was an occasional codeine-based product for headaches, he'd had to change his mindset.

In his spare time he had dug through every recorded piece of information he could find about her. Her psychological reports and school records had proved the most interesting. Her IQ was way higher than average, bordering on genius, she had the same photographic memory Esther had had, and she had been categorized as gifted with painting.

When Morell's assets had been impounded, he had made a trip to the house at Seacliff in San Francisco to take a look. He wasn't a psychologist or a criminal profiler, he just went on the facts, but when he'd stepped into her old room and had found a closet full of paintings, Rina had come into abrupt focus.

When he'd studied the canvases, he'd experienced the same feeling he got when he stepped out onto open prairie. Looking at what she had painted as a ten-year-old child, he had understood her on a level that had nothing to do with profiles or medical reports. The things that had been done to a child capable of that kind of creativity and insight had made him feel sick.

Over the past few months of researching her background, the picture of what had actually happened, as opposed to what had been visible on the surface, had become clear. Rina had been blinded in the accident that had killed her mother, then virtually imprisoned while Lopez had waited for Rina's memory to return so he could get his money back. Just over two years ago, he had stepped in and married her to make sure no one else could slide in under the wire and get the information if she did begin to remember. When he had her isolated from Cesar and any other family and friends, Lopez had attempted to reproduce the trauma that had caused the amnesia in an attempt to get the account numbers.

Rina's escape into WitSec had left a lot of loose ends dangling for Lopez. Aside from the fact that her testimony would put him behind bars for life, he knew she had recovered her sight. In theory, with the blocks in her mind dissolving, she was closer to remembering than she ever had been—just when she had slipped from his grasp. The fact that he had taken the risk of putting a price on her head—a move that could expose him—demonstrated just how badly Lopez wanted her back.

JT pulled in at a gas station, filled up and bought coffee and painkillers. Before driving out, he booted up the computer, punched in his PIN and accessed the GPS system. He waited while the system searched. Seconds later he had his signal.

Swallowing a couple of painkillers, he chased them down with a mouthful of coffee and turned back onto the highway.

Rina checked into a seedy motel in the Tenderloin, a run-down section of San Francisco just west of Union Square filled with budget accommodations, bars and an eclectic mix of cheap cafés. She signed the register using a fake name, paid in advance with cash, and when the clerk asked for ID, she slid two twenties across the counter. As she tucked change into her purse, she noted the time on the clock behind the reception desk. Six p.m. It had taken her almost twenty-four hours to reach San Francisco.

After she and Baby had caught the bus in Beaumont, following the advice of the driver, she had gotten off at a shopping center near the airport. The shopping center was open twenty-four hours, and she'd found everything she'd needed there: coffee, food and a rental car. Asking the bus driver for advice had been a risk, but she had been aware that the driver would be questioned, anyway, and it was highly unlikely he would forget a blind passenger with a Seeing Eye dog boarding an almost empty bus after dark. To put Marlow, JT and anyone else making inquiries off the scent, she had told him she was catching a flight to Dallas.

She'd stayed on the Beaumont Highway all the way to East Houston, then pulled in at the first motel with a vacancy sign. After snatching a few hours' sleep, she and Baby had gotten back on the road, but instead of heading for Dallas and its busy air terminal, she had driven to San Antonio and caught a flight out from there.

Flying at all had been risky, but she hadn't been able to afford the time driving to the West Coast would take. She had minimized the risk by using her credit card to pay for a flight to L.A. When the flight had gone, she had paid cash for a second flight that was boarding, this time to San Jose. As extra insurance, she had worn a dark blond wig she'd bought in Houston and Baby was checked on as pet cargo. That way she had been able to board and exit the flight as an unaccompanied passenger, not the woman and Seeing Eye dog combination the authorities, and Slater, were looking for.

A phone call before she boarded the flight to a kennel in San Jose had provided the solution of what to do with Baby when she reached San Francisco. She didn't want to let him out of her sight, but together they were too visible. For an extra fee, the couple that ran the kennels had agreed to collect Baby from the airport. Rina had paid ahead for a month's stay, nonrefundable, with the rider that she would collect him within a week. When they had requested contact details, she had provided a friend's address and phone number in San Diego. If she didn't survive the trip, Elena would make sure that Baby was cared for.

Now that she was just hours away from Eureka, her plan was simple. Once she located Radcliff's place, she intended to call Bayard and tell him she and Baby had been taken hostage and were being held there. The fact that she had gotten to a phone at all would make her call suspect, but that was exactly what Taylor had managed to do, so the idea was plausible. In any case, Rina planned to terminate the conversation before questions could be asked, leave the line to Bayard open, and plant the phone on the boundary of Radcliff's property. With any luck, Bayard would jump at the bait and whoever it was who had been sabotaging the FBI busts wouldn't have time to compromise this one.

She had tossed up simply calling Bayard from San Francisco, but she couldn't risk the fact that he might be able to locate the origin of the call whether it was a cell phone or a landline. The fact that she was asking him to invade a senator's residence, an action that could put his job on the line if she was wrong, added to the need for her to be physically close to Radcliff's address so that at least that part of the call would be validated.

After unpacking in her room, she walked toward Union Square. She needed to buy a number of items, including clothing. One of the things Esther had taught her was that if she dressed right for an occasion, she was more likely to get what she wanted, and with less fuss. In this case, she needed a more formal outfit that would help her blend in with the business community, and she couldn't buy those clothes from any of the shops she had used to frequent. She had never been that well known in San Francisco, courtesy of her blindness, but she *was* known. Reclusive or not, the fact that she was Cesar Morell's only child had always guaranteed that.

The mall she finally settled on had a clutch of mid-range boutiques and, according to the site map, an Internet café, which was her other requirement.

Before she drove to Eureka she intended to retrieve the contents of Esther's safe-deposit box; she couldn't risk leaving that particular job incomplete, in case she didn't make it back.

According to the FBI, if Esther had compiled evidence against Alex, they had never found it. Knowing how meticulous her mother had been, Rina was certain she would have collected evidence and stored it in a place Alex couldn't reach. She was equally certain that was what the safe-deposit box held.

She needed to find out about the protocol for accessing the safe-deposit box before she walked into the bank. By now there would be an APB out on her. She would only get one chance at retrieving the contents of the box and she didn't want to be turned away because she lacked the right documentation.

The Internet café, situated centrally in the mall, was easy to find. After a brief tussle with an unfamiliar mail program, Rina was online. She accessed the Web site of the bank she needed to research, and saw that the bank was a subsidiary of the Swiss bank Esther had used to work for, Bessel Holt.

The guidelines for safe-deposit boxes were straightforward. When you rented one, you rented space in the bank vault. The person renting the box, and anyone else they wanted to have access, had to sign a card. Every time the box was opened, the signature was compared with the signatures on the card. It took two keys to open the box, one held by the owner of the box, the other held by the bank. The bank didn't keep a copy of the owner's key, so if that was lost, the box would have to be drilled open. In the event that the person who rented the box died and there was no other signatory, a death certificate and a power of attorney were required.

That explained why Esther had placed the power of attorney in with the key. The only thing she hadn't been able to supply was the death certificate.

When a copy of the deposit box information had printed out, Rina did a search on Senator Radcliff. A string of news articles came up. She struck gold with an older magazine article about Radcliff's ex-model wife and their award-winning designer home. The article had been published before his recent election to the Senate, but even so, the magazine had been careful, not allowing any detail of the house plan itself to be published and only photographing tantalizing glimpses of the exterior and the interior decorating. However, the names of both the architect and the interior designer were supplied. Rina hit the print button on the article, then terminated the session.

An hour later she had everything she needed: the pages she'd printed and something to wear. The low-key beige pantsuit, cream camisole, beige shoes and matching handbag were classic. Combined with her jewelry, the outfit would look much more expensive than it had been. She also bought a new watch, perfume and makeup.

By the time she unlocked the door on her motel unit, she was exhausted and hungry. With all the shopping she'd done, she hadn't thought to get food. In the end, she settled for a pizza delivered by a franchise that had an outlet in the small shopping center that backed on to the motel. When she had eaten, she hung her new clothes in the bathroom so the creases would smooth out while she showered.

Just before she drifted off to sleep, she set the alarm on her clock. First thing in the morning, she needed to pay a visit to Carlton and Sykes, the Morell family solicitor. Directly after that, she'd head to the bank, then Radcliff's interior designer. She had considered visiting his architect instead, but the likelihood that an architect would let her look at the plans of the senator's house was remote; they would be very conscious of his need for security. The interior designer, with the emphasis on paint schemes and furniture, was a better bet.

She needed to be out of town before ten if she could manage it. Time was tight; Marlow would be looking for her, and so would JT and Bayard. By now, with the bogus flight to L.A. turning up empty, they would have discovered she had taken a second flight to San Jose Municipal and would be searching the San Francisco area.

She stared at the light strip of skin on her wrist where her watch had been. Not for the first time, it occurred to her that cutting that link with JT could mean she would never see him again. After the night they had spent together, the thought was hard to accept, but there hadn't been any other way. JT had his agenda, and she had hers.

When it was all over—if she was still alive—she would have time to rethink. She knew his name, she knew a little about his family, but her only real reference point was the CIA. It wasn't much of a basis for a relationship. She wasn't sure if she could see herself phoning Langley and asking for the number of the agent who had been working her case.

She turned off the bedside lamp, the absence of light soothing. Maybe JT had no idea that she was tired of being observed and judged, while everyone else got on with their lives, uninterrupted. She was just a part of their job. Destroying that last link had been liberating—for the first time in her life she was out on her own—but it hadn't stopped the ache of loneliness. And it hadn't stopped her wanting him back.

She was certain he would find her, eventually, even without the transmitter. If he had broken WitSec's security once, he could break it again. Nothing had been said between them, nothing confirmed, but when it came to men and women, she had an idea that JT was as uncomplicated as he was about his work. The day she had received her driver's license was a case in point.

If he still wanted her, he would have to work for it.

Twenty-Eight

At 9:00 a.m. the following morning, Rina strolled into Carlton and Sykes. When she made her request the receptionist gave her a startled look. After a flustered moment, she asked Rina to wait while she checked to see if either of the partners was available. Neither Henry Carlton nor Richard Sykes usually saw clients without an appointment, but in this case…

Seconds later, Rina was shown into Henry Carlton's office. Rina had never seen him, but his voice was recognizable and he knew her well enough. He had been handling her family's affairs for as long as she could remember, and he was likely to be handling them in perpetuity. Cesar's assets and accounts had been frozen, pending the outcome of an investigation into his links with the Chavez cartel. Apart from the more serious criminal charges, the side issues of money laundering and tax evasion were likely to tie up the estate for years.

Within a matter of minutes she had a copy of Esther's death certificate. Instead of catching a cab, she walked a block to the bank, which was situated on California Street.

Bracing herself against the scrutiny of the security cameras, she stepped through the doors into the cool, air-conditioned interior. The reception area was spacious and minimalist in design. Contemporary works of art dotted neutral walls, and large panels of frosted glass screened a number of cubicles where people could be glimpsed working at desks. The effect, apart from the security cameras, which sprouted from the corners of walls and gleamed from behind lush arrangements of potted plants, was soothing and serene.

Hooking the strap of her purse more firmly over her shoulder, Rina continued toward the information desk. A pretty dark-haired woman glanced up and smiled.

Rina made her request. Seconds later, she entered an interview room, took a chair and waited while a bank officer, who had introduced herself as Melinda, collected the relevant file. Seconds later, Melinda took the chair opposite her.

She opened the file, and the pleasant expression on her face slipped. After Cesar's death, the Morell name was high-profile enough that recognition was guaranteed. "The box is owned by Esther Morell."

"That's right. She was my mother."

Just saying the words touched an unexpected chord. When the memorial service for Esther had been conducted, she had still been recovering in hospital and had been excluded from the final rites. She had never gotten to say goodbye, or to even talk about Esther, because Cesar had refused to let her mention Esther's name. The reasons behind Cesar's behavior were now clear, but twenty-two years ago they hadn't been. To the ten-year-old child she had been it had felt like Esther hadn't so much died as ceased to exist.

But she *had* existed. No amount of skullduggery on Alex's part, or Cesar burying his head in the sand, could change that. Esther had been her mother, and after years of limbo, it was a relief to publicly state that fact.

She produced the death certificate and the power of attorney. The woman looked a little disconcerted as she read through the documents and made notes on the file. Rina felt shaky herself.

Melinda smiled. "Wait here. I'll get the bank's key, then take you into the vault."

Minutes later, battling an eerie sense of stepping into a role that had once been played by Esther, Rina was cleared through security and stepped into the vault. Melinda walked along the rows of numbered steel boxes and selected one. She laid the box on a table, which was set to one side of the room, inserted her key and withdrew it. She indicated the security guard standing just outside the door. "When you want to leave, Joe will ring through to me, and I'll take you back to reception."

With fingers that weren't quite steady, Rina slid the key into the second lock, turned it and opened the box.

A manila envelope lay on top of a sheaf of papers. She glanced in the envelope; her heart thumped hard in her chest. It was filled with cash, neat bundles of one-hundred-dollar bills. There had to be upwards of one hundred thousand dollars. Twenty-two years ago, that had been a great deal of money. Today it was still a substantial amount.

Closing the envelope, she lifted out the stack of papers and skimmed over a few pages. They were copies of bank records, sheets and sheets of transactions, some listed under Alex's name, most for a Michael Vitali. A penned note on one of the sheets made her go cold inside.

Michael Vitali/Miguel Perez.

Los Mendez.

In the weeks after she had been moved out of Winton she had researched the Chavez cartel, obsessively reading anything and everything she could find. One of the most brutal and publicized events had been the massacre at Los Mendez.

Included in the papers were financial reports for a number of companies and a handwritten précis outlining the paper trail Alex and Vitali had used to exert pressure on the Morell Group. With Esther's banking background, she would have known what to look for, and she had obviously found it.

Another much smaller envelope was in the bottom of the box. The envelope contained a cassette, and suddenly the connection to the past was immediate and visceral.

Heavy traffic. Fog everywhere, rolling in, wreathing the traffic lights.

"Lopez is a problem, isn't he?"

Esther's gaze was sharp. "What do you mean?"

"I heard him and Dad talking. Don't look so surprised. Just because it looks like I'm not listening, it doesn't mean I'm not... They thought I was listening to my Walkman... You want to hear?"

Esther braked for an intersection. "Hear what?"

"The tape. I told you, I wasn't listening to music, I was taping."

Fingers shaking slightly, she slipped the cassette she had been searching for in Winton in with the cash. Like the bank records, the tape was evidence. The conversation she had recorded couldn't help Cesar now, but it would prove that he had been set up and coerced.

Light glittered off something in one corner of the box. Rina picked up what she had at first thought was an earring. Beneath the harsh, white lights of the vault, the pink diamond ring flashed with a soft fire. Her chest swelled. If there was one piece of jewelry she associated with Esther more than any other, it was this ring. Esther had worn it more often than any other piece of jewelry other than her wedding and engagement rings. She had no idea what it was worth, but for Rina its value lay in the message of the ring. Pushed to the edge, Esther hadn't had time for notes or goodbyes. Determined to defeat Alex, attempting to save Cesar, she had done what she could. She had left the ring, a gift from mother to daughter.

Locking the now-empty box, Rina gathered up the papers, the envelope and the ring and exited the vault. A short phone call later by the security guard and Melinda escorted her back to the interview room.

"Would you like an envelope for those things?"

"For the papers, yes."

Opening a drawer, Melinda produced a large manila envelope. Rina slipped the stack of papers inside, scribbled a note to Marc Bayard and addressed the envelope. Maybe she was overreacting, but she didn't want to hold on to the papers any longer than she had to, in case something went wrong. Esther had literally risked her life to obtain this information. She would mail the documents off to Bayard as soon as she left the bank.

"Would you like an envelope for the ring?"

Rina stared at the pink diamond, her chest knotting. "No. Thank you. I'll wear it."

After posting the envelope, she caught a cab to the prestigious Pacific Heights district and stepped out onto a street that featured an array of designer boutiques. St. Marie Interiors occupied an impressive amount of ground-floor real estate. After negotiating acres of elegant furniture and fabrics, she found a retail assistant, introduced herself as Rina Morell and requested a consultation.

Within seconds, Hebert St. Marie himself was on the floor and directing her into a large, lushly appointed office. Rina sat down on one of the comfortably padded brocaded chairs positioned around a gleaming rosewood coffee table. St. Marie's gaze settled on the pink diamond. The fact that she had to lie didn't sit easily with her, but in the small hours of the morning, she had come to the conclusion that she had no option. She swung into action, her delivery as smooth as she could make it given that her nerves were strung so tight that if she hadn't folded her hands together they would be visibly shaking. She dropped Cesar's name, with a delicate mention of his estate being finalized, capped off by the information that she had just bought a beachfront property near Eureka. "A rather large house, actually."

St. Marie murmured condolences about her loss, his expression fascinated as his gaze slid back to the ring. He had read the newspapers; he knew the scandal; he could smell the money. "I take it the house needs some work."

"It's modern." She named the architectural firm who had designed Radcliff's house. "It needs redecorating. I never did like all that steel and glass."

St. Marie's assistant entered the room with a tray of coffee. While the coffee was poured and the tiny white cups handed out, she mentioned that she had seen Radcliff's house, leaving out the detail that it had only been in a magazine article. Calmly, she stated that she was very interested in seeing the complete design layout that St. Marie had done.

St. Marie set his cup down, his inner struggle brief. Rina was Cesar's heir. He knew an investigation was in progress, but money was money. If Rina inherited even a fraction of Cesar's assets, she would be one of the richest women in the country. "It's not normally done, but in your case, since you've already seen Senator Radcliff's house…"

He stepped out of the room. Moments later, he came back with a portfolio and began spreading the sheets detailing the design of each room. He didn't pull out the final sheet, which was a blueprint of the plans for the house, but Rina only needed a glimpse to imprint the layout of the rooms and read the address on the bottom of the page.

Twenty-Nine

Rina reached Eureka just after three in the afternoon.

She had picked up a rental in San Francisco. Even though she had paid cash, she was aware that her ID would be traced, although not as quickly as it would have been if she had used a card. She was counting on the few hours it might take for the ID to be picked up to give her enough time to get up the coast and get the car off the road before the highway patrol started looking for the plate.

Once she had checked into a motel and the car was parked out of sight, she let out a sigh of relief. She was hot and sweaty, and the drive north had been nerve-racking. Every time she had seen a patrol car or a motorcycle cop, she had expected to be pulled over. It hadn't happened, but the constant anticipation had wrung her out. At least now, for the few hours it took until it got dark enough for her to leave for Radcliff's house, she had the security of knowing the car wouldn't be spotted.

After eating a sandwich she'd bought earlier, she showered, changed into dark jeans and a sweater, then sat, studying a road map of the area, keeping an eye on the news programs on television and periodically dozing beneath the cool draft of a fan.

When she was ready, she repacked the car, locked the unit and left the key underneath a nearby pot plant. It was possible she would spend the night in the motel, but not likely, so she wasn't about to leave any belongings there. When she straightened, the conviction that she was being watched made her tense.

Careful not to betray that she was aware of anything out of the ordinary, she strolled toward her rental, fingers sliding into her purse to retrieve the key in case she had to make a run for the car.

A faint movement caught her eye. A Doberman, its slanted eyes intent as it tracked her progress, was leashed in an enclosure adjacent to the parking area. She let out a breath. The dog obviously belonged to the owner of the motel and was trained to guard the premises. She didn't know what she had done to set him on edge, although maybe it had been as simple as her own tension.

The sun set beneath a heavy mantle of cloud as she turned north onto Highway 101, leaving the evening cooler. She flicked her headlights on. The beams cut through the gloom. With the absence of the moon, or even starlight, the night would be darker than usual.

Twenty-five minutes later, she turned onto a steep coastal road rimmed by precipitous cliffs and dotted with expensive properties. Radcliff's house was situated in a cul-de-sac at the end of the road. According to her map, the cul-de-sac occupied one of the highest points in the area.

As she cruised up the steep gradient, she studied house numbers. There weren't many, because the properties were large and mostly spaced out. Her stomach sank as she located Radcliff's house, which was protected by a high masonry wall and a wrought-iron gate.

Radcliff's beach hideaway might be out in the country, but no expense had been spared on security. She would put money on video surveillance, with the possibility of sophisticated infrared and laser systems. Finding a place to call Bayard and plant the phone wasn't promising. The street frontage was bare and garishly lit; the area around the gate was devoid of any ornamentation. If she put the phone down on the sidewalk anywhere in the lit areas, it was possible surveillance cameras would pick it up.

Briefly, she considered throwing the phone over the fence, then dismissed the idea. If the phone didn't get damaged or accidentally switched off on landing, the chances were strong that the movement would be picked up on camera and the phone located almost immediately.

In contrast to the sterile sidewalk, the house itself was almost completely obscured by tall trees. She glanced over her shoulder at the property she had passed just before Radcliff's. The house was visible behind its masonry wall, but instead of wrought iron, the gate was solid timber. Planting the phone there would be just as risky.

Headlights glowed behind her. She slowed, allowing a low-slung Porsche to sweep past. At this time of night she had to expect some traffic. It was late, but anyone living here and commuting to either Winton or Eureka would get home about this time.

The masonry wall turned into a wrought-iron fence as she turned a corner, and the garish street lighting was dimmed, blocked by overhanging trees. She caught the glow of taillights as the Porsche disappeared between open gates. She glanced at a plaque inset into one of the masonry gateposts. The name etched into the bronze was clearly visible. *Eady.*

Heart pounding, she cruised past the gates. The car parked outside the garage was Diane Eady's.

She had always known Diane had a beach house, although she hadn't ever known exactly where it was. Now she knew.

If she had doubted it before, she didn't any longer. She was in the right place.

Diane Eady closed her front door and walked through to the kitchen, flicking lights as she went.

She reached for the phone and dialed. "I just saw a woman in a dark gray rental driving past your house. I'm almost certain it was Rina."

"It's okay." Slater's voice was smooth. "We've had her under surveillance since she turned onto Cliff Road."

Diane didn't try to keep the acid out of her voice. "That's a relief."

"Did you shut your gate?"

Diane's gaze narrowed at the curt tone. Lately Slater had become increasingly arrogant. She walked through to the front door and checked. In her hurry to get to the phone, she *had* left it open. "I'll close it now."

"Leave it open."

Rina drove as far as the beach lookout, turned around, then drove back the way she'd come, pulling over to park just short of Diane Eady's house. Every instinct she had told her she should leave while she still could. If Diane lived next door to Radcliff it was possible—no, probable—that other houses were also occupied by Alex's people.

She stared at the glowing windows of the houses lining either side of the road. They were all nestled together, isolated from the string of beach cottages and the small village farther along the beach. Maybe she was being overly paranoid, but, given that Alex was the head of a Colombian drug cartel, she couldn't ignore the possibility that the entire enclave was a cartel fortress situated on United States soil.

In which case, time was a luxury she didn't have. Each house had its own security system and it was also possible the road in and out was monitored. But if that were the case, a security guard should already have checked her out, and she hadn't seen anyone who looked remotely official.

Diane's gate was still open.

Adrenaline surged. All she had to do was make the call and tuck the phone out of sight. There were enough shrubs and trees on the front lawn that she wouldn't have to walk more than a few paces onto the property.

Grabbing her handbag, she extracted her cell phone, then locked the car and walked briskly toward the open gate, hugging the deepest shadows.

Headlights swept the road. Heart pounding, she pressed into a clump of shrubs as the car cruised past and disappeared around the bend, heading for the lookout. Long seconds passed while she waited to see if the vehicle would turn around and cruise back past her. When it didn't, she short-dialed Bayard's number, stepped out of the shadows and walked into Diane Eady's driveway. Slipping behind a thick hydrangea, she crouched down and waited for the call to be picked up. If Bayard didn't answer, she would go to plan B and ring JT. If he could track her using military satellites, he shouldn't have any problem locating the signal from her phone.

The phone continued to ring, the sound amplified in the silence of the garden.

"Stand up slowly, disconnect the call and hand the phone to me."

Slater.

Rina straightened and handed over the phone just as Bayard picked up. Slater terminated the call and slipped the phone in his pocket.

A flickering movement drew her gaze.

Slater smiled. "That won't help. I've got two men either side of the gate."

A cold click changed the expression on Slater's face. A dark shape separated itself from the trunk of a tree. The glare from a streetlamp caught the distinctive line of JT's profile. "Past tense, Slater. You had two men. Drop the gun, then kick it onto the drive."

For long seconds Slater didn't move. JT moved a step closer, the handgun now fully visible. Like the night he'd gotten her out of Winton, he was dressed in dark clothing. He was also wearing a lip mike and body armor, which meant he had come prepared with backup. Slater's mouth twisted when he registered those details. With slow movements, he complied.

A red dot appeared on JT's chest.

Rina stared at the dot. "JT—"

Diane Eady stepped out from behind a shrub edging her driveway, with what looked like an assault rifle cradled at her shoulder.

JT didn't shift his weapon from Slater. "Eady. This gets better and better."

A split second later, two shadowy forms materialized on either side of the gate. The crack of gunfire split the air. The red dot jerked upward. Time seemed to slow, stop, as Rina dived to one side.

She was aware of movement, a blur as Slater lunged, further shots as two weapons were fired simultaneously. Slater made a high-pitched sound. The place that Diane had been standing was empty. She realized Diane was lying sprawled on the ground. The first shot had taken her out.

A split second later JT was crouched beside her. "Are you all right?"

She pushed to her knees. Her palms were stinging and her hands were shaking again. Maybe in a year, living in a very small, quiet, isolated town where she had nothing more dangerous to do than paint, she would be all right. "I'm fine."

One of the dark shadows flowed past and crouched next to Diane. "She's dead."

Slater, who was lying on the ground curled in a fetal position clutching his shoulder, groaned. The second shadow was holding a gun on him.

"Stay down." JT searched Slater. He pulled a handgun from an ankle holster, ejected the magazine and slipped it into his pocket. He did the same with the first weapon he had taken off Slater, then threw both handguns into a thick clump of shrubs.

Motioning her to her feet, he kept her behind him as he checked out the driveway. Gun in one hand, his free hand at the back of her neck, keeping her low,

they ran for the cover of the gate. One of the men
who had covered JT ghosted along behind them as
they moved down the street.

Rina's car was where she'd left it. Parked directly
behind it was the car she had seen drive past earlier.

JT pulled a set of keys from his pocket and deactivated the locks on the second car. His gaze caught
hers. She realized that as unruffled as he seemed, he
wasn't calm at all. "What were you going to do?
Take on Slater and Eady on your own?"

"I was trying to call Bayard."

A pulsing sound registered. Seconds later, sound
and light exploded as a helicopter rose above the
cliff's edge and swept in low, spotlights sweeping
the enclave as it hovered over Radcliff's house.
"*That's* Bayard. When I knew where you were
headed, I put the call through."

A second helicopter appeared. Dark figures
were momentarily visible, swarming down ropes
onto Radcliff's lawn, before the helicopter disappeared from view.

"What about Taylor?" A burst of gunfire punctuated the compressed whine of rotor blades.

JT's hand landed in the small of her back as he
hurried her toward the car. "I told you there was
someone in Winton. He's been surveilling Eady, but
until she turned up in Beaumont and shot Wendell, he
didn't have anything solid enough to warrant an
arrest."

The fact that Wendell had been killed by the

therapist who had been treating her since she was a child should have shocked her, but after watching Diane climb over her back fence, her threshold for being shocked had shrunk to zero.

Lights flicked on in the house across the street. Farther down the road a car engine revved. Gunfire erupted from Radcliff's place.

JT pulled open the passenger-side door. "Get in."

"When I've got my stuff." Rina already had the rental unlocked. Leaning in, she grabbed her knapsack. Any delay was dangerous, but the knapsack contained all she had left of her old life and her family. She hadn't carried it this far to leave it behind.

JT took the knapsack from her and shoved it on the backseat, then climbed behind the wheel. "Fasten your seat belt."

She dropped her handbag on the floor, then belted herself in. After everything that had happened, the detail of fastening the belt seemed ridiculous and a little mundane, but if JT said she needed to, then she would do it. She noticed that the agent who had accompanied them was no longer on the street. At some point he had probably rejoined the agent who was holding Slater.

Within ten seconds she understood why she needed the belt. When they reached the bottom of the hill, they ran straight into a roadblock and a second FBI SWAT team, every one of them armed with submachine guns.

With slow, careful movements, JT flipped open his badge.

A grim-faced agent shone his flashlight in the window, stared at their faces, then examined the badge. After checking Rina's ID, and a brief conversation into a handheld radio, he motioned them on.

When they had cleared the barrier of FBI and both state and county police cruisers, JT peeled off his lip mike and picked up a phone. A brief call later and he went back to driving. "Taylor's in the clear. Bayard had her choppered out to the nearest hospital. She's unhurt, but Lopez had her under sedation. They picked up Slater and a number of other smaller fish. Lopez either escaped or he wasn't there."

Relief that Taylor was safe eased some of her tension, but she couldn't repress a shudder at the thought that Alex could have been in the enclave. As much as she wanted him caught, she didn't relish the thought of coming face-to-face with him again. The memory of the cold way he had executed Cesar was still too fresh.

JT slowed for an intersection, then turned right, heading south. Sometime over the past hour the heavy clouds had cleared away, and now it was a beautiful night. The moon had just risen over the coastal hills, spreading a silvery light over the landscape and giving the sea a limpid, metallic sheen.

JT reached over onto the backseat, found a jacket and handed it to her. Rina draped the buttery-soft leather over her legs. Now that the cloud cover had gone, the temperature was cooler and crisper, a big change from Beaumont.

Warmth seeped into her legs. She relaxed a little more, letting the rhythm of the car soothe her. She glanced at JT's profile. "How did you find me?"

He sent her an enigmatic look. "There was a second transmitter in one of your photo frames. You were also tailed by one of Bayard's boys from the airport. I took over when I got into town. I just missed you at the bank, then the interior design place. I picked you up again when you got the rental and headed north."

She stared at his profile. A second transmitter. No wonder she hadn't been stopped. The realization that she had been tailed since she had left Beaumont was sobering. JT and Bayard hadn't reeled her in for a reason: she had been too useful.

Thirty

JT pulled over into the brightly lit area out in front of a motel. He stepped out of the car and peeled off the body armor, black T-shirt and his weapons belt, and stowed them in the trunk. Reaching into the backseat, he extracted a fresh T-shirt from a nylon gear bag, pulled it on and slid back behind the wheel. "You've got two options. You can call Marlow and get out now, or you can come with me."

Rina hadn't expected to get a choice. "Isn't that breaking the rules?"

His gaze locked with hers. Suddenly they were back in relationship territory, and it was…complicated.

He leaned forward and kissed her, taking his time. "Does that make it easier?"

"I can't promise to do everything you tell me."

"You're going to have to." He put the car in gear

and nosed back out onto the highway. "Two days ago, the Chavez compound in Colombia turned into a crater. The press is blaming the military. The military are blaming a rival cartel. I haven't received confirmation yet, but we think the missile is one of a batch of scrapped warheads that Lopez was in the process of smuggling out of the country, in which case the hit was very personal."

Rina frowned. The thought that someone wanted to kill Alex so badly that they had used a missile was bizarre. "Who wants to kill him?" She was certain there was a long queue, but using a missile put whoever had launched it right at the front.

"The people who have been using Lopez. They brought him into the country as an adolescent, gave him a new identity and helped him set up in business. Lopez has been importing cocaine into the States, exporting guns and ammunition and brokering terrorism for a group known as the cabal ever since. He's their primary link into Libya, Afghanistan and Pakistan. A few months ago the stakes went up, when they asked him to move missile components.

"The missiles were an exception to the rule. Normally, they don't pull that kind of stuff. The manipulation has usually been high level and subtle—influencing armament contracts, inserting key personnel into foreign postings, manipulating information to keep the war machine turning over and the money flowing into their pockets."

She stared at the cold landscape they were passing

through, bare hills and miles of open sea. She knew what a cabal was, a group involved in political intrigue. The term was old-fashioned, but the crimes were up to date. "Just who are the cabal?"

"They're the children of Nazis who escaped from Germany on a ship called the *Nordika* a few weeks before Berlin fell and took refuge in Colombia. That's where Marco Chavez came in. He hid them for a price."

The connection with Nazi Germany raised gooseflesh. It was another layer, another weird twist she hadn't seen coming.

She must have fallen asleep. When she woke, JT was still driving and the night sky was once again shrouded in a bank of cloud, blocking out the moon and stars. The clock on the dash said it was after one in the morning.

Rina stretched, ironing out the cricks in her neck. "Where are we going?"

"You're going to San Francisco. I'm going south."

She sat up. "How far south?"

"New Mexico. I've booked a flight out of Oakland airport. I get into El Paso at six."

Getting details from JT was like extracting blood from a stone, but eventually she got what she needed. The same South American informant who had previously supplied information about Alex had tipped them off about a party that was being thrown as a cover for a meeting Lopez was having with a cabal member. According to the source, Alex had had his appearance surgically altered since the bust in Winton—a process he had started when he had left Colombia as a teenager. Apart from the surgical alterations, he would also be in disguise.

The party itself was being thrown by a charitable organization to celebrate the opening of an art exhibition of "lost" works that had been recovered by a private collector. The tickets ran to five figures, and counting.

Rina stared at the ribbon of road ahead, caught in the powerful beam of the headlights. El Paso was right on the border, the perfect meeting place for criminals, with a quick escape into Mexico just minutes away. The thought that Alex would slip away again made her stomach clench. She needed to be there. She needed to make sure he was caught. "I'm coming with you."

JT's glance was cool. "No. I'll meet up with you in a couple of days."

"Without me, you'll lose him. Even if he's disguised, I can ID him for you. Pull over, and I'll show you."

Five minutes of tense debate later, JT pulled over into a deserted picnic area. With the headlights off, the night was pitch-black, but not dark enough.

"Now blindfold me."

A spare T-shirt from JT's bag, folded so it formed a pad over her eyes then tied tightly, served as a blindfold. Rina turned to face the road and directed him to walk into the shrubs that fringed the picnic area and position himself so she couldn't see him.

When she turned back, JT was instantly visible. Despite being mostly hidden behind shrubs, he glowed in the dark. A bright turquoise around his head flowed into a deep, pure blue around his shoulders and chest. The colors were clear and distinct, nothing like the murky hues around Slater and Eady or the unusual bisection of black and red that marked Alex.

Slowly she walked toward him, taking care, because while she could see JT with her eyes closed, she couldn't see anything else. "You're partially hidden by the sign, but your colors are clear and distinct." She walked up to him and planted her palm on his chest. "I can find Alex for you. No matter how much he disguises his physical appearance, I'll be able to see him."

Rina avoided a waiter with a tray of champagne and the press of expensively dressed guests in favor of drifting past the impressive walls of paintings.

Wearing a blond wig and an elegant black gown, and wired for sound and video with a set of state-of-the-art earrings, spectacles and a brooch, she should have been too tense to notice the "lost" art. But the works, mysteriously recovered by a reclusive European collector, were mesmerizing: Gainsborough, Chagalle, a breathtaking oil by Turner, and a previously undiscovered set of dancers by Degas.

JT's hand tightened on her elbow. They'd been mingling for more than an hour, drifting between the garden and the beautifully appointed reception room of the large private mansion in which the party was being held. So far the only positive IDs made had been of an A-list movie star and his entourage, and a long list of the financially advantaged.

JT bent close to her ear. Wearing a mustache and spectacles, his hair artificially grayed at the temples, he looked fifty-plus, but the fiction was periodically blurred by the fluid way he moved, and the fact that the tux couldn't disguise the set of his shoulders. "I'm going upstairs. Kurt thinks he's spotted one of Lopez's men. Wait five. If you don't hear from me, walk to the car and stay there."

Rina checked her watch as the seconds crawled by. Stepping outside, where there was less of a crush, she did another circuit of the pool, then paused in the shadowy lee of a statue situated directly opposite the open doors of the reception room. Closing her eyes, she tried to sort out the confused mass of color. Singly, people were easy to "see." In a crowded room, it was like trying to search for colors in soup—everything blended.

"Waiting for someone special?"

Her eyes popped open. There were a lot of men at the party; they outnumbered women by a ratio of about three to one. Her blond wig had attracted plenty of looks, but so far she hadn't had any approaches because JT had been with her. In a white tux, his hair caught back in a sleek ponytail, this guy had to be a member of the movie star entourage. "Sorry, you're not him."

He shrugged and walked on. She checked her watch. Two minutes to go.

A voice jerked her head around. She caught a glimpse of movement in the shadows of a gazebo, the unmistakable outline of a heavyset man. A gleam of light flashed over a profile that, thanks to the gallery of photos Bayard had shown her shortly after she had been moved out of Winton, was shockingly familiar. Edward Dennison.

The improbability of Dennison's appearance here, now, knocked her off balance. He had been working for Alex twenty-two years ago when Esther had been murdered. Since then he had disappeared off the scope. According to Bayard, his new job had been running Alex's Colombian operation after the death of Marco Chavez. Since then, Dennison hadn't been seen on U.S. soil, but, with the destruction of the Chavez compound in Colombia, he had plenty of reason to return home. If Dennison was here, it was a certainty that Alex was, too.

Touching the jewel on her brooch that activated her mike, she relayed the information to the communications center, which was a catering truck parked out on the street. Stepping past the statue, Rina fell in behind a couple strolling up the patio steps, and trailed Dennison into the crowded reception room.

Dennison moved into a long conservatory-style

gallery dotted with lush palms, its doors flung open to the garden. This room was packed, and most of the guests were men. Suddenly she felt a lot more conspicuous than she had been in the main reception room.

A waiter offered her a glass of champagne. She refused the drink, stepping around him to keep Dennison in sight. He was walking with purpose, not stopping to make conversation, or to eat or drink.

Her unease sharpened. An unsettling feeling, as if someone was watching her intently, made her spine tighten. Paranoia—maybe. She hadn't felt this way since she had been at Winton.

With a shudder, she kept moving, sliding between knots of guests. Dennison had merged with the sea of black tuxes and disappeared. She glanced around the room, just in case he had changed direction or doubled back behind her. It was possible he had stepped back out into the garden. One thing was certain, he had come inside to find someone.

The feeling that she was being watched, very specifically, coalesced into certainty. Suddenly she was sure that Alex was here. He was in the room, and he had seen her.

Stomach tight, she threaded past a large mixed group, high on champagne, and ducked down beside a small forest of potted palms. Seconds later, she had removed her blond wig and tossed it behind a palm. The most singular thing about her appearance had been the wig. Aside from that, she was dressed to blend in black. If Alex had been using the wig to keep her in view, he had just lost his point of reference. Bending, ostensibly to adjust the fastening of her shoe, she relayed the information that Alex was in the gallery.

The order came back to stay where she was until JT or one of the other agents could get to her. She lifted a glass of champagne from a waiter's tray and hovered at the edge of the large, partying group, making herself even less conspicuous as she scanned the crowd.

She caught a glimpse of Dennison. She studied the men around him, looking for a match for Alex in height and build. Hair color was unreliable. If she could wear a wig, Alex could, too—or alter the color of his hair.

Closing her eyes, she tried to see colors, but this room didn't look any different to the way the main reception room had looked from the garden: soup.

A door to her left popped open. JT, Kurt and a third agent stepped into the gallery. The instant JT's gaze locked with hers, she knew something was wrong. He lunged toward her. Time seemed to slow, stop. He caught her side on, sending her tumbling. The champagne glass smashed on the tiles, and a muffled spitting sound froze the blood in her veins. The potted palms behind her shivered, leaves shredding as JT's weight crashed down on her. The spitting sound came again, followed by the heavier detonation of a gun that wasn't silenced. Screams erupted, and the gallery became a stampede of panicked guests. Seconds later, the room was plunged into darkness.

When JT didn't immediately move, panic surged. She could smell blood. The gunfire had been aimed at her, but aside from a bruised hip and elbow she wasn't hurt.

JT's weight shifted, pinning her more securely. "Stay still."

His voice was flat, almost unnaturally calm; he wasn't hit, just making sure she didn't get to her feet.

She picked up the faint static of JT's mike and snatches of his almost-soundless replies, enough to know that Dennison had been hit, and someone had pulled the fuses.

Seconds later, JT rolled off her. Oxygen flooded her lungs. His fingers gripped her arm and she found herself back on her feet and moving. Her hair, now loose from the clips that had held it flat beneath the wig, tumbled around her face and shoulders.

Her shoulder brushed a doorjamb. They rounded a corner, then another. The narrow beam of a flashlight flickered over richly embossed walls. "Where are we?"

"Just off the main hallway." JT opened a door and pushed her inside a room. The brief skim of light identified it as a library, with a bank of French doors opening out onto yet another garden vista. "Wait here. Don't move."

The command made sense. The gallery, the hall

and the main reception room were awash with panicked people. The chance that someone would get hurt, or even accidentally shot, was high. Added to that, the possibility that Alex would attempt to grab her under these conditions was remote, but it couldn't be discounted.

Moving farther into the room, she located one of the leather wing chairs she had seen when JT had checked out the room with his flashlight, and sat down. Silence closed in on her. The sounds of panicked voices became muffled and distant.

The tick of a grandfather clock in one corner measured time. Minutes only, but sitting in the dark, it felt longer.

A footfall sounded. The door opened. Relief flooded her. For a split second she thought it was JT and she almost spoke, then a shadowy figure glided past her, close enough that she caught a faint whiff of masculine cologne.

Her stomach jolted. She had a glimpse of a peculiarly bisected aura, the murky red dissolving into black as he opened one of the French doors, stepped out into the garden and merged with the night.

She stared into darkness. *Alex.* He *had* been here and she had seen him, but only with her secondary vision.

Backing toward the door that opened onto the hall, she touched the jewel on her brooch and relayed the information. Feverishly, she tried to remember the men she had noticed around Dennison before the shooting had started. A lean man with a cigar, an intellectual with wafer-thin spectacles, any number of black-and-white tuxes, but she couldn't recall anyone who had looked remotely like Alex.

As she stepped out into the hall, the beam of a flashlight pinned her. JT's gaze locked with hers, the faint shake of his head said he couldn't leave her for a second.

"He went out through the French doors." She jerked her head at the room. A shudder rolled through her. If the house hadn't been plunged into darkness, Alex would have seen her.

JT checked out the room and the garden beyond. She noticed he'd lost the tuxedo jacket, the fake glasses and the mustache.

The lights came back on. Simultaneously, static erupted from a handheld radio. His gaze connected with hers. "A man was seen trying to scale the garden wall on this side of the house. Bayard's got a team tracking him. They've got him cornered."

Kurt stepped into the library. "One of the house security guards and a guest caught bullets. Other than that we're okay. Dennison's down, and one of Lopez's soldiers is dead. We've rounded up another couple out by the pool. There's no sign of Radcliff or any of our high-level friends."

"Or Lopez." A black woman dressed in the feminine version of a tux poked her head through the French doors. "He must have pulled a switch, or he was never here, because the baby-faced guy they picked up is twenty if he's a day." She turned away, then poked her head back in again. "By the way, a body's just been located in the gazebo. Double-tap to the head. Looks like a professional job."

"Any ID?"

She raised her hands. "I couldn't get close. All I know is that this one's been dead long enough to go cold. Bayard's already moved on him."

JT glanced at Kurt. "Get over there. I need an ID and anything else you can dig up." He already knew who the dead man had to be. After the bombing in Colombia—a clear signal from the cabal that they wanted to cut their connection to the Chavez cartel—Lopez had been here to negotiate terms. Senator Radcliff had been representing the cabal, but the fact that he had been executed before the meeting with Lopez added a new twist.

A helicopter with the insignia of a prominent news network decorating its underbelly skimmed overhead. The rhythmic chop of the blades and the spotlight sweeping the cordoned-off areas underlined the fact that they had a mess on their hands.

JT watched as Radcliff's body was loaded into an ambulance. Two murders, in excess of two hundred suspects, more than half of whom had left the scene, and the press were already calling Radcliff's killing an assassination. The homicide, combined with the fact that Radcliff had gone live about the missile strike on the Chavez compound just days ago, and they had enough fuel to stir up every conspiracy theorist in the country. JT wasn't so sure they would be wrong.

He checked out the cops and bureau personnel keeping the press at bay. Rina was sitting in one of the bureau cars, a ball cap Kurt had managed to borrow from one of the house security staff pulled down on her head, shading her face. The press hadn't spotted her, they were too focused on Radcliff, but JT wouldn't relax until he had gotten her out. She had been in the garden when Dennison had found Radcliff in the gazebo. As close calls went, it was too close for him.

Kurt joined him as the ambulance left. "What's the estimated time of death?"

The helicopter moved in for another pass, dipping low.

JT waited out the noise. "Radcliff's been dead for two hours, give or take."

His killers had transported his body to the scene, set it up in the gazebo, then either left before the stampede of guests or else used it as a convenient cover. JT would check the video-surveillance cameras set around the house and grounds and the FBI surveillance tapes, but the likelihood that he would be able to find anything conclusive was slim. Whoever had shot Radcliff had been slick and professional.

"A catering van's been located abandoned a couple of streets away."

And when it was processed for prints, JT was willing to bet it would be clean. Another dead end.

The cabal had made a mistake with the missile components, and with Lopez, but the trap they had set had been clinical. Lopez, out on a limb with the base of his South American operation destroyed and with Bayard on his heels, had taken the bait the cabal had dangled. He had been here to deal, but he had been outmaneuvered. The cabal had executed Radcliff. The only thing they had failed to do was kill Lopez and implicate him in Radcliff's killing, thereby neatly tying off the loose end that Radcliff and the missile components had presented.

If they had succeeded, the military and the government would have had their traitor and the bureau would have gotten Lopez and enough evidence to keep it busy for months. The time lag between Radcliff and Lopez's deaths would have been a detail. As damage control for the cabal, it would have been effective—if it had worked.

A burst of static distracted JT. He lifted the radio to his ear. A second later, he put it down, his expression grim: a perfect ending to a perfect night. "Dennison's missing."

Thirty-One

A jolting movement, and the sickening burst of pain that went with it, brought Dennison to. He was being dragged. The buttoned neckline of his shirt gouged his trachea with every step. His fingers and heels trailed over damp grass as he was pulled along by the bunched fabric of his shirt and jacket.

The forward movement stopped and the pressure on his windpipe eased. The back of his head smacked onto the ground.

He became aware of movement around him and the fact that he was lying beneath a huge phoenix palm tree that blocked out the stars and most of the lights from a string of houses.

When he had passed out from the wound he had thought he was dying. He didn't know why Lopez had bothered to drag him anywhere. Leaving him to bleed to death was more in character, and quite frankly, Dennison would have preferred that. Since Anne had passed away, the thought of his own death had lost the power to scare him.

Distantly, he could hear sirens, which meant they weren't far from the house party.

The soft thud of a spade refocused his attention.

The smell of freshly turned earth overrode the thick scent of his own blood and an irrational panic gripped him. Lopez was going to bury him while he was still alive.

Long seconds passed while Dennison feverishly calculated his chances of escape. Back at the house, he had managed to crawl a few feet and roll into one of the gardens before he had lost consciousness. Now he was past that point. His body felt like lead, his breathing was shallow and too fast and he kept blacking out.

He knew the symptoms; he had read the medical facts often enough. With the loss of blood, he had gone into shock.

A thud as Lopez dropped the spade sent adrenaline twitching through his veins. Dennison was jerked into motion. Automatically, his stomach tensed. The resulting flood of pain sent him back into darkness.

Dennison's lids flipped open. His stomach was on fire. He was lying sprawled on the backseat of a moving vehicle. If he had survived this long, he decided, he would probably live…if Lopez got him to a hospital in time.

With an effort of will, he lifted one hand and gingerly felt around the region of his stomach, recoiling when his fingers brushed something wet and glistening. Lopez hadn't bothered to apply a bandage or even attempt to cover the opened area, but the lack of care wasn't surprising. Dennison wouldn't trust the murderous bastard to apply a Band-Aid, let alone attempt first aid for a seeping intestinal wound. Septicemia was a horrible way to die, but he guessed it was marginally better than being buried alive.

The fact that he wasn't rotting in a shallow grave meant that Lopez had either dug up or buried something. Dennison would put money on the second option.

Lopez might have ditched the identity he had been using and his weapons, so he could slide through whatever security cordons the feds had put in place. Judging from the roughness of the potholed road they were driving over, he had succeeded and they were across the border. No mean feat when he had counted at least ten feds at the party—courtesy of the information he had supplied them. And this time Lopez had escaped from two traps, not one.

Radcliff's death had confirmed that Lopez had outlived his usefulness with the cabal, and any doubt about who had launched a missile into the compound at Macaro was gone. The cabal had missed vaporizing Alex and himself by mere seconds. Dennison had actually witnessed the destruction from the air as Alex had skimmed his private helicopter over the hills on the flight in from Bogotá. If they had left the airport on time they would have been killed, but they had been delayed for a few minutes.

Tonight had been the cabal's second attempt but, like the first, this one had backfired.

The car hit a pothole and jumped sideways. Pain washed through him as he braced himself against another bone-shaking series of jolts.

Lopez was silent as he drove. There was no one else in the car, so Dennison knew Lopez had been the one who had manhandled him into the backseat. He had to be close to one hundred and eighty pounds. Unconscious, he would have been a dead weight. The fact that Lopez had gone to so much trouble to keep him alive wasn't comforting. It meant he must need him for something.

The burning pain in his stomach increased.

If Lopez still needed him, that meant it wasn't over yet.

Thirty-Two

Mexico, six months later

Dust swirled around the truck as JT pulled up at a sprawling farmhouse set on a plain that stretched to a range of blue hills in the distance. The house was nestled close to the only source of water Rina had seen for miles, a river that snaked across the dry land like a jewel-bright ribbon of green.

The second she opened her door, Baby surged out and, nose to the ground, began following scent trails. JT stepped out of the truck, a quiet settled expression on his face that told her that he had made his choice.

When JT had entered the Witness Security Program with her, he'd decided to sell the ranch he'd owned for several years. In the interim they had lived in rental accommodation until they could find exactly what they wanted. For the past few weeks they had looked at real estate on the Internet, and for the past month JT had been viewing properties.

She could see why he liked it. The place had a desolate, windblown aspect. It was exactly the kind of ranch she had pictured him owning, but that wasn't what captured Rina.

Climbing out of the truck, she breathed in the dry air. She felt an instant affinity for the bronzed, wild landscape. Down here, even the air tasted different. Esther had been half-Mexican, and maybe that was what made the difference: the place was in her blood.

JT's arms came around her, pulling her back against his chest in a loose hold.

Their relationship had settled into a pattern that was more comfortable than she had ever imagined. They were planning on a wedding, eventually. They were even considering starting a family, although it would take a while for either of them to relax into that final commitment. JT had walked away from his job with the CIA, but he hadn't given up searching for Alex and the cabal. Rina could understand the obsession, even if she wasn't comfortable with it. She wanted Alex and the cabal out of her life, but more than that, she wanted JT, so she was prepared to wait it out.

His hold tightened, as if he'd picked up on the thought. "Do you like it?"

She stared at the intense blue sky, the contrasting ochre of the earth and the hot, wheaten glow of seed heads rippling in the wind and felt something unfold in herself—a sense of expansion, of…contentment. JT fitted here, and so did she. "I love it."

An hour later, after looking through the house and a collection of outbuildings, which included a huge barn and stables, she hooked her fingers through JT's and dragged him down to the river. Here the landscape was different, more lush, softer and very green, with shady trees arching over the water. Just below the house the river broadened out nicely and looked deep enough for swimming.

JT picked up a stick and threw it out over the water. Baby ploughed into the river and began to paddle.

Rina watched as the current caught the stick, sending it spinning lazily downstream. A memory of another river flickered, this one shrouded in mist…something white—a piece of paper, floating, the ink dissolving.

Not a piece of paper. A notepad with numbers written on it.

Emotion almost buckled her knees.

JT caught her. "What's wrong?"

"My mother…"

The car tumbling through the air. Blood everywhere. A gun. The notepad. Numbers.

Esther's gaze: fierce, urgent. "The first set is for the police, no one else. The second set is for you, only you. Do you understand?"

Tears squeezed from between her lids, her chest burned.

"Yes."

Esther's hand closed on hers and gripped hard. *"Good girl. I love you, baby."*

Emotion—loss and the tearing, dispossessed grief of a child—poured through her and this time she didn't attempt to block it. Esther had been murdered. She had been there. It was past time to feel it, time to let go.

The breeze picked up, rustling through the trees. JT continued to hold her, silent and steady, until she had finished crying and her breathing evened out. Exhausted, she turned her head on his shoulder, stared out over the smooth flowing water and let her eyes drift closed.

The first set is for the police, no one else. The second set is for you, only for you.

And the numbers floated up out of the darkness....

* * * * *

Turn the page to read an exciting excerpt from the sequel to
DOUBLE VISION, KILLER FOCUS,
available December 2007.

Prologue

October 12, 1984
Portland, Maine

The powerful beam of a flashlight probed the darkness, skimming over breaking waves as they sluiced over dark fingers of rock. Hunching against an icy southerly wind and counting steps as she picked her way through a treacherous labyrinth of tidal pools, a lean, angular woman swung the beam inland. Light pinpointed the most prominent feature on the exposed piece of coastline, a gnarled, embattled birch that marked the beginning of a steep path.

Breath pluming on the chill air, she followed the track that led to the rotted remains of a mansion. The building which had once commanded the promontory, had burned down almost thirty years ago to the day.

Memories crowded with each step, flickering one after the other, isolated and stilted like the wartime newsreels she'd watched as a child. The wind gusted, razor-edged with sleet, but the steady rhythm of the climb and the purpose that had pulled her away from a warm, chandelier-lit room and an ambassadorial reception to this—a mausoleum of the dead—kept the autumn cold at bay.

Thirty years ago, the man who had hunted her, Xavier le Clerc, had almost succeeded. The Jewish banker-turned-Nazi-hunter had tracked her and her father and the *Schutzstaffel*, the SS officer who had been tasked with caring for them, through a series of international business transactions. Somehow le Clerc had broken through the layers of paper companies that should have protected them and found their physical address.

Dengler had shot him, but not fatally. In the ensuing struggle le Clerc had turned the tables on Dengler, wounding him. Then he had shot her father at point-blank range. She had no doubt le Clerc would have killed her, too, if she hadn't barricaded both Dengler and le Clerc in the ancient storeroom where they were grappled together, and set it ablaze.

The fire had been terrifying, but it had served its purpose. The two men and her father's body had been consumed within minutes. In the smoking aftermath, any evidence of gunshot wounds the skeletal remains might have yielded had been wiped out by a substantial cash payment to the chief of police. The weeks following her father's death had been difficult, but money had smoothed the way. At eighteen years of age, she had been old enough to conclude all of the legal requirements and make arrangements to secure herself.

Ice stung her cheeks as she paused by a small sturdy shed and dug a set of keys out of the pocket of her coat. A gust flattened stiffened oilskin against her body and whipped blond strands, now streaked with gray, across her cheeks, reminding her of a moment even further in the past.

Nineteen forty-four. She had been boarding the Nordika.

She shoved the key in the lock, her fingers stiff with cold. She had been…seven years old? Eight?

She didn't know why that moment had stuck with her. After years of heady victory, then horror, it hadn't been significant. The wind had been howling off the Baltic, right up the cold alley that Lubeck was in the dead of winter, and it had been freezing. Aside from the lights illuminating the deck of the *Nordika*, and the dock in direct contravention of the blackout regulations—it had been pitch-black. After hours spent crouching in the back of a truck, sandwiched cheek-by-jowl with the other children, the lights and the frantic activity had been a welcome distraction, but hardly riveting.

And yet she had remembered that moment vividly. A crate had been suspended above the ship's hold as she'd walked up the gangplank, the swastika stenciled on its side garishly spotlighted, the crane almost buckling under the weight as the crate swayed in the wind. The captain had turned to watch her, his eyes blank, and for a moment she had felt the power her father had wielded. The power of life and death.

Stepping inside out of the wind, she pulled the door closed behind her, slipped the key back in her pocket and engaged the interior locks. She played the beam of the flashlight over the dusty interior of the shed, then reached down and pulled up the hatch door that had once been the entrance to the mansion's storm cellar. Flashlight trained below, she descended to the bottom of the ladder, crossed a cavernous, empty area, ducked beneath a beam and unlocked a second door.

Here the walls were irregular, chiseled from the limestone that had formed a natural series of caves, some that led down almost to the sea. The beam of the flashlight swept the room. It was a dank and cold museum, filled with echoes of a past that would never be resurrected and a plethora of unexpected antiquities.

A dowry to smooth their way in the New World and ensure their survival.

Moldering uniforms hung against one wall. For a moment, in the flickering shadows, they took on movement and animation, as if the SS officers to whom they had once belonged had sprung to life. Her father, *Oberst* Reichmann. *Hauptmann* Ernst,

Oberleutnant Dengler, *Leutnants* Webber, Lindeberg, Konrad, Dietrich and Hammel.

It was a terrible treasure house. But despite the fact that by right of her genetic heritage she had become the custodian, she wasn't locked in the past; the future was much too interesting.

Provided they were never discovered.

She'd studied the news reports over the years as, one after another, their kind had been cornered and killed or imprisoned in various countries, but she was too disciplined to let emotion or bitterness take hold. She was nothing if not her father's daughter.

Crouching down, she unlocked a safe. Her fingers, still stiff with cold, slid over the mottled leather binding of a book. Relocking the safe, she set the book down on a dusty table and turned fragile pages until she found the entries she needed. *Names, birth dates, genetic lineage, blood types. And the numbers the institute had tattooed into their backs.*

The older entries, written in an elegant copperplate hand, had faded with time. The more recent additions, the false names, IRS numbers and addresses, were starkly legible.

The nature of the link they all shared, portrayed in the book, was an unconscionable risk and a protective mechanism. They were all ex-Nazis and illegal aliens; the surviving *Schutzstaffel* were gazetted war criminals. Collectively, they were all thieves. They had stolen the spoils of war from a dozen nations to cushion a new life, and murdered to secure it.

Every one of them was vulnerable to discovery. The agreed penalty for exposing a member of the group, or compromising the group as a whole was death.

She turned to the last section of the book, and the half-dozen names noted there, and added a seventh: Johannes Webber, now known as George Hartley. It was an execution list.

Slipping a plastic bag from the pocket of her coat, she wrapped and sealed the book, which was no longer safe in this location, and carried it with her when she left. She would make arrangements in the morning to relocate the rest of the items and destroy those that couldn't be moved.

Cold anger flowed through her as she locked the door of the shed and started down the steep path, hampered by the powerful wind and driving sleet. She hadn't used the book for almost a decade. But then, as now, the need to use it had been triggered by a betrayal. Webber, the old fool, had talked.

After all these years the *Nordika* had been located.

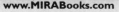

REQUEST YOUR
FREE BOOKS!

2 FREE NOVELS
FROM THE ROMANCE/SUSPENSE
COLLECTION PLUS 2 FREE GIFTS!

BOB07

FIONA BRAND

32289 BODY WORK   ___ $6.99 U.S.   ___ $8.50 CAN.

(limited quantities available)

TOTAL AMOUNT	$ _____
POSTAGE & HANDLING	$ _____
($1.00 FOR 1 BOOK, 50¢ for each additional)	
APPLICABLE TAXES*	$ _____
TOTAL PAYABLE	$ _____

(check or money order—please do not send cash)

To order, complete this form and send it, along with a check or money order for the total above, payable to MIRA Books, to: **In the U.S.:** 3010 Walden Avenue, P.O. Box 9077, Buffalo, NY 14269-9077; **In Canada:** P.O. Box 636, Fort Erie, Ontario, L2A 5X3.

Name: _____
Address: _____ City: _____
State/Prov.: _____ Zip/Postal Code: _____
Account Number (if applicable): _____

075 CSAS

*New York residents remit applicable sales taxes.
*Canadian residents remit applicable GST and provincial taxes.

MIRA®

www.MIRABooks.com

MFB1007BL